W9-BGZ-291

HEADBANGER

Other books by Hugo Hamilton

Surrogate City

The Last Shot

The Love Test

Dublin Where the Palm Trees Grow

Hugo Hamilton

HEADBANGER

Secker & Warburg
London

LIBRARY OF
THOMAS FOX

The author would like to thank David Collins
of Samson Films for his generous support
and encouragement while writing this book.

First published in Great Britain in 1996
by Martin Secker & Warburg Limited
an imprint of Reed International Books Limited
Michelin House, 81 Fulham Road, London SW3 6RB
and Auckland, Melbourne, Singapore and Toronto

www.secker.com

Copyright © 1996 by Hugo Hamilton
The author has asserted his moral rights

A CIP catalogue record for this book
is available from the British Library

ISBN 0 436 20418 5

Phototypeset in 11 on 13 point Plantin
by Intype London Ltd
Printed and bound in Great Britain
by Clays Ltd, St Ives plc

For Mary Rose

LIBRARY OF
THOMAS

Coyne was a father figure to the city of Dublin, holding his paternal arm around its suburbs, protecting its inhabitants like a family. He was a member of the Garda Siochana, guardian of peace; a cop, pig, rozzer, fuzz, bluebottle, who drove the squad car with both hands on the steering wheel, alert and ready for the next situation. His navy-blue Garda cap lay on the ledge beneath the back window, along with that of his colleague, Garda McGuinness. Now and again, the voice from headquarters broke in over the radio, drawing attention to the city's emergencies, traffic accidents, little rust spots of criminality. It was a bright autumn afternoon, a day on which nothing much had happened yet, and beside him, McGuinness was going on about golf, explaining at length how he had to let Superintendent Molloy win a game.

Molloy couldn't play golf to save his life, McGuinness was saying. It's an act of charity. I had to turn my back and pretend I didn't see him putting the ball back.

But Coyne was only half listening to this golf tirade because he was more concerned with the state of the world outside, observing every tiny detail in the street, waiting for something suspicious to turn up. Coyne – the real policeman – a massive database of ordinary facts and figures, licence plates, faces and social trivia. No detail too small.

Coyne saw the woman in a motorized wheelchair moving up the street. He saw the security van pulling up outside the post office and one of the uniformed men getting out carrying a steel case shackled to his arm. The reassuring emblem on the side of the van, like a Papal insignia – two crossed keys and a slogan underneath saying: vigilant and valiant. At the traffic lights, Coyne scanned the faces at the bus stop as though they were all potential criminals. Everybody looking mysteriously down the street like a bunch of weather vanes to see the bus coming. On the pavement, the usual chewing-gum droppings stuck to the ground in their thousands; flattened discs of dirty off-white or off-pink gum-pennies that people spat out before getting on the bus.

Garda Pat Coyne would be in a position to reconstruct every faithful detail in evidence. Your honour, the youth was seen spitting a grey substance in the direction of the oncoming bus. Your honour, the lady at the front of the queue carried an upturned sweeping brush. When the time came, Coyne was in possession of the facts.

Vigilant and valiant. Somehow, the words applied more to Coyne himself. Mind you, he'd come across some fairly peculiar slogans on the sides of vans lately. Signs like: East Coast Glass – Your Pane is our Pleasure. Or else: Personal Plumbing Services – day and night. And the oddest one of them all was the 'Dip–Strip' van, boasting all kinds of stripping services. I mean, how were you to know it was furniture they were talking about? Were the people of Ireland trying to look like complete eejits or what? Somebody should go up and point out how absolutely absurd they looked. 'Embibing Emporium' was another Dublin idiosyncrasy that sprang to mind. As a Garda, Coyne took an interest in the precision of language, and one of these days he would walk straight into that pub, slap a concise Oxford down on the bar counter and say: you pack of right honourable gobshites, you can't even fucking spell. Look, it's I, not E. Imbibing.

These were the things that mattered to the sensibilities of a cop, not who could or could not strike a golf ball. Whatever way you whacked the thing, it was predestined to seek only one conclusion, that was to go down a hole.

Molloy might as well be playing golf with a shovel, McGuinness went on. He's got this fabulous Ping driver and he keeps hacking the fairway with it. I swear to God, you'd think he was cutting turf.

Coyne remained silent. His attention was drawn instead to the window display of a lingerie shop. He examined its contents of bras and knickers; a purple camisole; an amputated leg doing a solo cancan; a dismembered female torso cut off at mid thigh and squeezed into a beige corset; a black plastic bust wearing a white lace bra and a large sign, written in red capital letters, saying: BRAS REDUCED. Another sign saying: NIGHTWEAR 20% OFF.

What are they talking about – bras reduced?

Coyne slapped his hands on the steering wheel and for a moment, both men were staring intensely at this new shrinking phenomenon. As though the women of Ireland were heading into some kind of physical recession. *Erin go Bra* – that great cry for national freedom would have to be reassessed.

With the afternoon sunshine sloping across the city, he turned the squad car down the street towards the sea and saw a band of water shimmering like a cool blue drink at the bottom of a glass. Even though it was autumn already, Coyne could vividly remember the summer and the people walking along with rolled-up towels, ghettoblasters on their shoulders; prams with parasols; girls who had forgotten to turn over and went crimson on one side of the face, or crimson down the backs of their legs. Now there was nobody except an old man leaning over the granite wall staring out at the ferry.

The kids were back at school, but Coyne still carried with him the rather sad summer image of an upturned ice-cream cone with a white pool spreading out along the pavement, and a crow with tattered charcoal wings tilting his beak to drink from some child's misfortune. To Coyne it was a symbol for all the invisible tragedy that lurked underneath society. He was there to make sure that the enemies of happiness were banished. Somebody had to deal with all the brutality and misery. And Coyne was going to kick ass, as they kept saying on TV. He was going to sort out some of these bastards. Blow them away. The Dublin Dirty Harry. He had a list of names in his head, like a top ten of local criminals.

Every muscle in his body was spring-loaded and ready for action. He was in a state of cataleptic readiness, lying dormant like a lethal virus that was going to rain down on some of these characters. He had put some of the hoors away before. And he wasn't finished yet either. You know, Coyne thought, while McGuinness was still going through every stroke on the Straffan golf course, life wasn't meant to be stationary. Life was more than a series of shagging holes on a green landscape. It had to have momentum, like music. Coyne wasn't the kind of cop with the cap tilted on the back of the head. No way.

Then it came: the situation. The familiar voice on the radio speaking with precise eloquence.

Ballsbridge area. Armed robbery in progress. Newsagent cum post office. We believe the raiders are still on the premises.

McGuinness picked up the radio mouthpiece and got

4

the exact details, the very post office they had just passed by five minutes ago. Coyne swung the car around. With the siren on, they howled through the streets, blue light flashing back at them from doors and windows as they passed. Maybe this time they would really punch the clock. They arrived just in time to see a motor bike skidding off the pavement out on to the road. Hey Joe, where would you be going with that bag in your hand? Coyne was on the ball, only fifty yards behind.

We have them, Larry, he said. And as he caught up with them, he could have knocked them down with a tiny shove, only that one of the raiders on the back of the bike turned around and hurled a hatchet at them. Coyne took evasive action. Braked and skidded. But the hatchet came crashing through the windscreen like a shark through the side of an aquarium. Glass everywhere. Diamonds cascading all over their laps.

Jesus Christ, McGuinness said, his eyes open wide, staring at the hatchet stuck in the windscreen as if it were alive.

Coyne broke through and cleared away some of the glass with his elbow, then accelerated once more. He hadn't lost them yet, and after the next junction, he caught up with them again, just as they were heading into a small laneway at the end of which the raiders dropped the bike and jumped over the wall into the gardens, engine left running and the back wheel continuing to spin out like roulette. Coyne brought the car to a halt.

Don't be crazy, McGuinness urged.

But Coyne was going after them. No wonder they called him Mr Suicide back at the station. In the attempt to apprehend the raiders he jumped over the wall and came close to being savaged by a dog. He crossed the gardens like an obstacle course. Almost severed his leg from the knee down on a wheelbarrow and, in the end, very nearly got himself killed by the passing DART when he tried to give chase across the railway line. Jumped back just in time.

Bastards. Forced to give up the chase, Coyne limped back to talk to a woman who was standing in shock at the centre of a vegetable plot with her gardening gloves clasped as in prayer. They both faced each other suddenly, as though they were at a shrine together. Coyne out of breath and half kneeling to examine the footprints across the trampled leeks. He was embarrassed that he could not recover his breath more quickly. His chest was so badly out of condition that it felt like he was playing the accordion with himself. A tiny E flat note whistling through the air passages like a bent reed.

There had always been a sort of imaginary audience in Coyne's head. After all, a man's life was a performance. At this moment, the reaction would have been a short, modest applause, tailing off to silence, everybody waiting for his next move. Now and again, at crucial moments, he would talk to his audience, justifying his motives. Now and again, his audience merged with the real people he knew – his wife Carmel, his late father, his mentor Fred, and his friend Vinnie Foley. God knows who else was there in Garda Pat Coyne's audience? His friend Billy who had emigrated to Australia. Even his enemies maybe. And the top ten victims were always there in the front row admiring his tenacity in the face of all odds.

The Novena in the garden. Coyne looked like he'd come for a miracle, inhaling furiously. When he finally regained his breath, he asked the woman if she had been able to identify any of the raiders. She shook her head. But Coyne already had his own suspicions and began to lift some of the soil up in his hand, trying to ascertain if it was organic.

6

Yes, the woman nodded. Totally organic.

Back in the patrol car, with the sections of laminated glass all over the floor, Coyne thought of his own safety for the first time. He had lost sight of any personal fear and stopped acting like a man with a wife and three children. He was being heroic and suicidal again. More like a younger man trying to impress his friends, or his girlfriend, with nothing to lose.

Pat, you're a mad bastard, McGuinness crooned in his Tralee accent. You're going to get yourself killed.

I nearly had the fuckers, Larry.

You nearly had yourself mangled, you mean.

It's that bastard, Perry. I know it. He hasn't seen the last of me, the little savage.

McGuinness held the hatchet in his hand, and you'd think he was going to burst into song, some kind of Kerry golfing ballad. I don't want something like this in my skull, no thanks. It would be a terrible handicap on the golf course.

Garda Coyne was in his mid thirties, medium build and a narrow, handsome face. More handsome than he knew himself. He had a good smile, but more often bore an expression of great determination which made him look worried, or furious, or just stunned. Like he'd just been whacked on the back of the head with a newspaper and was ready to turn around and retaliate. A man who had his mind made up. A man who knew exactly what had gone wrong with the world.

He was a dedicated cop. Above and beyond the call of duty. He was following invisible goals, set by his own father, by his wife Carmel and by her mother, Mrs Gogarty. One day he would reach the rank of superintendent or commissioner. But Coyne was interested in more than that. He was a crusader and the streets of Dublin had gone out of control, simple as that. He was answering an inner mission to reform the society and clean up the city. And somebody was going to have to do something about the shaggin' environment as well.

The world was fucked, basically. The problem was that Coyne frequently found himself making his case to empty houses. Nobody wanted to know. He was explaining his views to an uninterested audience at a matinée, with popcorn left all over the place and sticky patches where they had spilled Coke in the dark. People with nowhere else to go. There he was, telling them about the kind of world he wanted his wife and children to be able to live in, and the audience would just walk out on him, leaving only the cleaning staff with the sound of their buckets and brushes, letting in a brash blast of daylight, flooding the place with the banal sound of traffic from outside.

At home, Carmel was getting ready to go to her art classes – Painting for Pleasure. The brochure from the local night school had been hanging on the notice board for weeks, beside the gas bill, and surrounded by calendar pages of Chagall and Egon Schiele. Some of her own new paintings were also beginning to take over the kitchen wall.

Carmel was slightly younger than her husband. Small build, blonde hair and a round face. She had sad, light-blue eyes. In her own way, she was full of determination too, and looked like she was fond of arguing, but also ready to laugh at any minute. She wanted to go places. Do something interesting with her life. She was maternal but fiercely independent, and in a modest way, proud of her looks, especially her legs. She knew she had talent.

Her mother was in the kitchen with her, drinking tea. The children were playing in the hall: Jimmy trying to arrest his two little sisters, Jennifer and Nuala, persuading them that they had to go to prison in the cupboard underneath the stairs. He was reading them their rights – You have the right to remain silent, but everything you say will be taken down in evidence. Look, there was nothing to be afraid of, he reassured them. He allowed himself to be incarcerated first.

Carmel was packing her art materials, throwing pencils and brushes into her bag. Made her feel she was seven years old again. Held up the fattest of her brushes and pretended to use it as a blusher. They laughed and her mother almost choked on a mouthful of bitter tea, bringing tears to her eyes, not so much because of the inhaled liquid but because of a sudden sense of pride in her daughter. She blew her nose: a mixture of snot and tears and tea, remembering the little flat tins of water-colour paints Carmel had used as a child. Squares of magenta and scarlet and purple that became mixed into a brown mess after a few days.

You were always gifted, Carmel, she wanted to say, but there was a scream from the hallway and Nuala came running into the kitchen crying, sniffling, sitting up on her grandmother's knee.

There you are, pet, Carmel's mother said, wiping the child's face. That'll teach you never to marry a Guard.

Ah now, Ma. There's no need for that, Carmel said, giving her mother a look.

At the station, Joe Perry had been taken in for questioning and Garda Coyne was pulling him apart over the raid on the post office. He was a young lad of seventeen, with milk moustache still clinging to his upper lip. He was wearing wide jeans and a hooded jacket. Just the kind of generic description they often put out on *Crimeline*. He seemed terribly casual as he was brought into the main office, looking around and smiling as though he was being ushered in for some kind of talk show, waiting for somebody to come and clip the little mike to his lapel. There was a kind of swing in his walk. The Ringsend swagger. He sat right underneath the cannabis poster – 'you've got the wrong man' written all over his face.

Coyne knew how to deal with these clowns. That grin didn't fool him one little bit.

So it's hatchets now, he said, leaning against a filing cabinet like it was the mantelpiece at home. But you could see Perry saying to himself: Yah thick Garda gobshite. What do you expect me to say, yes?

Coyne approached Perry and jabbed him in the chest.

Chief Running-Foot, he said, waiting to see if the joke worked. You won't be running very far now, you little savage. Coyne got the hatchet from his desk and held it up to Perry's face. Exhibit A. Did you leave this behind by any chance? His personal audience roared laughing.

I done nothin', I swear.

Let's see your footwear then. Perry's sneakers had massive tongues; maybe they were meant to make him look like one of those mythical horses with white wings on their hooves.

Come here, Pegasus, you little bastard. And Coyne made him stand up while he examined the soles like a blacksmith.

Organic soil, eh?

I want to speak to my solicitor.

Coyne dropped the hoof and Perry's shoe made a tiny squeak on the tiled floor. But he wasn't finished, and Coyne then produced a small bag of soil.

Exhibit B, he shouted triumphantly as he pushed the soil bag into Perry's face. What was happening? Was it the adrenalin from the chase still surging like a narcotic

10

around his head? Coyne suddenly lost his patience and began trying to feed Perry some of the soil, stuffing it into his mouth as though he was concerned about some nutritional deficiency, until some of the other Guards came over to restrain him.

You've made your point, Pat.

Perry was spitting out the black mixture of clay and saliva, proclaiming his innocence. Grimacing at the taste of wholefood.

At this point, Coyne felt a bit of a shit. He was only dealing with small fry. He had let himself down and felt his audience had suddenly switched over to *Come Dancing* in utter desperation. McGuinness even handed Perry a Kleenex, for God's sake, and Coyne held his palms out to his inner public, appealing that he was only human too. There is only so much a man can take. But his ratings had plummeted and his audience were all passed out on the sofa, yawning, half watching a couple strutting around in a high-bottomed tango.

As usual, the real crime was happening somewhere else. Public enemy number one, Berti Cunningham, was driving a spanking new Range Rover through the streets of the city. Just about the same time that Coyne was carrying out the special feeding programme at Irishtown Garda station, Berti Cunningham, his younger brother Mick Cunningham and their chief accountant Charlie Robinson were stopping briefly along Baggot Street so that Berti could pick up a kebab. They were the untouchables. Nobody could lay a finger on them. Berti strolled into Abrakebabra inhaling the smell, drawn to the counter like a fly to a ketchup stain. He had a thin, wiry sort of frame as though he had been underfed as a child. Raised on sliced bread and jam. Chip sandwiches, maybe. Where other crime lords needed a drink before they went out on a job, Berti Cunningham, or the Drummer as they all called him, needed some really evil piece of food, something that would set off a vicious clash of gastric fluids, leaving him with the stench of a tannery on his breath and a slight disfiguration at the edges of his mouth that only barely concealed the boiling bile.

His brother Mick was a little less ugly. Small goatie beard and a reversed baseball cap. He sat at a table with Chief, a stout man with a shaven head, wearing a kind of happy, vegetarian shirt, with lots of colours. It was more like a pizza really, with braces holding up his jeans. They had left Drummer's two Rottweiler dogs in the back of the Range Rover, panting with their tongues hanging out. They and sat looking up at MTV – three women standing knee deep in the sea singing: *Don't go chasing waterfalls*, whatever the fuck that was supposed to mean. Right underneath a sign that said: No alcohol allowed on the premises, Chief cracked open a can of beer while Drummer ordered three kebabs, one for himself with lettuce and garnish, and two plain kebabs for his Rottweilers. Abrakebabra. Sure it was only dogfood anyway.

Carmel sat at the back of the class, listening to the art teacher, Gordon Sitwell, with vocation written all over her eyes. An unfinished painting was spread out in front of her and she was mixing up some paint, spellbound by eagerness, soaking up every word that Mr Sitwell uttered as though he was carefully distributing some precious linseed oil you could not afford to lose even one drop of.

Sitwell was a gentleman with a grand accent that somehow went with all that art talk. He had a squat build and wore a green corduroy jacket. He seemed to draw inspiration from his earlobe, which he squeezed gently as he spoke. He was there to spout erudition and to urge his disciples on to greater things. He kept walking up and down the room, talking as though he had a direct link to the great masters, stopping occasionally to hold up his index finger, knocking against an invisible urn and waiting to hear a faint musical note. He was just the kind of art teacher Carmel had expected, somebody with grey temples who was utterly lost in culture.

Sometimes he made eye contact with her, just to see if she understood what he was saying, and she automatically nodded. Once or twice he smiled as he wandered around the classroom, leaving behind him an intoxicating whiff of aftershave, which had to be called something like 'Renaissance' or 'Rubens' and must have been made with some ancient musk extracted from the entrails of a mythical animal. A sphinx or a unicorn. It curled around Carmel's nostrils and inspired her to carry on working on an evening sky over the sea, with a tree to one side. Nothing too fancy. Keep it simple.

Nice, gentle brush strokes, Sitwell was saying. Let me see the brush swing a little in your hand. Remember that painting is like telling a story. The colours are your words.

He turned his back and walked away as though he was leaving the room, then swivelled round dramatically and stopped to look everyone in the eye, individually. Some of the people had come back for a second year and knew by the sleepy grin on his face that he was about to say something funny.

Remember, ladies. It's not a powder puff you're holding, and everybody laughed in recognition as though they had heard this one before. It's an instrument of self-expression.

And when he came up behind Carmel the next time, he leaned over with his medieval musk and urged her to use some more dramatic colour for the sky. Something really sensuous. A fiery cobalt, perhaps?

13

That's how it started, Coyne was telling the lads at the station. With tribal rituals.

He was writing in the details on the arrest sheet and stopped for a moment to tell the other members one of his little anthropological facts. Sergeant Devaney was listening with a sceptical smile on his face, buttocks perched on a desk. Life on Earth, with Pat Coyne.

That's how all that art and culture began in the first place. This tribe of people where all the men go out together to have a communal crap.

You're taking the piss, McGuinness said.

I swear, Coyne insisted. Every morning, all the men go out and leave these little sculptures on the landscape. Defecation missions they called it. I read all about it. It's only much later that they began to use materials like wood and paint.

Coyne could not remember where he had developed this obsession with facts. Probably at school, as a form of protection. To fit in with the schoolboy hierarchies. It resulted in a real interest in nature, and he still borrowed books and anthropological videos all the time. He still bought the *National Geographic* and was deeply committed to the environment; anything that affected the future. But none of his knowledge ever brought him closer to people. He had difficulty communicating his vision of the universe to his colleagues. He was not one for bending reality to the demands of story-telling, and in the end, always found himself alone, staring out from his own mind as though he sat on a raft that would never reach the shore. It seemed as if the other Gardai in the station were all listening to him from the far bank.

You wanker, Coyne. You're making this up.

I'm telling you, it's a well-known fact, these lavatory

parties in the forest. Can't remember the name of the place.

But Coyne saw them all gazing at him incredulously, as though he was beyond rescue this time. Out of reach. At the mercy of a tide of Garda realism. Maybe it was the way he told it. But as usual, he felt the awkwardness of drawing an unspoken comparison between the actions of tribal men and the toilet-trained men of Ireland with whom he worked. Telling them the unenhanced truth. We're all a bunch of civilized shitters when it comes down to it, each one of us proclaiming our identity, marking our space in the world through waste. It was clear that nobody had any idea what the hell Coyne was going on about. Where was the joke?

Out in the real world, Drummer Cunningham and his gang were making their way along the canal down to Percy Place. Mick Cunningham had taken over the wheel of the Range Rover to allow Drummer to finish off his mobile meal. The Rottweilers had already inhaled theirs. As they pulled up outside a house in flats, Drummer got out and threw the kebab wrapper on to the pavement as much as to say: This is my city. I'll throw my shite around if I like.

Upstairs, in a small apartment facing on to the street, Naomi Keegan was lying in a heap along the bed. She was still in her dressing-gown and the ring on the doorbell was her first contact with the outside world that day. Up to then she had successfully been able to remove reality by watching MTV. Her mind was a sponge, soaked in senseless images, heaving with the endless motion of limbs and lyrics. She went to the window, opened it and threw down the key. Then went back to lie on the bed again with a litre bottle of Ballygowan. Not so much to drink it but to hold it like a teddy bear or some kind of comfort toy that offered a vague notion of innocence and purity.

She was around twenty-five and had been a student of architecture at one stage. A drawing board in the corner of the room was submerged under a pile of clothes and personal items. It had also been misused more frequently as a surface from which she snorted whatever substance Drummer brought to her. A rolled-up James Joyce note was stuck in a penholder as the most essential implement. She was the architect of her own misfortune was the last sentence she heard from her South Dublin parents. To them, the sight of their daughter with an ear-ring in her eyebrow and black fingernails was the end of her education. Not to mention the tattoo on her backside. That was a step beyond.

She could smell the kebab coming up the stairs and finally decided it was time to take another drink of water to recover some real sense of purity. Drummer came in and gave her the shite and onion smile. Looked around with disgust at the state of the room and pushed a mug away with his foot. *Can I touch you there* was on MTV at that moment. Michael Bunburger Bolton floating down some tropical river in a white suit, looking for some woman washing her hair in a waterfall for fucksake. Drummer made a little joke about the lyrics which Naomi ignored until he passed her a tab and she began to perk up. Then he went to the wardrobe and chose some clothes; a gold skirt and a thin black pullover.

I've got a job for you, he said.

Berti, please. Don't ask me. I'll do anything.

Just a little dance, baby. That's all.

She looked at him, and he smiled as though there was a VIP lounge in the back of his head that nobody ever got into. Even in matters of sex there was a Bluebeard room in Drummer's mind which you didn't want to investigate. Some young one had been turned into a kebab and hidden under the floorboards in the past maybe. A challenge to all women. Please discover me. Try and get into my last VIP lounge and find out what no woman has ever seen before.

He was already pulling her off the bed, taking the fizzy water from her and forcing her to get dressed. Slapped the tattoo on her backside just a little too hard to pass for affection, and while Naomi got dressed, he began to dance to the music on the TV. Some kind of profane jerky movements that made him look like he was suffering a mild form of tropical tarantism. He was a shite dancer. It was Tai Chi meets Michael Jackson, holding his crotch and thrusting forward like he'd just received a kick in the sphincter. His body just mocked everything that was aesthetic.

Carmel's art class was coming to an end. Everybody was beginning to wash brushes and put everything away while Mr Sitwell stood behind her, commenting on her tree.

It looks like a chestnut, or an oak, he said. Perhaps you could give it a little more body. Make it look stronger, more muscular. If you get my drift?

Carmel looked up. She didn't know what he meant.

Try a bit of maroon or burgundy, he said, taking her hand and guiding the brush towards the paints, dabbing and mixing with great skill, then applying thin downward lines of burgundy along the tree trunk.

Brilliant, she thought. He had transformed the painting and was already walking away again, talking to the class in general.

Every object has its own personality. Every object has its own dark, romantic secrets inside. When you draw an oak tree, it should look like a mystery man. A tall, handsome, muscular body. You should want to hug him, ladies.

They all laughed. Carmel blushed. The cheek of him.

Superintendent Molloy was in a strange, elated mood that evening. With good reason. He had finally broken through the wall of silence which surrounded Drummer Cunningham's deeds. He was excited by the fact that he now had a conviction in sight. A key witness, Dermot Brannigan, had turned police informer and was prepared to talk in court. Not so much a supergrass as a disaffected former associate of Berti Cunningham's who had given Molloy more than he needed to end the Drummer's reign.

When it came to the armed robbery and the case of Joe hatchet-man Perry, that was a different matter. His lawyer came into the station ranting about his client being assaulted. Superintendent Molloy said there was no harm done and he was happy to release the suspect to show that the Gardai were being reasonable about the whole affair. The lawyer was standing in the office with a long face on him, you'd think it was he who had been force-fed the organic muck. OK, Coyne had gone a little too far on the high-fibre diet, but after risking life and limb to arrest the little bastard, Molloy was now deciding not to have him charged.

He was just helping us in our enquiries, Molloy said.

He has his rights, you know, the lawyer complained. I'm considering a case of serious harassment.

Not at all, there's no need for that, Molloy brayed. We'll be releasing him right away. We're just going through the formalities.

My client has suffered deep distress, the solicitor added.

Well, he shouldn't be waving his hatchet around the post office then, Coyne said, finally losing his head.

What are you talking about, the solicitor fought back. My client was visiting his sick grandmother this afternoon.

So that's where he got the muck on his shoes. That bastard is guilty and you know it.

Coyne found himself pointing his finger straight at the lawyer. But it was like touching an electric fence. Once again he felt his audience had deserted him as though the only person in the world who would understand him was his wife, Carmel. She was there in the audience, about five or six rows back with her crisps and her toffees; a devoted fan with her knees up against the seat in front encouraging him. But Coyne had already gone too far and Superintendent Molloy was urging him to calm down.

Everything is under control, he said.

Coyne couldn't believe it. What was the point in him half killing himself running over those garden walls. As far as he was concerned, the legal profession only interfered with the administration of justice.

Just keep him away from my client, the lawyer said.

And afterwards, when the lawyer was gone, Superintendent Molloy took the opportunity to make a little speech of his own. Telling Coyne he wasn't up to it any more. He had lost his balance and needed to relax. Should go down the country for a few days.

That's not the way to go after these fellas, Molloy said. You can't take any short cuts.

Like Coyne's own father, Superintendent Molloy came from West Cork. Those county by county alliances throughout the Garda ranks had once established a bond between them, protecting Coyne, keeping him in sight of promotion. Molloy was taking on the role of a lost father figure, using the same tired country clichés.

Superintendent Molloy was a true redneck Garda. His hair crossed over from one side of his bald head to the other, like a lid or a trapdoor that had to be put back in place every time he went out in the wind. A hair-door is what it looked like, with a hinge at the side of the head, just above the temple. And Coyne stared at the mole just under the super's nose thinking, how does he shave? He imagined Molloy shaving the mole off and a fountain of blood gushing out. Moleshaver Molloy, walking around all day with a plaster on his face with the blood still seeping through.

You've got to play by the rules, Moleshaver said like a mantra.

I'll get him one of these days, Coyne vowed.

Look, Coyne. We've gone through this before. You can't lean on a suspect like that. Everybody knows he's guilty, but he's got a smart lawyer. Works for big-time sharks like the Cunninghams as well. Lay off until you've got something concrete.

Molloy leaned back, touching the tips of his fingers against each other, shampooing some invisible head in front of him. Coyne could see his own father, with the braces, and the rings holding up the sleeves of his shirt. He could smell the ancient tube of shaving cream, as though it was against the principles of the new republic to change to foam shaving lotion. Molloy took in a deep breath and leaned forward again, with purpose.

A word of advice, Pat. It's like a fart in the sauna. Unless you catch the fucker at it, forget it. It's the legal system in this country. He didn't get away with much anyhow.

That's not the point, Coyne snapped back in amazement. We can't just let him go.

Forget Perry, Molloy insisted. We've got Brannigan talking. He's under protective surveillance at the moment. You know what this means, Pat.

The Drummer.

Moleshaver looked across his desk with great Garda pride. Then he got himself ready to deliver an even more profound piece of advice.

You see, you've got to be able to connect the shite back to the arsehole it came from, he said.

Now that was ten per cent extra talk. That was the new improved formula language. As though Moleshaver had put forward the greatest ecological message of our time. The solution to pollution. Connect the shite back to the arsehole it came from. Molloy winked, and Coyne could not help being impressed by the impact of this new visual illustration. He liked it. It rounded off the faecal discussion earlier on. An inspiring concept which had a crisp cinematic feel to it, like the final words before a deadly subversive mission. Go for it, men. There was nothing to add, only action.

Coyne drove home along the seafront. Over the rasping sound of his own car, the tape deck was playing the blues. A brilliant red sky over Dublin had begun to fade away and it was getting dark. The red glow on the granite walls was gone and there was a pure white moon up in the shape of a half-masticated host. There was a hint of winter in the breeze, which swirled up dust and leaves and sweet wrappers together along the pavement.

Coyne laughed to himself. It was the most inappropriate reaction to the day. But he felt light-headed and washed over by a kind of dangerous exuberance. He saw everything in black and white. It always came down to this – the two directions: top road or bottom road. You could blame the world or blame yourself. You could try and change the environment and the circumstances around you, or you could try and change yourself. Coyne was certain that he was right and they were all wrong. He would show them all one of these days.

Carmel's mother was at home, putting on her coat as soon as he arrived in the door.

Your dinner is in the micro, she muttered.

Chicken Chernobyl, Coyne muttered back.

He felt like doing something outrageous. Like pulling down his trousers and exposing himself to her back; that ridiculous wide hairdo on her, the cloud of Lancôme and the chiffon scarf, for God's sake. Tried the chiffon scarf test lately, Gran? Sorry, Baroness von Gogarty. He made a grimace at the back of her head, pretending to come up and open the door for her. But she caught him.

I can see what you're doing, she said, letting herself out instead. Spinning around on her hind legs to throw him a filthy look. He watched her walking out the driveway, waiting to see if she would allow herself one more vicious look back. Yes.

Jennifer, one of the children, stood at the top of the stairs saying she couldn't sleep. So he went upstairs and found them all awake, waiting for him to tell the stories. He was much better than Gran.

She just tells girls' stories, Jimmy said. And Coyne felt appreciated, knowing that he could re-invent the whole universe for his family audience at least. He was back once more in the bubble of his own home, laughing at arcane little jokes that no other family would understand. Insulated by the warmth of his own group as though the world depended on them to begin all over again.

At other times, Coyne felt he had become his own audience entirely, watching himself on closed-circuit TV; a silent blue figure shifting around in a semi-detached house on a Dublin housing estate, carrying his children into bed, telling them bedtime stories about forsaken places under the sea.

And then the underwater man with no eyelids brought the little pink fishes to a place where they could hide. He lived in a sunken ship where they would be safe. You see the mackerel were smart because they had white tummies and they swam up high where the shark couldn't see them against the light. But the coloured fishes had to find a place to hide.

The children were gathered all around him in one of the beds. Nuala hiding all her furry toys under Coyne's arm, as if to act out the story. Jennifer holding her eyes open with her index fingers.

And even though the underwater man had no ears, he could hear everything. Every tiny sound. He could hear a bubble bursting a hundred miles away. So he could hear the shark coming back.

Coyne almost fell asleep himself when the story was over. Coyne the real father, tucking them in, rubbing his hand over his son's forehead, stalling to pick up a sock near the door, walking down the stairs lightly. Coyne eating his dried-out dinner. Coyne stealing biscuits in his own home.

Relaxing in front of the TV, he was still wearing his uniform, tie undone, watching the men of Papua New Guinea re-enact old tribal rituals. Above all else, he was concerned with extinction; the disappearance of legendary people. Last men belonging to ancient and pure civilizations which had clashed with modernity. Men and women like the Blasket Islanders.

Half-lying across the opulent floral sofa which Carmel had picked out on the advice of Mrs Gogarty, he watched the warriors jumping around, preparing for battle. He was almost asleep again when he saw one of the men running towards him with a hatchet. He jumped up. Kicked the dinner plate on the floor with his foot thinking he was dealing with Perry again. He found the remote control and played it back again and again. The warrior wore nothing but a purple jacket and a felt hat. Chest bare. White curly hair. The braided jacket looked like part of a hotel porter's uniform which had somehow become separated from the trousers. Maybe it came from some famous American Hotel, like the Waldorf Astoria, and made its way right out to Port Moresby, sold and resold, only to be worn in ceremonious battle with a painted face and bare painted legs underneath. The warrior's white teeth bared as though he was smiling, waiting for a tip. The hatchet came up in the right hand, just like Perry.

Suddenly Coyne thought everything he had done and said that day was entirely unbalanced. Out of control. The volume turned up too high. He had overdone it with Perry. Coyne had to get smart. He should try to be more cool. A balanced cop, calmly tracing the shite back to the arsehole it came from.

It was Gordon Sitwell who held the door open for Carmel when she was going home. Her painting rolled up like a precious scroll in her hand, smiling like a child. But he was laughing to himself and shaking his head.

Got a dash of paint on your nose, he said.

Oh really, she said. But when she tried to wipe it off, he held up his hand as though she was about to rub away a secret sign.

No, no. Leave it there, love. It's proof that you were at your art classes and not in the pub.

Adieu, he said, and then walked off briskly in the direction of the car-park.

When she got home, Coyne was already in bed, sitting up reading a magazine. Bare hairy arms outside the duvet. There was an explosion of talk; so much to catch up with. He exaggerated the chase, and the hatchet. Vowed he would get his revenge as though it was Carmel herself who had been placed in danger and he was expected to uphold a bond of chivalry on her behalf.

She pinned her painting up on the dressing-table and asked: What do you think?

Good, he said.

But Coyne was absolutely amazed. It was the sky he had come home with earlier on; the fading, yellow and red furnace which hung over the city that evening when he drove out along the coast road. The end of Coyne's day, looking like an old bruise over Dublin Bay. Her painting contained such honesty, such complete understanding of Coyne's mind that he felt he was looking into some kind of new mirror through which he could look back along the day and see everything radiating with burning violence, down to the wine-red glow along the side of the trees. Coyne was afraid to say it was brilliant. Angry that she could be so accurate. You didn't fucking do that yourself; no way, he wanted to say.

She got undressed, talking about the art class, still watching as if to make sure nobody would steal her painting. Slipped a giant T-shirt over her head and stood before him for a moment, a headless, naked woman struggling to come to the surface. Then she drew lines of white cream on her face and her elbows like a female warrior about to take part in a fertility ritual.

Do you think the tree is muscular enough, she asked?

Muscular. Yeah, I suppose so.

But Carmel was unhappy that he could so easily dismiss her work.

God bless you, Pat. You're such a headbanger.

I said it was muscular, didn't I.

You're a philistine. She smiled cheerfully.

Coyne mistrusted this new language. He stared at her until she got into bed and kissed him. He dutifully kissed her back, like a man tiptoeing around the intimacy of words. For a while they sat up in bed, Coyne reading, Carmel squinting at her own masterpiece. The voices from next door drifting softly in through the wall. Light switches being flicked. Water running. The Gillespies moving around and speaking to each other, asking final questions, offering final assurances, perhaps sitting up right there on the other side of the wall, in the same position, back to back, like a mirror image of Pat and Carmel Coyne in their bed.

Come on, Pat.

Come on what?

You never headbutt me any more.

So Coyne got up and switched off the main light, while she turned over on her hands and knees. He pulled back the duvet, though he could see nothing and stumbled against the end of the bed. It was pitch black, and in that moment of blindness, the unspoken aim was that she would keep shifting around like a moving target, while he would score by crashing his head against her bottom. Again and again, bashing his skull like a young buffalo into her soft rump while her shrieks went out the window.

Drummer Cunningham drove the Range Rover up to a small Corporation estate in the north of the city. He had left the dogs at home. There was a bit of business to settle with Brannigan. Like Coyne, he was dedicated to his work, beyond the call of duty. He had never once been out of the country and boasted about it as though it pointed to some extreme loyalty towards his own piece of turf. Leaving even for a short holiday to Ibiza would be a major act of betrayal, surrendering the sovereignty of his ground to others. He'd come back to find his territory and his followers subsumed into some other gang.

Drummer usually wore a gold bracelet with his suit. He occasionally brought a set of rosary beads, just to mock his victims. Praying over them and blessing them before they were done in. The nickname, Drummer, had stuck to him from a long time back so that nobody really knew its origins, except his victims, who said they heard drums whenever they faced him. Otherwise, Berti Cunningham was ordinary in his taste for night-clubs and let on he was the king, holding a mobile phone, surrounded by a whole load of other boneheads in suits. Now Drummer had even bought a night-club of his own.

Coyne's ex-Garda friend and mentor, Fred, had given him a lot of these details on the gang. All the stuff the Special Branch knew but could not prove in court. Fred was close to the source and in a position to pass on sensitive information to Coyne. Two men had been shot or beaten to death in Dublin in the past six weeks, both of them attributed to Drummer. It was clear that Drummer was trying to transform himself into a respectable night-club owner while at the same time reasserting his authority over the underworld. There was nothing the law could do about it. But wait till Coyne started dealing with him. One of these days, Coyne would wipe the floor with that bum-fucking primate – stick him back in the serious offenders wing of Mountjoy zoo.

Outside Dermot Brannigan's home, two rookies from the Serious Crime Squad were keeping a vigil when Naomi

Keegan came walking towards them. Her gold skirt, leather jacket and long legs drew their attention. She appeared to be dancing down along the pavement almost, and just as she got past the two detectives, she screamed. When they looked around they could see that she was being assaulted. A youth trying to take her bag. They jumped out of the car and ran towards her, but the youth had already disappeared without the bag, leaving the men there to try and comfort her.

Around the back of Brannigan's house, Drummer and his chief accountant were already dragging their victim down a laneway towards the blue Range Rover. Brannigan was trying desperately to shout for help but uttering no more than a minimal squeak under his gag. It was no use. He had been delivered up to Drummer's court of justice. Brannigan was shittin' bricks. Nervous as an albino rabbit staring into the eyes of a starving ferret. Obediently got into the Range Rover and found himself going for a little drive out to Brittas Bay, after they drove around to pick up Naomi and Mick again.

She sat in the front seat listening to a Walkman all the way, occasionally slapping her hands on the dashboard in time to the music. Mick had taken over the wheel while Drummer and the Chief sat on either side of Brannigan in the back. Berti making the sign of the cross and taking out a luminous set of rosary beads. *In nomine Patris et Filii et Spiritus Sancti.*

Amen, said the Chief Accountant, laughing.

Moments later, Berti almost broke his mobile phone, jabbing it into Brannigan's groin because he wouldn't answer his question. By the time they got out to Brittas Bay, Brannigan had sweated a gallon of crude oil out through his forehead and there was condensation all over the windows.

At a boathouse, Drummer kicked his pleading victim around for a while until he got tired. Brannigan inhaled and tasted the sweet terror of his own blood as he swallowed. With the headlights of the car shining on him, they began to staple Brannigan to the door by his jacket. In crucified formation he hung in his clothes as the Chief Accountant whispered into his ear, telling him he was going to heaven and he would be well looked after up there, speaking with the gravitas of a liquidator to one of his doomed shareholders.

You're surplus to requirement, pal.

And Brannigan kept looking at Drummer as though he hadn't even heard Chief. Please, Berti, Jesus, please, he repeated, grimacing through his pink teeth like he'd been eating loads of raspberries. But Drummer just got tired of listening to this whining and told Chief to replace the piece of packing tape over his mouth. Then he went over to put some music on the car stereo.

Come out and do your thing, he commanded. Naomi had hardly seen anything of what was going on because she was lost in her own narcotic fantasy.

Berti, don't ask me to do this, she said.

But there was no way of refusing, so she got out and began to perform a sort of liturgical dance in front of Dermot Brannigan. Right there with the waves crashing in on the shore and the sand dunes all round shaped into smooth bellies and thighs behind them. A light breeze stirred the bristle of reeds. The car stereo blasted out across the deserted landscape with Chris de Burgh: *Don't pay the fucking ferryman* – the most appropriate musical murder to emphasize the tackiness of life and death. Brannigan stared with open eyes at the girl swinging her hips with wonderful accuracy, pointing all the fluid narrative of her physical attributes at him in order to take away the pain of his imminent departure. He felt the self-pity of a dying man. Duped by desire. Legs, hips, breasts and smiles; the supreme icons of compassion, warmth and self-preservation dancing in front of him. A dance of mercy in which she began to uncover herself, bit by bit, turning to show glimpses of her body that made Brannigan wish he was already gone. It was like sex had become a rehearsal for death. She danced until he could see a strip of black pubic fur, which seemed to be stuck on at the top of her legs with velcro. Her discreet tattoo looked like she had Taiwan stamped on her right buttock. It entered Brannigan's eyes and slipped into his unlocked mind along the secret passages of desire, sitting like a silent cat beside the furnace of his fear.

That's all they allowed him to see. He had tears in his eyes when they put a black refuse sack over his head. They stood around smoking and watching the sack moving in and out with his breath.

Naomi pulled on her clothes again, but instead of getting back into the car, she walked out towards the sea as though she had done her life's work and was now ready to depart herself. Chief had to run out and drag her back to the car at the last minute.

You didn't say you were going to kill him, she kept pleading on behalf of Brannigan as though the dance had turned her into a carnal companion.

Drummer was ready for this and gave her a syringe. Put on the light inside the Range Rover and helped her to send the cool blast of smack into her arm. All the venom of Berti Cunningham's law flooding into her veins. She slammed her head back against the side of the car. Her eyes rolled around her head.

She'll remember nothing, Drummer muttered and then went over to make sure his victim was nailed up properly.

With a hammer and two large nails he crucified Brannigan one last time. Blood rolled down from the palms of his hands in long red lines along the flaky, light-blue door of the boathouse. There was no sound of pain, just Brannigan looking like a monk and a martyr, bowing his head all the time under the black plastic hood.

Fuckin' mouth, Chief said as though he was speaking for Drummer. As though the silence was too much and something had to be said in the presence of such violence. He won't fucking talk again, that's for sure. The next time he'll talk is when he's begging to be let into the big night-club in the sky.

Drummer laughed but said nothing.

The words were surplus. They stood back and watched the bag moving in and out. Chief looking at Drummer and waiting to see if he should take the bag off again. But Drummer remained silent. The victim's hooded head sank forward and the breathing stopped. Then they left.

Brannigan's body was found early in the morning. The Special Branch were all over the beach, combing the sand for clues, erecting Garda crime-scene tape to keep possible onlookers away from the location of the murder. The discovery had been made by a group of early-morning pony trekkers. A woman had to be sedated on account of the shock.

Superintendent Molloy was pacing up and down, knowing that he had not only lost a valuable witness but that he was also, in a way, responsible for it. His personal war with the Drummer gang had come to a pitch. An incident room had already been set up at his own station at Irishtown. They were following a definite line of enquiry, they announced, but that was all bullshit. What they really needed was somebody tough like Coyne. Somebody who would sort out Drummer and his followers once and for all. People like Molloy and the Special Branch would be too scared even to put a parking ticket on his car, for fucksake.

Coyne played with the children after breakfast, letting them jump down from tables and cupboards, catching them in his arms all morning. It was like bungee jumping for kids. Nuala was absolutely fearless. Threw herself off any surface down into the safety of Coyne's embrace. They all trusted him, but Nuala went a step further and liked to throw herself backwards, with her eyes closed.

Carmel didn't like it. To her, the game was childish and dangerous. She was afraid they would throw themselves off somewhere when he was not there.

He's teaching them to commit suicide, was Mrs Gogarty's attitude.

But Coyne urged his kids to go higher and higher, to find new peaks of fearlessness, and to hurl themselves off the roof of the car, right in front of the neighbours. Carmel inside trying to draw her mother, who was looking out through the window and shaking her head all the time with shock and horror.

He's showing them how to kill themselves. That little grimace around her nose as though she was constantly caught fighting back a bad smell.

You're such a headbanger, Pat, Carmel said when he finally stopped and came inside. Why don't you build them a swing instead. That would be useful. More normal too.

You call that useful, Coyne responded, looking at the half-finished painting of Mrs Gogarty looking all flushed and red in the face, like she was asphyxiating.

Coyne went into the kitchen. Underneath that instant surge of aggression, he reflected on his role as a father. Felt that he'd failed his kids. Of course they should have a

32

swing. It wasn't a lot to ask for, and maybe he was desensit-
izing them to feelings of fear with his games. They were
deprived kids and he vowed he would build the swing. A
really good one. But he wasn't going to do it on orders
from Carmel. He wasn't going to do it for Mrs Gogarty,
the voice of righteousness. No way. So he sat in the kitchen
and stared with contempt at the pictures of Chagall and
all the others on the wall.

Shag off, Chagall, he muttered.

Maybe it was the way Coyne was brought up. Maybe it
was the passionate severity of his father that made him the
way he was. His father had come to Dublin from West
Cork to claim his part in the making of a new Ireland. An
Irish, Catholic Ireland. With his job in the Civil Service,
Coyne's father began to involve his family in a personal
crusade for the language. He would shape the new Ireland
through his own kids, turning them into native Irish
speakers. Making them speak Irish on the buses, like aliens
in their own land. Coyne could see that his father was
right, but too late. By the time Coyne was growing up,
rock 'n' roll had already taken a grip of his intellect. The
Irish language could never work in neon. It was unsuited
to the electric guitar. Unsuited to commerce. It was like
jumping off the roofs of cars.

Coyne was sent to the Gaeltacht in Connemara at the
age of nine where he learned how to smoke. The old
woman in the house gave him Sweet Afton for his sweet
asthma. *Puffail siar air sin*, she said. That will make you
cough it up, and it took him twenty years to give it up
again. He could still hear the song of her voice calling out
on the wind, the chickens proclaiming newly laid eggs, and
the sound of enamel buckets, slopping with milk. Coyne
loved Irish Ireland, the warmth and non-judgemental

33

nobility of the west. At Colaiste Mhuire, the all-Irish secondary school where Coyne was educated in the city centre, the Christian Brother idea of education was nothing but decolonization, lash by lash. The panic of a young nation. They had nothing in common with the Blasket Islanders, or the famine cottages of West Cork.

Now it was Coyne's turn to shape the nation. Only that it was changing again and all the old historical landmarks would be eclipsed by new outrageous shrines of crime. As a Garda, he saw it all coming. Murder at the Rock of Cashel. Armed robbery in Enniscorthy. A paedophile priest at a summer camp in Glendalough. The old Yeats poem, 'Come away, Oh human child . . .', took on a whole new meaning. The sacred places of Irish history defiled by new atrocities. And now it was murder in Brittas. Crime was the nation's biggest growth industry.

Back in the squad car that afternoon, Coyne was casually telling McGuinness what he had read in one of his nature magazines the night before. They were crossing back over the toll-bridge at the time. The green river backing up into the city, bridge by bridge.

Come 'ere, Larry. You know something I found out about scorpions last night.

What?

You know they have a sting in the tail and all that.

Yeah!

Well that's not all they have. Did you know they have a disposable penis?

McGuinness laughed. But Coyne remained serious, looking for some sense in his own words, some new allegory he could pin on to his fellow humans.

I'm not joking you, Larry. One shot. Then they grow a new one.

Coming back into Ringsend, they passed by a convoy of police vehicles. In the back of one of them sat Drummer Cunningham, who was being taken in for questioning. Molloy sat in another vehicle waiting to extract a confession from his man. But Berti Cunningham had a special grin on his face as though he was enjoying the journey. Behaved like somebody on a state visit.

Somebody should impale that fucker, Coyne remarked.

He's the real Teflon criminal, McGuinness responded with the usual lethargy. No evidence will ever stick to him.

I wish his mickey would fall off, Coyne said, waiting for his turn to deal with Drummer.

But Coyne's life revolved instead around petty crime and they were soon called to the scene of a mugging, where an old woman stood bewildered at the side of the street, outside some shops, holding a strap in her hand.

I seen them do it, a bystander kept saying, as Coyne got out of the squad car and went over to them. I seen her holding on, the poor thing. Dragged her along the pavement so they did.

It was this kind of situation that Coyne had to deal with. Some junkie out of his mind taking the price of a fix off an old woman and nearly putting her into the grave in the process. There she was, lost and shocked, just passing the strap of her bag along in her hand like a set of rosary beads. Shaking and crying.

We'll run her up to the cemetery, McGuinness said, and they led her gently towards the car. Drove up along the canal to see if there were any new bags floating along the surface. Then stopped at a place under a railway bridge which they called the handbag graveyard. A place full of handbags and other rubbish. They brought the old woman out to see if she could identify her own.

What colour was your handbag, Mam?

Tomorrow, she answered.

What colour, Coyne tried again.

Wednesday, she said. My appointment is Wednesday, isn't it?

Animals, Coyne muttered to McGuinness.

Come on, we'll take you home, he said, leading the old woman back to the car. And as he placed her in the back seat, Coyne began to think of his own mother. He should review the security arrangements before anything could happen to her.

Coyne saw it all. He saw the pigeons pecking at dried vomit and discarded chips. He saw the victims, culprits – the lucky and the unlucky. Coyne could tell you more about the nature of society than anyone else. The kids sleeping rough. Boys for sale. It was difficult not to be whipped by compassion. But that was Moleshaver Molloy's golden rule to all Gardai – you couldn't allow it to get to you. Never entertain your emotions.

Coyne had witnessed everything. The amount of people he brought to Focus Point; women with their entire families on the move in the middle of the night. Whole families of junkies. Beatings, muggings, suicides. Shopkeepers held up with syringes. The distress of a woman after rape. They dragged a man in his pyjamas out of the canal one night. Found a well-known politician in a car with a young boy. Once helped to contain a riot near the British Embassy. Yobbos. Paedophiles. Alcoholics going downhill year by year. Rich kids acting the fool as though they owned the city. And the endless succession of car crimes. Road accidents.

Coyne saw the filth and the funny side of the city. In broad daylight, he once had to restrain an old traveller woman standing in the middle of a busy intersection with an oar, beating the cars and buses as they went by. A boy who had accidentally shot an arrow into his mother's neck. A burglary where the criminal called the Gardai to save him from a snake. A car parked suspiciously, only to reveal a woman's naked arse in the windscreen. And all of this had to be interpreted for the larger public audience. Each incident had to be put in official words, for the records, and for the press. Gardai at Irishtown received reports of a man interfering with himself on the canal bank. Drunk and disorderly youth, barking at the punters in Shelbourne Park. There was a lot of repetition. Lots that Coyne didn't even remember offhand. Or care to. The foreign tabloids across the water frequently had more spectacular stories, but this was Dublin. And Dublin had everything. He tried not to make a political judgement. He had his own ideas on how the society should be run, but he was only concerned with justice and fair play. Coyne's Justice.

Mick Cunningham was arrested in the snooker hall. When members of the Special Crime Squad walked up to table number five, he looked around and said: Wait till I take this shot. The Gardai ran and lunged forward to prevent him potting the last red. Under interrogation, he got them back, however, by making total fools of them. One detective after another went in to listen to Mick talk like a cross between an garrulous DJ and a pro-life spokesperson, droning on in a kind of pseudo-legal gibberish, The term 'You have the right to remain silent' took on an entirely different meaning. We beg you to remain silent and stop fucking going on about article this and article that of the constitution.

Chief was arrested at his home. He was sitting there with a two-day stubble on his face, trying to get his girl-friend's cat drunk. Devising new sources of delicious cat food that could be marinated in alcohol to deceive the suspicious animal. But the feline hangover must have rated among the world's worst. And when Chief answered the door to two detectives in plain clothes, the cat made a dash for it.

Drummer Cunningham and his gang were finally sitting in various interview rooms at Irishtown Garda station. Drummer surrounded by Superintendent Molloy and top members of a special unit that had been set up to deal with this case alone. In the yard of another station, the Range Rover was being examined carefully by forensic experts, sweeping little bits of dust and sand particles into plastic bags. Moleshaver Molloy, with his jacket off, was there leading the enquiry, asking lots of questions and getting no answers. Like his brother and understudy, Mick, Drummer put into effect his strict policy of obfuscation, saying something utterly daft back to them – something domestic, something philosophical that would demonstrate clearly what a waste of time it was. Then Molloy would start all over again.

OK, Cunningham. That's all very interesting, but let me ask you a simple question. You filled the Range Rover with petrol in the afternoon. Next morning it's empty. That's a lot of mileage, Drummer. Can you explain that?

You went for a drive, isn't that so? one of the other detectives added. A midnight beach party maybe.

Who was with you, Berti?

But Drummer just smiled. You could see that it was all very amusing to him. They were trying to get into the select VIP lounge at the back of his head again, so he just stared at the wall.

Gentlemen, is all he would say. Because even trivial answers would help them. He rarely gratified them with anything. It was only when Superintendent Molloy seemed to lose his temper and start shouting the same question at him again and again that Berti Cunningham decided it was time to give them something.

All right. I'm going to tell you something. Just to keep yous happy.

Cunningham began to talk to them about his new night-club, offering invitations to the stunned detectives. They had to hold themselves back. And secretly, they were also curious, as though there might be some hidden clue for which they dutifully had to listen.

My club, Drummer said. Opening up next weekend. Bring the missus.

Molloy glared back. Refused to entertain the joke and remained serious. In order not to lose face, he immediately lashed back with another question. A crucial one that would get Drummer worried. Looked like he was going to beat the living daylights out of him. Came right up close to him, breathing mint and black pudding breath over his face, staring straight into the whites of his eyes and speaking in a quiet, eerie tone of voice.

What's the sand doing all over your car, Cunningham?

Drummer seemed to be caught out by the question. He was smiling with pride, and suddenly went serious. Looked up with a kind of new-born innocence and came up with the most straightforward answer.

The dogs, he said. I walk the dogs on the beach every day. They need the exercise.

Coyne was on duty that night. There was hardly any action except the usual complaints: dogs barking and drunk driving. A youth pissing against the railings of the American Embassy; somebody puking right up against the window of Pizza Hut, like an action replay for the diners inside; break-ins, car thefts and loads of domestic stuff. It was not until the early hours of the morning, just before they went off duty, that they received an unusual call. A girl on the railway line. Tight-rope walking along the tracks in some kind of death-wish. With the first DART due any minute, she was impervious, treading along one of the silver rails in her bare feet like some angel of commuter despair.

Coyne parked at the level crossing. And while McGuinness stayed with the car, he ran down along the sleepers, behind the terraces of the Lansdowne Road grounds. Coyne had begun to see certain moments like this in sharp relief, like a symbol of what had become of his life, running along the railway line wheezing. This is where he had ended up, his friend Vinnie Foley would say.

He shouted but the girl didn't hear him. When he got closer, he discovered that she was humming, or moaning. She wore starry purple shorts and a loose belly top, holding her shoes in her hand. Some young one dancing as though she had lost control of her intellect altogether.

What are you trying to do, kill yourself, he shouted.

A glazed blue trance occupied her eyes and she was shivering, mouthing a frantic, silent refrain that reminded Coyne of Lady Macbeth. Fucked-up on smack or something. He then realized that she was trying to top herself.

What's wrong, love. Why don't you come with us. Everything will be all right.

He took hold of her bare arm, feeling the soft, creamy white flesh in his hand. He was miles away from the squad car and had to walk her all the way back along the line. She didn't even realize that he was guiding her, she was so stoned out of her mind. Trembling with the chemical imbalance in her blood. Deeply unhappy, stopping every now and again to fret and clutch her shoes to her chest.

Not far to go now, love, Coyne said, coaxing her along

like a father bringing a child to the bathroom in the middle of the night. But then she suddenly pulled away and ran towards some railway huts. He followed her, calling after her until she stopped in the shadow of one of the huts. And when he moved towards her, she pulled up her jumper exposing her breasts to him. He stalled a moment to look at them. The nipples and their dark aureoles were staring at him. Challenging him. Women like that gave him a fundamental feeling of inadequacy, because he felt a duty to go after them. It brought out all the hard man talk at the back of his mind. I'd love to drink your bathwater, missus. *Suas do Guna, Una.* She lunged forward to embrace him, kissing and crying at the same time, trying to make him place his hand on one of her breasts. But Coyne jumped back.

Pull yourself together, he said almost to himself as much as to her. He drew her top back down again.

What's your name?

Naomi, she said in a melancholy voice, as though to indicate that he was another failure.

Well look, Naomi. We've got to go home now. Come on.

Lights were coming on in the nearby houses. Silhouettes in bathrooms. Kettles boiling in kitchens with built-in pine cupboards. You could see right down into the houses, and through one window he saw a duvet pulled back on a bed. Somewhere else just a naked bulb lighting up a bare room. Dawn seeping across the city like a great sadness. It crept along the railway line, all the way from Wexford, emptying out a steady blue-white flood of solitude on to the dewy sleepers. Dublin-lonely. The night was dying and a blanket of cold reality claimed back the illusion, bit by bit, reaching in under bridges, along the empty streets and down the long narrow gardens below. Dogs were barking somewhere. Soon there would be people everywhere.

He had brought junkies to the methadone dispensary before, but this was like his own daughter. When he got back to the squad car, he opened the rear door and placed her in the back seat.

Jesus – she's like Madonna on oysters and Guinness, he whispered to his colleague.

By morning, Moleshaver Molloy had been forced to release the Cunningham gang. There was no evidence, nothing they could pin on them. Drummer emerged from the Garda station triumphant, shaking hands with his solicitor, thanking the forensic experts for cleaning all the sand out of his Range Rover.

Coyne was there to see Mick Cunningham and Chief being released some time later. Made the Gardai look like a whole bunch of flowerpots. The law was an asshole. And on the way home, Coyne dropped in on Fred Metcalf, his older, ex-Garda friend who now worked as a security guard at premises in Dublin Port. Fred kept saying it was time to get tough. Somebody was going to have to get dirty. Rules had to be broken.

What do you expect, Pat. Criminals have taken on designer status. No question about it. It's Kilkenny Design. Look at this place here. Gurriers coming in here every night to see what they can rob or smash up. It's the dogs of illusion, Pat.

The dogs of illusion, Coyne said, puzzled.

Fred had guru qualities. He knew the city like the back of his hand. He was an encyclopaedia on crime and Dublin anthropology. Knew the background circumstances on every court case and every personality involved. Fred had taken early retirement from the force, though Coyne never found out why. There were various excuses, but it was too late to ask. And Coyne was his protégé, in a sense; destined to succeed where Fred had failed.

It was to Fred Metcalf that Coyne looked for real guidance. With his grey moustache and his slow, deliberate movements, he provided great encouragement. Coyne admired the way Fred could follow a line of enquiry by simply going in and talking to local newsagents, butchers, car mechanics. He just talked for no reason about the weather, football, the government; anything that could sustain a subtle little question here and there about the local suspects. Fred was a natural born local, no matter where he went.

Whenever Coyne tried make some of his own discreet investigations, the result was always uneven; either he got on too well and revealed more about himself than he gathered, or else the conversation got stuck on the weather. An old woman in the local shop just going on about the wind, saying it was penetrating, and Coyne just walking off thinking about the choice of word: penetrating.

Fred was such a talented investigator, he could only have been hounded out of the Gardai by some injustice. Lack of promotion perhaps. Fred had a way of being invisible. A good listener who offered little titbits as bait. The great Irish trade of information – give a little, take a little. Somebody's always dying to talk, he'd say. Fred and Coyne had already built up quite a dossier on many of the top criminals.

How's Carmel? Fred asked over tea and Kerry Cream biscuits.

She's gone mad on this art business, Coyne replied.

Fred also played a role in Coyne's moral and intellectual well-being. Liked to listen to Coyne talking about his kids. Took an interest in Carmel's latest craze.

Won't last, Fred pronounced. I can tell you that straight off.

That reflexology thing lasted long enough, Coyne insisted. I'm telling you, Fred: she's gone nuts about this painting business. She's at it all the time now. Day and night. All over the kitchen she's got this calendar of Chagall, or whatever his shaggin' name is.

Won't last. There's too many at it. All that self-expression lark. There's too much expression and too little understanding, Fred thought.

Not Carmel. She's hooked.

Have you thought of taking her away? Fred asked.

Away?

Coyne considered it. Since when had they been away together like a couple, without their kids? In fact, Coyne was afraid of that. Afraid in a way that they would have to face each other, some kind of imaginary family court where everything would come up in evidence between them. He was afraid of the honesty of a weekend trip with Carmel.

Think about it. A weekend in the west. Be good for you, Fred said.

Inevitably, however, the conversation would return to crime. And as Coyne accompanied his mentor on his tour of the compound, shining his torch under parked trucks, lighting up the deadly shadows behind containers and checking the razor-wire-topped walls of his fortress, Fred came up with a theory.

Will I tell you what's causing all this crime, Pat?

What?

Cars! That's what. The private car is what's doing it. You see, all that privacy is no good for people. Alienates everybody. Makes them unfriendly. A sick society. There should be no such thing as private cars.

We'd be walking around in the rain otherwise, Coyne remarked.

What's wrong with taxis? There should be nothing but taxis and trains. Far more sociable. It would give people things to do. And reduce the crime. A nation of taxi drivers and delivery men.

And squad cars, Coyne added.

It's the dogs of illusion, Pat.

Drummer Cunningham was a man of few words. Within hours of his release he was walking around his new night-club on Leeson Street as though nothing had happened. He wasn't even being triumphant, or celebrating his release like a primitive criminal. He just got on with his business and nodded quietly as the builder, Brendan Barry, explained how they would be finished in a day or two.

We're just putting in the spots, then we're ready to roll.

Rock 'n' Roll, Drummer echoed.

The workers were busy carrying out the last-minute renovations. A DJ was already trying out the new sound system and two Go-Go dancers were shifting around on the dance floor with mechanical movements.

Chief was there too, looking busy with a little pocket calculator. And Mick Cunningham leaning up against the new oval-shaped bar. Drummer looked a little concerned as he stood back and squinted at the dance floor. Liked everything to be dead on. Felt he knew something about architecture since he had a former student of architecture as a girl-friend. With his new-found talent for interior design he gave the builder some minimal instructions. Then started looking around in a suspicious way as though something was wrong.

There's something missing here, he said, and Builder Brendan instantly became a ball of nerves.

What, Berti? There's nothing missing.

Something isn't right here, Cunningham insisted.

I swear. There's nothing gone out of here, boss. You can search us.

No, I don't mean missing, Drummer said. I mean, there should be something else here, like a fountain.

A fountain? The builder smiled with relief.

Yeah. A fountain would be nice.

Where?

There, you know, Berti said, waving his hands in the general direction of the dance floor and then moving on to inspect the lights and the mirrors, leaving the builder to ponder the sheer lunacy of erecting a fountain at such short notice. A fountain would require a water supply. That meant pipework, ripping up the floor again; a nightmare. And while Drummer was walking towards the DJ, Chief whispered discreetly into the builder's ear.

Put in a fuckin' fountain, he commanded. I don't care where you get it. I want to see a bleedin' fountain there by tomorrow.

Some days later, Coyne found an opportunity to deal directly with the Cunninghams. Just to let them know that even if the Special Branch had given up on them, the whole business with Brannigan wasn't over yet. They hadn't come across Coyne yet. Be afraid, was the message he was trying to get across.

Coming around the corner towards the canal at Percy Place, Mick Cunningham drove the Range Rover through the city, showing the world and his mother what an excellent driver he was. Should have been a stunt man, doing wheelies maybe. Except that Coyne happened to be driving the squad car from the other direction. A conversation with McGuinness about why he didn't go to the cinema had to be postponed. Coyne felt there was far too much escapism. The streets of Dublin were like one big movie anyway, something that was borne out like an instant illustration by Mick Cunningham, lashing around the corner at high speed.

Coyne was just in time to switch on the blue light and pull out to stop the oncoming car. Got out and discovered he had stopped Mr Big Time's brother Mick. Should have known not to proceed any further because it was a sensitive case. But Coyne was beginning to see it as his own personal crusade, a kind of tacit competition with Moleshaver Molloy to see who would put these boys behind bars first. The Cunning brothers, he called them.

Out, he shouted, McGuinness standing right behind him with a torch.

Mick Cunningham was the calmest person you could ever meet on a dark night. Thought he was being arrested again, so he didn't put up any struggle. He was like the Pope, waving his hands up and down in slow motion like a wind-up doll. Wearing his reversed baseball cap, and bomber jacket with a mobile phone in the pocket. Clean shaven, number one haircut, with highlights. Coyne was staring into Mick Cunningham's eyes, just to make him understand who was who around here. The air laden with silent aggression.

You think you can get away with the Brannigan murder, Coyne said. Well, wait till you start dealing with me.

Coyne lifted up his baton as though he was going to beat Mick Cunningham to a pulp in the street. McGuinness anxiously shifting around in the background, hoping this would go off peacefully.

You can't touch me, Mick Cunningham said.

That's what you think, Coyne said, instinctively throwing Cunningham up against the car, showing him the baton.

47

Have you ever shat one of these before?

You'll have to ask my solicitor, was Cunningham's slick reply.

Coyne laughed. McGuinness coughed in the background as though he wanted to pass on some urgent message to Coyne but was afraid to interrupt.

Are you in the VHI? Coyne asked, holding Cunningham by the throat. The voluntary health?

He got no answer, just a stunned look. Coyne released his grip and turned away, satisfied that he had delivered his message. He knew he had gone too far. It was not the right time yet. That day would come soon. But Cunningham was even more amazed that he was being let go. Looked at Coyne with great surprise.

You better be in the VHI when I deal with you, you *glick* bastard. Plan fucking D.

Coyne began to walk back towards the squad car. He turned again at the last minute to add a final warning, pointing his baton at Cunningham once more.

'Cause, I'm going to get medieval on your arse, boy.

Back in the squad car, McGuinness was uneasy about the incident.

Take it easy, Pat. You're shittin' yourself.

But Coyne was still furious, as though everything had broken loose inside him. He was all over the place. These Cunningham brothers had it coming. Coyne's Justice was on the way.

That was mild, Larry. They're going to get it. They'll wish they were born scorpions.

I don't like it. We've nothing on Mick Cunningham. It's not our case.

You have to connect the shite back to the arsehole it came from, Coyne announced.

But McGuinness was starting to act the psychologist, telling Coyne he should relax. Had he ever thought of taking up golf.

Piss off, Larry. Golf is for emotionally disturbed whackoes.

Even before the shift was over, Superintendent Molloy sent out a message over the radio asking Coyne to come back to base. Molloy was hopping.

For Jesussake, Coyne. What are you up to? he barked. Threatening a suspect in the middle of a murder enquiry.

I was keeping an eye on him, Coyne offered.

Keeping an eye on him? Do you fancy him or something.

Molloy looked like he was going to start foaming at the mouth like a wounded horse. Yellow teeth all biting the dust. He was squinting up as though he was going through a particularly difficult gastric experience. Mouth curled up into an O of incomprehension. His hair-flap all out of place.

Look, Coyne. You lay off these guys. Ignore them. They don't exist. Are you watching too much of feckin' television or something? You're a plain and simple Garda on the beat, no more. This is Special Branch stuff, stay out of it. Got that?

Yes, Coyne agreed.

Molloy was staring up at him as though he'd had his stomach lanced by a pike, horse intestines spilled out all over the place. Moleshaver Molloy crawling away from the agony of his own bowels.

What the hell has got into you, Pat? Relax. You should take up golf. It would calm you down a bit.

Coyne stared back with great indignation. Golf? Coming from Moleshaver, that was a good one. You think you can solve Dublin's crime with golf. Coyne was no ordinary cop.

49

They would see. Coyne's Justice was coming. He had nailed down some of these bastards and was keeping an open mind on a lot more. He had solved a few minor mysteries and put a certain Brian Quinn behind bars. And Sergeant Moran had become the station's best-known alcoholic, leaving Coyne directly in line for promotion. All he needed was one big case. One big crap which he could bring back in a plastic evidence bag and put on Superintendent Molloy's desk.

Coyne's Justice referred to an incident at school. A concept of fair play that wasn't without regret, as though justice was always accompanied by a certain guilt and compassion for those who were condemned. Even as a child, Coyne had wondered about the cruelty of Divine justice. I mean, how the fuck could God get away with burning people for ever. Bet there were a whole load of innocent people in hell too, people stitched up on spurious confessions. Coyne knew all about the innocents. And Coyne's Justice referred to Brother O Maolbheannaigh, and his little dog Bran, who came to a bad end on behalf of his master. O Maolbheannaigh's innocent little terrier took the rap for all the beatings dished out to the pupils over the years in school.

Every Wednesday, Coyne went out to the playing fields along the Liffey in Chapelizod for hurling. Next to the Garda rowing club as it happened. Health of body, purity of mind. There was no way out of it. Hurling was compulsory, even if you were an utter gobshite with no sense of direction, wielding the hurling stick like a sword or a *Claimh Solais* around your head as though you were after a wasp. The fastest game in the world. The first time Coyne ever tried to hit a ball he nearly decapitated Proinsias De Barra, otherwise known as 'Spunk', with an almighty blow to the back of the head.

O Maolbheannaigh was always there on Wednesdays, extolling the virtues of the air. Seagulls everywhere, waiting for a new delivery at the dump on the far side of the river. Flocks of them milling and screeching as the bulldozer turned over the city's rubbish for them. And the playing fields were usually covered in sheepshite. The Brothers let out the fields to a sheep farmer through the week, and on Wednesdays the lads were lifting *sliotars* of dried black dung and whacking them into the air. Boys stuffing great lumps of it into each other's nicks, forcing each other's faces down on to the grass to eat it. Oh you boyo. Flying sheepshite everywhere until O Maolbheannaigh came out with the real ball and his little dog, Bran. Sometimes he would send some of the goodie boys down to get a bar of Aero for the dog.

There was always a smell too, Coyne remembered. From the river. From the dump. From the Guinness brewery. A mixture of rot and ferment drifting across the playing fields, like O Maolbheannaigh's breath, shouting at everyone all the time: Go, boy. Go, you moke, or else I'll take a big *sceilp* out of you with my bare hands. It was never clear whether the players were inspired by the ball or by the fear of O Maolbheannaigh, who sometimes chased after a player and gave him a clout for not doing what Christy Ring or Jack Lynch would have done. He treated the little leather *sliotar* like a museum piece, holding it up in the air as though it was the one used on the grassy slopes of ancient Ireland by the fucking Fianna.

And one day, Coyne's Justice took over. Coyne took his revenge for all the casual beatings that O Maolbheannaigh had given out. Struck a blow back on behalf of his friends and all the other pupils. He got O Maolbheannaigh's dog. Bran was always there on the sidelines, looking for rats, everybody dying to use him as a *sliotar*. Coyne could not

51

recall ever hitting the ball, except for one day when he was required to take a seventy-yard puck. Ten minutes whacking the clear daylight with the stick until O Maolbheannaigh came over and said: Right, me bucko. In fear, Coyne attempted one last time, throwing the ball up gently and finally making contact, sending it into infinity like a legendary puck from the Ulster Cycle. The impact of the ball shuddering back through the ash and stinging his fingers, all the way back through his arms, down to his groin. The ball went sailing out over the perimeter fence towards the river and O Maolbheannaigh instantly rained clouts and punches.

You clod, O Maolbheannaigh shouted, giving Coyne an almighty kick in the arse that almost sent him over the perimeter fence as well.

They carried on with a tattered back-up *sliotar* while Coyne searched in the reeds and bushes along the banks of the Liffey. Bran searching too, and before he knew it, the dog was somersaulting through the air down into the green water. Bran surfaced and tried to swim, even though the chocolate was holding him back. He got to the shore, but Coyne was there throwing stones at him, pushing him back out again with his hurley, running along the bank to make sure. And then Bran started going down, Coyne watching from the side, feeling a new sense of compassion for the innocent dog. Maybe for O Maolbheannaigh too, who was going to be the loneliest bastard in Ireland without his partner. Coyne felt awful. Tried to rescue the dog, wading out into the muddy water and almost drowning himself, but it was too late and the limp, upturned corpse floated down the river, mouth open, teeth bared in the agony of defeat. Coyne's Justice.

Carmel was sitting up in bed sketching, the noise of the

pencil on the paper scratching at Coyne's brain. He stood by the window, looking out over the gardens, and saw Mr Gillespie next door playing golf in darkness. There was only the light from the kitchen illuminating the tiny garden in which the neighbour was swinging his iron. Each swish followed by a small pock of the plastic golf ball against the back wall.

Gillespie, you're a sad case altogether. What's this, the Irish Open or something? You wanker. Who do think you are, Bernard Langer?

Carmel continued sketching. The time on the digital clock was 12:12. It always came back to those even numbers again and Coyne thought he was going mad, surrounded by all the tiny signals of suburban melancholia. Swish, pock, scratch, flush is what his life amounted to. It was at moments like this that Coyne became aware how trapped you could be by noise. The trademarks of his home. It was this shaggin' art business. She was as bad as the nocturnal golfer next door. Every night she sat up in bed with her sketch pad, scratching away like a chicken while Coyne drifted off into sleep. Fruit bowls, baskets of flowers, trees, children's faces – the whole house was already infested with drawings. Everything had to be recorded in art as though it was in danger of evaporating. And how many times in the past month had Coyne heard her repeat the story about Matisse, how Matisse could not afford to eat the fruit he painted. How he would work away in a cold studio because he was afraid the heat would make the fruit go bad. Again he saw Mr Gillespie placing the plastic golf ball on the grass and shuffling up, getting ready to tee off in his little suburban dog pound of a garden.

Everybody's gone golf mad, Coyne muttered, and Carmel ignored him because she had just had a brilliant idea.

53

Pat, why don't you let me paint you?

Give me a break, Carmel.

Please, Pat. As a special favour?

What, like this? He almost conceded. He was standing in his boxer shorts and a vest.

No, silly.

You mean in my uniform.

No, Pat. In your nude. With no clothes on.

No way, Coyne retorted immediately, turning around towards her. She could put that out of her head immediately. No way was he going to become part of this running archive in art. He wouldn't be trapped on canvas. And certainly not in the nude. Whatever about living in reality, he was sure as hell not going to allow himself to be immortalized in fucking art.

And you better give up those ideas, Carmel. You've gone far enough. This art business has gone to your head, love.

The art teacher, Gordon Sitwell, said Carmel was very good. Week by week he watched her making great progress.

You're coming on very nicely, Carmel. I think you've got real talent.

At the end of the class, when most of the other students had already drifted on home and Carmel was gathering up her materials, Sitwell leaned on a table and said he had been meaning to talk to her.

I'm impressed with your work.

Thanks, she said. But she wasn't going to allow herself to be flattered too much. She was a married woman with three children, afraid of letting the whole art thing get out of perspective.

And you're not getting quite so much paint on your nose any more, he joked. Carmel instinctively ran the back of her hand over her nose to check.

54

Only joking, Sitwell said. I seriously think you've got what it takes. Look at the skies you paint. They're really quite . . . visceral.

I've never really done this kind of thing seriously before, she said. Only with the children at home. You know, crayons and stuff.

Sitwell was disappointed. Didn't like her downgrading her own talent like that. Wanted his students to think big. To let go of all the emotional domestic traps that held her back from real self-expression.

You speak the language of colour, he said. I run a workshop from time to time. Only for the really talented, mind you. I think you would be good on portraits and human form.

A workshop, Carmel stammered.

Think it over. I think you could make a career of it.

Oh no, Mr Sitwell. It's only for pleasure.

Maybe they were right. Coyne needed a break. Over the next few weeks he tried to take things easy. Tried to get closer to his family. He wanted to get back to basics with them. He got a call from one of his old drinking companions, Vinnie Foley, but he put the binge on the long finger. Most of Coyne's friends had disappeared or moved out of reach somehow. He went for pints occasionally, but he was more inclined to devote his life to his work and his family. Vinnie Foley was an advertising executive now. Look where we've all ended up, Vinnie would say before he went on his own public relations monologue. And you couldn't talk to somebody who was constantly reviewing life like it was a comparative study.

Coyne had too much to do. He had to look after his mother, who lived on the outskirts of the city. Make sure she was safe. His sister was in England. His brother Jim lived down the country, so it was up to Coyne to protect her. He drove out there to erect wire grids on the downstairs windows at the back of the house. He had the sudden feeling that his mother was in great danger and prone to attack. She stayed indoors all the time now, just watching TV. He put a massive, ugly bolt on the back door and felt better after that. It eased his conscience as he walked away from his old home with the feeling that he had left his mother locked in safely behind him, like the *Sean Bhean Bhocht* – the old woman of Ireland besieged and incarcerated by wire grids of immobility.

Coyne felt he was on top of things. He achieved moments of deep intimacy with his family. One day, he just told everyone to get into the car. He was going to buy them all chips. Jennifer and Nuala giggling in the back of the Escort, touching tongues until Carmel told them it was disgusting. The local chipper was closed, so Coyne just drove on as though he was going to drive for ever.

Left or right, he said at each junction, and they all said different things until they eventually arrived far away in Bray, at the amusement arcade on the seafront. They bought chips and went on the dodgems. Carmel and Jennifer versus Coyne and Nuala. Jimmy in a car of his own. There was nobody else around and they had the whole place to themselves. Jimmy drove in a figure of eight, looking up at the sparks on the electric cage, colliding with everyone. Nuala's bag of chips hopping up in the air out of her hand, making her cry. Flattened chips all over the dodgem track. Carmel laughing like she'd never laughed before, head jolting back, hair bouncing up around her head like she was in some shampoo ad.

For once, Coyne heard nothing but the sound around him of the dodgems and the video machines and the camel race. No inner voices telling him to carry out some impossible goal. He smiled at the woman in a cardigan inside the glass office with the towers of tenpenny coins. The sound of a pop song was hanging over everything like a soft duvet, eliminating the past as well as the future, pinpointing just one feeling of warmth, love and utter joy. *Can't live, if livin' is without you – Can't live, can't live any more.* Coyne had lost consciousness. He was entertaining his emotions, afflicted by a great longing to be swallowed up in this comic bubble of happiness for ever.

Then they moved on to play the Tin Can Alley, where the whole family threw coloured balls into a red dustbin from which a woolly cat peeked out every few seconds. Coyne with all the remaining chips stuffed in his jacket pocket, lifting up handfulls of balls to bring the score up so that they would win a free game and be able to stay there for ever, game after game. Jimmy like his dad, serious and determined. Jennifer and Nuala throwing one ball every minute between them. And Carmel just leaning on the rail in weakness, unable to breathe with the pain of laughter.

Do you want to go away? he said to her that evening when they got home again. He had eventually built up the courage to ask her, and she looked up to see what he was getting at. What possessed him?

Away to the west. A break. Just the two of us.

Like lovers? She laughed.

An autumn break, like. I just thought we should try and get away together more often.

Out to the west. Brilliant, she said.

Carmel had already begun to imagine the trip as a great art excursion, giving her a chance to do some outdoor work. Mountains, coastline, bogs; provided it wasn't raining. He let her make all the plans. She phoned up the tourist board looking for a cheap hotel. Bought an easel so she could stand and paint the sun going down over Galway Bay.

And so they were off. Late one Friday morning, Mrs Gogarty waved goodbye from the door as Carmel and Pat drove away. The children had been bribed with sweets and promises of new toys. The last beep of the horn seemed so final.

They drove through Ireland with the blues on the car stereo. It was the first time in ages that Coyne and Carmel had actually listened to music together. My God, why hadn't they thought of doing this before? How green everything was. They had been out of touch with nature. Carmel thought she was looking at cardboard cut-out cows. All the familiar landmarks from the hitch-hiking days – Newland's Cross, Newbridge, Kinnegad. They were heading west, into the sun. Subliminal blue flashes of the Atlantic already appearing in their minds like holograms of past journeys. They stopped for lunch in Athlone and on the last part of the journey Carmel changed into a teenager. Sang along with the songs on the car radio, giggling. It was as though the glass of wine at lunch had gone to her head and she tried to dance in the front seat, moving her shoulders; embarrassingly happy; happy beyond any of her wildest dreams.

At the hotel in Galway, the receptionist apologized for the renovations. There was dust all over the place and dirty footprints of workmen on the carpets where the plastic sheeting had shifted. Walls had been broken through in some places. In others, new plasterboard walls had gone up. But the bar was still in business as usual. The dining-room had a massive sheet of plyboard over the window holding out the wind.

They were led through a maze of corridors and little steps going up, down, then back up again into an extension

58

which was not finished. In some places, the roof had not even gone up yet. Smell of paint and bitumen everywhere. Men hammering and whistling all around. A sign in the hallway apologized for the inconvenience on behalf of the management. Right beside it, an attempt to restore the sense of hospitality with a gilded print of a child playing with a kitten. All covered in dust. At the end of the corridor, they were shown into a room overlooking the Corrib river. The smell of fresh paint was intoxicating and a new picture of horses galloping through canyons at night hung on the wall. The bathroom was all in pink. And Coyne's Garda obsession with time noticed that the ever-present digital clock stood at 4:44. Enjoy your stay.

It's a shagging building site, Carmel.

It doesn't matter, Pat. We got twenty-five per cent off.

Carmel threw herself across the bed. There were men passing by the window, clanking down the steel emergency staircase outside in their boots. Coyne closed the curtains and threw the room into a tropical yellow and green forest interior. The duvet had apple blossoms and red apples at the same time. Above them, the men were hammering, shifting pieces of felt and plyboard, whistling and laughing. Soon they would be knocking off for pints, which increased the urgency in their work.

Come on, Cowboy, Carmel said.

Coyne pointed at the ceiling. Indicating the audience above. But she pulled him down on the bed beside her. Unzipped his trousers in such a hurry that he thought she was looking for money or something. Pulled up her dress to show him that she was wearing no underwear, and had come all the way from Dublin like that, arriving in Galway with the Atlantic breeze whistling around her thighs. What if a gust of wind had blown her dress up? At the hotel as she got out of the car? Was she going to walk around like that all weekend? Until she met an almighty squall up on Eyre Square and ended up looking like an inverted umbrella, exposed to the entire western world. But there was no sense in trying to talk because somebody had started using a drill outside and plunged the whole place into a sound-shadow. She began to kiss him. With the noise of the hammering and sawing and shouting, they made love. She drew him on top of herself, on the apple duvet. Smothered him with her tongue and pinned his buttocks down with her hands. In front of all those workmen, you could say. All that violence and passion on a Friday afternoon. The noise around them urging on the fury of love. His breathing like that of a labourer. Her shouts merging with the shouts of men outside, beating the last Friday afternoon nails into the timber planks above.

They fell asleep with all that clamour in their ears. A deep afternoon sleep from which they would never wake up. They might as well have been dead. No amount of noise could raise them out of the torpor of this love-drugged sleep. It was only after the men had gone away that Coyne eventually roused himself out of the coma in a great panic, sweating, as though he'd been left behind in utter emptiness. He had never experienced such absolute silence before.

When Carmel woke up, she found Coyne naked at the foot of the bed, his hair all wet, rubbing his back with a towel. He had just come out of the shower and she reached up to slap his buttocks.

There was a naked man in my room, your honour, she laughed and ran away into the bathroom before he could lash back with his towel.

Pat Coyne was the most complicated man in Ireland. He bore that slightly troubled expression of a man with an indeterminate mission. He was no messer. He was waiting for a crisis, some apocalyptic occasion when he could really come into his own. 1916 might have been a good year for him, but he was born half a century too late, looking ahead to the next major event and resenting the complacency around him, as though all that humour and laughter in the country was denying the presence of real disaster underneath. Right from the beginning, Carmel could see that he was devoted to sorting out the world.

Stubborn as hell too, he was. And full of contradictions. Always coming out with his own notions on the way things should be done, even down to the small details like whether to go for wooden or plastic clothes pegs. The kind of man who would remind you of what gear you were in, and give you firm instructions on the most direct way from A to B. The kind of man who could fix the washing machine as if he was dealing with a broken heart, and interfere with the buttons of your blouse with the detachment of a gynaecologist. Stopping to admire the design features of the bra strap.

He was no pain in the arse, though. And there was a soft side to him as well. A gentleman, who occasionally allowed people to talk him into things. Her man, protective and courteous, drawing on chivalry from a bygone age.

He was afraid of affection, however. As though affection was always something progressive, leading up to a goal. Making love was one thing, but affection was really scary. Ireland was not a very tactile country. It was a place where people touched each other with words. Songs. Jokes. The kind of verbal intimacy of islanders. And Coyne was not a groper, or a poser, or some kind of bedroom hero. His advances came in the shape of ideas. Thoughts. Observations. Pronouncements on the environment. Projections about the future. He touched her with words and silent spaces between words.

In a way, you didn't marry one person, Carmel always said. You married a place, an era, a set of pop songs and world events that all merged into a general drift towards one person. You were in love with a gang. In love with the pubs you drank in, the cafés, the arch at Stephen's Green, the taxi driver who once let you off with half the fare. It was group consciousness. She recalled the clothes, the way she wore her hair, the clumpy high heels, the expressions everyone used at the time. The jokes, the repetition, and Vinnie Foley's stories in which they all appeared like characters in a soap opera. Billy Burke's enigmatic laugh. Deirdre Claffey's father's car. All the other friends who had now emigrated. And Pat.

She had come away with Pat. She had married a Garda. A good man. Could have been more ambitious and ended up in a right mess with Vinnie Foley. It was only later on that you realized your luck. Even though she remained loyal as ever to that collective feeling, to whatever song was in her head at that time, to the Lakes of Ponchartrain, to the Rolling Stones, or even the Bee Gees, she had now become an individual. Somebody with biography. Only years later, with three children and a unique memory, had she thought of doing something for herself. And she would not allow that moment of individuality to be consumed by her family. She was determined to become an artist.

That night they sat over dinner in a Galway restaurant as though they had gone right back to the beginning, the first moment alone together. A dangerous moment. With the silence left behind by workmen still ringing in their ears.

She had the Chicken Butler Yeats, with its golden, crisp breadcrumbs. Coyne almost exploded when he saw the T-bone Bernard Shaw on the menue; wanted to rant at the factual sloppiness of the management until she told him to calm down. They were on holidays. And who cared if Shaw was a vegeterian.

Later, Carmel was shifting the last crumbs of chocolate gateau around on her plate, listening to Pat talking about consumerism. He hit her with a wave of statistics. Did she know how much Coke they drank per capita in Iceland. Did she know that they drank more Coke in Northern Ireland than they did in the south. He was about to come to his conclusion, his vision of the future. It all culminated in cataclysm, in pollution – the end of the world. But he was so enthusiastic about it, so committed to that vision of miasmal disaster, that it came across the table to Carmel like words of love. If the universe came to an end that moment, Pat Coyne would say: what did I tell you, Carmel?

Do you realize what they pump into the lakes, he went on, with light radiating from his eyes. And the sea. Look at the Irish Sea, full of nuclear crap.

Pat, don't start getting worked up on the ecology again, she said.

Coyne poured more wine.

Look at the Black Sea, he said. A cauldron of filth and gunge, like a thick soup with all these big lumps. Dead horses and that kind of thing. Islands of floating ordure.

Come on, Pat. We're eating.

The world is shagged, Carmel. I'm telling you.

Carmel looked wonderful. She was wearing a pearl necklace borrowed from her mother. Her hair was clamped up at the back with a spangle the children were afraid of, because she called it jaws and chased them around the bedroom with it, like teeth going up and down. In the light

63

of the candle, her face was illuminated by a kind of Mediterranean warmth.

But Coyne talked as if he had a big cardboard box around his head. Massive boulders of ice had come loose in the Arctic, he cautioned. Something was happening. The depth of the permafrost was shrinking each year. And did she want to know what was going to become of the melting ice caps? Rain. More clouds and more shagging rain. It was all going to be dumped on Ireland, that's what. I'm telling you, Carmel, he said, holding her under a spell of doom with the power of his forecast, there's going to be another flood soon. Wait till the water starts coming up to our front door.

In a feckless, end-of-the-world decision Coyne ordered two brandies. A sign of abandoned hope.

Come a day very soon though, he continued without a hitch in his delivery, when water will mean everything. Everywhere else will be suffering the biggest drought in history. The world will have its tongue hanging out and water will become as expensive as oil. Then we'll have the last laugh. Us here in Ireland and all the rain.

With a triumphant look in his eyes, he sat back, sniffing the exotic liquid in his glass as though he could measure it for toxic waste. He was thinking wooden barrels collecting rainwater at the gable end of each house. Rain-money. Water-sheiks. Selling bottled clouds from Croke Patrick to the tourists. He was drunk on a distant notion of future prosperity. Carmel looking across the table at him in solid agreement. Waiting for a moment where she could speak.

Pat, she whispered. I've never been so happy.

Yes, he said, as though she concurred with his predictions of chaos.

I really don't have words to say how I feel.

He reached over and held her hand: steady on there,

Carmel. Don't entertain your emotions in the restaurant. He had to lean sideways to look beyond the candle. Couldn't take it if she cried, because it would make him all soft and pathetic.

I've found something really worthwhile, she uttered through moist eyes.

Sure.

My art, she said at last. Doing something creative has given me something to live for, something to look forward to. I feel really fulfilled.

Coyne could not hide his disappointment. He was looking across the table of betrayal. Withdrew his hand and folded his arms to register his surprise. It was as though she had said something about the universe that disproved his forecast, some amazing revelation that meant he had been staring into a blind alley. The world was safe and he didn't know it.

What's wrong, Pat. I thought you'd be happy about it.

Carmel, there's far too much creativity in the world already. That's what's wrong with the place. Too much junk. It's only going to lead to trouble, believe me.

You don't understand, Pat. I need to do something with myself. I'm not the type to stay at home and make puff pastry and soufflés. Can't waste my talent on that.

Coyne took the opportunity to pay the bill. A climax of romantic illusion, shattered in an instant.

You're afraid I might improve myself, she said in an outburst of absolute lucidity, but Coyne wasn't listening any more. He was already planning a great future. A world without improvement where people could be themselves and not keep trying to be creative or paint pictures of each other.

Back at the hotel, he came to a peak of new ideas and suddenly asked an absurd question. Suggested they should move down to the west altogether, to the Gaeltacht, where the children would speak Irish, where they would be a part of the real Ireland. He would get promotion easily and become a celebrated Connemara cop; famous far and wide among the ordinary people; a kind of nobleman of the west. Out there with all that raw nature she wouldn't need any of that art lark. They would be content on the beauty of the rocky land, living an uncomplicated life between the bog and the sky. Nothing else. Maybe they would learn a few songs. And there was that business in water. They would start something with water, that's for sure.

But Carmel stared at him. Like he had made some outrageous sexual demand on her.

You must be out of your Vulcan mind, Pat, if you think I'm going to live down here and speak the *cupla focail*.

Then she started laughing again and calling him a teddy bear. Giggling hysterically while he remained utterly serious. As if something in her mirth pointed the finger straight at something in his doomed vision. As if her laughter was bringing the world to an end more rapidly than he had expected. And he could not see what was funny about it. His proclamation was in shreds.

Carmel jumped on the bed, bouncing up and down. Behaving like a child, not a mother. She put on the bedside radio – Daniel O Donnell singing *Whatever happened to old-fashioned love*. She danced on the spring-harvest duvet like she was in a field, running with her hair blowing back in the wind. Looked up at the painting with the white frame above the bed and felt she was galloping across the blue moonlit canyons with the horses. Coyne was the horse on his own, heading in the wrong direction. Inspired by a magnetic signal that nobody else was willing to answer.

Catch on to yourself, Carmel, he said.

But there was no point in talking to her. She was drunk

and disorderly. He had chosen the worst moment to put his daft dream of relocation forward because she had begun to perform a mildly erotic floor-show, laughing defiantly, showing him her new bottle-green knickers with white lace edging. He stared at them as if they were some kind of plastic carrier bag from Dunnes Stores. Refused to enter into the spirit of shopping, denying his instinct, cantering off towards a different moon.

You can take nothing seriously, can you, he said in pure Garda-speak.

Her hips moved at angles that contradicted any musical logic. She pouted and pulled the dress down off her shoulder, gazing at him with mock shyness like a calendar girl. A deadly sex kitten. Eyes radiating a comic impression of lust; something between deep trust and deep suspicion, between hatred and love, barely holding back the next burst of helpless laughter.

Coyne wasn't going to wait for it. He'd had enough and opened the door suddenly. Said he was going out because he needed to clear his head, leaving her behind with a look on her face like the moment the track begins to fade away on the radio. She had gone too far and it seemed he was about to set off right away to find himself a bothy or a disused cottage to spend the rest of his days in.

Had she misunderstood him? Had she not acknowledged his stark vision? Such consummate pessimism was like an act of faith, an act of obstinate loyalty to their love. All that talk of imminent catastrophe, all that irrational longing for a simple life in the west was just a way of stopping the drift away from the night they first kissed in public, at the bottom of Grafton Street, while everyone else was running for the last bus. One of her feet off the ground, toe pointing. Coyne had become obsessed with endings, with the futility of things carrying on and being repeated

67

into infinity. Once was enough of everything on his fevered plane of understanding. Things needed to come to a conclusion.

It had begun to rain. Buckets of rain. He was soaked already, walking through the narrow streets of Galway in his good jacket. To go back to the hotel for his coat would have seemed like an expression of immense hope and reconciliation. His hair was already plastered down on his skull. Rain in his eyes. Cool water running off his face, in around the back of his neck. He blew sprinkles upwards from his nose. Kicked water forward with his shoes. Jumped back in fright when he saw a couple huddled together in the shelter of a doorway. The rain drove people in Ireland into each other's arms, while back at the hotel, Carmel was already lying on the bed, face downwards, crying.

Coyne was right about the rain. The streets were like rivers and there was a sense that things had adopted the appropriate tone of emergency. Everyone had fled the deluge, and the sheer fury of the rain bouncing on the pavement had proved him right. Everything about rain was moving downwards to a glorious end. He saw the herringbone pattern along the gutter as the water rushed away into the shores. A saturated welcome mat. A car hissing along the street with the driver leaning forward and the windscreen wipers dancing. Rain sloping across headlights and street lights and small upstairs windows. Across the plains of Connemara and across the islands. The Corrib was in spate and he stood on the bridge of despair, looking down into that wild, single-minded frenzy as though it was his salvation.

Drummer Cunningham got his picture in the paper. On the same page as the headline – Farmers attack Taoiseach

– he was smiling at the people of Ireland from some charity function where he'd won the prize as best-dressed man. Coyne saw it the day he got back from Galway. It made the Irish legal system look like it had crashed into the side of a mountain in thick fog. One of its greatest adversaries on the loose, wearing the double-breasted suit of respectability. The benevolent face of Berti J. Cunningham: philanthropist; supporter of the blind; man of substance and owner of the Fountain night-club, his new laundry operation. He had become an overnight celebrity, laughing at the law with a grin that looked more like a slashed bus seat.

Whoever took the Drummer out of circulation was going to make legendary status. A real modern-day patriot. Superintendent Molloy's methods were no use. All Moleshaver could do was dance around his office in a great fury, like some new rap king, moving his arms up and down in a steady rhythm and repeating: The Gardai have their hands tied. Moleshaver, you're so funky.

There was little Coyne could do either. He was trapped in his squad car again like a shaggin' astronaut, listening to McGuinness giving him the membership rates on all the different golf clubs, still trying his best to persuade him to join. The Garda club at Stackstown wasn't a bad spot. What they needed, however, was a floodlit club for people on shift work. Fair play to the first person who runs a twenty-four-hour golf course.

Trust a Kerryman to think of that.

Give it a chance, McGuinness urged. You'd love it.

But Coyne dismissed it. His views on golf were well known; it was for failed psychopaths. He had already made up his mind to go for strength and speed. He had booked an appointment at the chest clinic. He was going to join up in some local gym and get into serious shape. There was going to be a showdown and he would be ready.

In his new role as businessman, benefactor and best-dressed man, Drummer seemed to be getting a taste for funerals and charity functions. The man who had sold smack to kids on the streets, robbed banks, snuffed out the lives of anyone who threatened his empire, was now transforming himself into a regular statesman. He knew the way to the hearts of the people. Go to the funeral. Offer your condolences. Shake hands. Put some money in the fund and turn up at a benefit concert for the young widow of Dermot Brannigan. How fucking cynical can you get? Front-row table for Berti and Naomi, Chief and Mick, drinking pints and buying all colours of raffle tickets, maybe hoping to win back the satellite dish Drummer had donated for the first prize. Drummer could be generous when the time came to demonstrate that he had a heart.

A hundred pounds' worth of satellite dish, the master of ceremonies announced every ten minutes. Kindly donated by Berti Cunningham. A hundred pounds' worth of satellite dish, ladies and gentlemen.

That's cause I couldn't get the rest of it off the roof, Drummer whispered discreetly to his friends, and they all chuckled.

He liked simple pleasures, and though he remained mostly serious and aloof, speaking only whenever he had to, he loved a bit of clean fun. He smiled and tapped his foot to the music. Enjoyed the sound of laughter. Felt the warmth of the community around him as they clapped and danced in their seats, singing along with the band: *Knock three times on the ceiling if you want me*. What a night! Drummer even danced with some of the girls from Crazy Prices. Invited them all to the new night-club. Then he laid into more egg sandwiches and Smithwicks, and watched a strippogram dressed in black leather and fishnet tights, cracking a whip and hauling two very embarrassed local men up on the stage for a double birthday celebration.

I'm gonna whip yes to death, she threatened, as the men dutifully knelt down on the stage to remove her red garter with their teeth.

It would be a brave woman who would get Drummer Cunningham to do that, because he was such a deeply private individual at heart. You wouldn't make a show of him. Only at your own peril. It would be like breaking and entering the VIP lounge in his head. People knew not to try that kind of thing on him, like you wouldn't try it on a priest, or a doctor, or a politician. Berti Cunningham was in a position of power, with influence over people's lives. He was too well respected.

Even the Special Branch had learned to respect him. They never troubled his ex-wife, Eileen, for instance. For security reasons, she and her two sons lived in an apartment in Ballsbridge, where Berti could play happy families whenever he wanted to. Christmas, Easter, birthdays and the occasional football international. Or whenever he felt like being the head of the family, and using his wife for a punch bag, leaving her with a few marks to remember him by. The two little Cunningham boys were going to a good school and Berti was obviously intending to break the cycle of crime that he had inherited from his own father. They were going to grow up like decent citizens.

Two senior detectives who once went around to the apartment to check it out got the surprise of their lives. Eileen rang her husband and Drummer got so angry that he sent a squad of young lads round to deal with the situation. That's not your car, is it? she then asked them,

71

and the detectives looked out through the window to see their car engulfed in flames.

That taught them to respect Eileen's privacy. The family flat was out of bounds for detectives. Just as Berti's house in Sandymount was out of bounds for his wife. Only his brother Mick slept there occasionally, as well as special guests and the most prominent members of the gang like Chief, and their women friends.

Fred was of the opinion that Drummer had insulated himself so well, there was nothing the Special Branch could do at this stage. He was in the process of going clean. Had some new friends in high places.

The whole thing needs to be tackled in a different way altogether, Fred said.

Yeah, like joining them.

It's time to get tough. That's the bottom line. I tried some innovations when I was in the Force, but it was all ahead of my time.

Coyne was waiting to see what Fred might suggest. Watched him pour milk into his tea in the small night-watchman's room. Then waited a while further as Fred dunked a Mikado biscuit and chewed as though he could extract some great new plan from its soft pink flesh.

Pat, somebody with your abilities should be actively beavering away. The person who nails that bastard will shoot up the ranks. You should be out there preparing your own dossier on these guys.

What do you mean?

Surveillance, Pat. In your spare time. Just keep an eye on them. Take away some of his privacy. You'll come up with something in the end, wait till you see.

What about the rookies from the CDU, and the drug squad?

Don't worry about them, Fred said. I have the contacts in there. I know for a fact that they've been ordered to drop the stake-out.

If the Super finds out, he'll go bananas.

Forget Molloy. He's got his head up his arse. You'll get the results, Pat. It'll take time, but you'll win if you persevere. Check out his new night-club.

Ah Jesus, Fred. My clubbing days are over.

Coyne could see it already. Girls in hot-pants – men with mobile phones and wedding bands in their pockets. Spiderwoman getting into the car and asking what the baby seat was doing in the back. Oh fuck.

Be worth having a look around some night, Fred urged. Keep a low profile, though. Stay incognito.

But instead, Coyne began a special surveillance of Cunningham's swanky home in Sandymount. Kept walking up and down Hawthorn Avenue in the early hours of the morning, staring into the window of Cunningham's cosy front room with its lampshades and floral wallpaper, all deluxe and delightful. Until he eventually saw Drummer coming out with his dogs. An overcoat slung over his shoulders, like he was fucking Napoleon or somebody, leading two Rottweilers up the pavement. The dogs were larger than life, straining on their leads, almost pulling Drummer up the street with them, as though they could smell the local Abrakebabra about half a mile away. Berti all cool and aggressive, smoking a cigarette and jerking the leads back violently.

Wait, ye fuckers.

Coyne had come up behind them, walking at a slightly faster pace, feeling the edginess of being on the same street as his enemy, posing as an ordinary suburban resident. He wanted to get a good look at his man, stare into the whites of his eyes. Get a sense of his stature.

But as he caught up with them, Coyne was surprised at how small Drummer really was. He was tough looking. But he expected a much larger man. And Drummer's hair seemed a little bit laughable; cut short at the sides and long at the back, like one of those really stupid haircuts that *Wrestlemania* stars wore.

As Coyne approached, Drummer stopped on the street to undo his fly. While the dogs were lifting a leg against one of the hawthorn trees, Drummer joined them, pissing in public to mark his territory. A gesture of contempt towards the people of Sandymount.

Like a normal, disgusted neighbour, Coyne took the opportunity to cross the street to avoid him. But he had made eye contact at last. Under cover he had managed to come face to face with Cunningham. You'll be pissing in hell soon, Berti. You'll be passing boiling urine with the dogs of the underworld to keep you company. Burning and barking into infinity. Just you wait.

In a new sense of reform, Coyne decided he was going to be more of a brick. The new Coyne would be all muscle and speed. He was going to get in touch with his body, so to speak. All he had to do was get his health cleared first. The lungs had been acting up quite a bit recently, so he found himself in Vincents, lining up for another chest X-ray. Felt he was back in short trousers with his mother, endlessly shifting from one bench to another to see the consultant and talk about the dinosaur in his chest. How is the bronchitis? Coyne with his indigenous lungs, rasping and coughing with the hollow bark of a seal until the tears stung his eyes. Lungs like a damp Irish cottage with the wind whistling and the half-door banging.

Once more he found himself walking along the polished corridors with a new pink card and big folder containing his skeletal upper half; humble ribs and air bags that had acquired their own medical fame over the years. It was like a homecoming for the nostrils – the disinfectant, the stuffiness, the heavy smell of hospital food rushing towards him like an old uncle, urging contrition and humility. The alarming clang of kidney bowls. Nurses squeaking along the lino in their white shoes, and the patients everywhere infecting each other with a deep sense of mortality.

Hard man? He felt about as hard as a globule of phlegm in a plastic beaker. Waiting outside the pulmonary lab, he listened as the others went ahead – could you please spit into this cup, like a good man. Who needs a tennis racket? An old man serving a high-speed green ace and Nurse Proctor saying: excellent, well done. Oh my God, call the Ghostbusters, what's this? Then they were proud of themselves, thinking of their record-breaking sputum being rushed away to a research centre where it was going to be tested for radioactivity, for fucksake.

Coyne observed fellow patients like the ghosts of his own future. Some of them were inmates from the wards. A thin man sat opposite him in his pyjamas, rib-cage showing and his whole frame heaving and droning like a set of human *uileann* pipes. Ivory feet stuck into a pair of tartan slippers and a bony hand holding on to a sort of metal staff on wheels, with a suspended see-through bag and a tube that disappeared up one nostril. His face was more like the Tolund Man they found preserved in the bog with a thin leather gauze pulled over the skull.

They were all so desperate to live on. Old women talking all the time about how long they had to wait. As though they had something urgent to do somewhere else. One of them urged Coyne to read something in *Hello!* magazine.

See how the other half live, she said. There's Burt Reynolds. He's coming to collect me after I'm finished here.

Then she threw back her head like a young girl, closing over the dusty pink dressing-gown and shaking with laughter, Jesus, you'd think she was holding back a chainsaw.

Coyne found no soul mates in *Hello!* Healthy bastards. You'll be coughing up daiquiris, you'll be spitting up Bailey's on ice one of these days, you fuckers. Burt, you big dickhead. Who do you think you're codding? You and your missus will be in for tests any day now.

Then St Patrick got up and shuffled in with his mobile crozier and there was a kind of hypnotic peace attached to the sound of his forerunner wheezing away to the chant of Nurse Proctor's voice. Proctor? Who Proct her?

Put your mouth around the nozzle for me, like a good man, and blow out all the way. Now take in a deep breath and blast it out – all the way, all the way, all the way, all the way. Excellent. When it came to Coyne's turn, he blasted all the way like a bricked camel. He was showing off, sending the indicator crazy, numbers on the computer spinning out of control trying to keep up with his carbon output.

But in the end he still came up with no more than a sixty per cent capacity. How did things get so out of hand? There was a lot of bronchial scarring on the lungs, the consultant tried to explain, pointing to pathetic white shadows on the X-ray. We're going to have to put you on an inhaler, and Coyne felt the elation of imminent death. I'm dying, he said to himself like a celebrity who had gained instant recognition.

There is no need to panic, the consultant said. Nobody is a hundred per cent. And people function perfectly on much less than sixty per cent. However, you'll need the inhaler to reduce the inflammation.

For fucksake. Coyne felt he had been cheated. He was

going to live after all. Whereas he wanted to go out in glory. Wanted to have something really serious, something that would make them all look up and take notice. Something terminal that would make his audience hiss. Not the same old half-arsed lung ailment that he would carry around for the rest of his life until he was walking around in pyjamas with a tube up his fucking nostril. In the middle of the action, Coyne would be stopping to puff on his little blue pipe. Vlad the inhaler.

Then he joined the gym. He was going to be as fit as a raver. He was going to be Keanu Reeves from the neck down. Carmel had been echoing his concern for his health, saying it was about time he started getting into shape. And there was nothing more irritating than somebody telling you what you've already made up your mind to do.

Do you want me to go down with you? she asked, maybe just to give him a bit of moral support.

Yeah, hold my hand.

I'm only asking. Just thought you'd like the company.

What's this, the first day at school or something? Come on, Carmel.

There were odd moments like this when Coyne became so embarrassed of his own family that he disowned them completely. As though they might blow his cover. Wanted only to be an individual, a lone ranger with a clean slate and an unquantifiable past. Even wondered if he had suddenly ended up just like his father and would one day overlook his own son in the street. As though his family was in danger of destroying any slender sense of mystery that might have been attached to him. Coyne the family man, they'd be saying. Whereas Coyne was a much more complex figure. A man of many permutations. Didn't even want anyone to know he was a Garda, and let on to the girl with the orange face at the desk that he was in advertising, like Vinnie Foley.

Done any trainin' before? the instructor asked bluntly.

Sure. I'm just out of the habit.

I thought so.

But it was obvious he hadn't a clue. Made the mistake of pointing to his chest when the talk was of deltoids. Got the biceps right and luckily didn't say anything about forceps. But from the way he eyed the gym equipment it was clear that Coyne anticipated some kind of human mousetrap that would fold up on top of him as soon as he touched it.

We're going to have to develop that chest, the trainer said after measuring him. He'd already used his first name about seven times. And Coyne kept looking down with a sense of awe at the trainer's industrial-size build.

Good job Coyne had chosen a quiet time of the day. There was a man at the end of the gym, letting out a terrible grunt every now and again. Agony beyond human endurance. He wasn't even doing very much, just looking at these barbells and flexing his fingers like he was going to get metaphysical on them. There were two more men working themselves to death on the machines. One of them suddenly began to beat the shite out of an invisible enemy in front of a mirror. The other walked around in circles shaking a leg. *Girl I'm going to make you sweat* on the sound system. Smell of armpits everywhere.

Punch my chest, the trainer commanded.

But Coyne was far too much of a gentleman. Didn't see what the point was.

Go on, Pat. Punch me. Like, hard as you can.

Coyne slapped a gentle fist against a faded picture of James Dean and dutifully pretended he had hurt his hand.

Know what I'm sayin'?

What?

This is you in four weeks. Guaranteed. On this machine alone. It's called the Pec Deck, Pat.

Coyne sat into the machine and couldn't help a little self-conscious smile. Here's me on the Pec Deck. Wondered what it would sound like if his name was Declan – here's Deck on the Pec Deck.

He looked at the poster of a girl on a similar machine, except that she was smiling and making it look like it had suddenly inflated her breasts. Coyne was out of breath within seconds. Broke into an instant sweat. Wanted to grunt like the man at the end of the gym but wouldn't let go of his dignity. He furtively puffed on his blue pipe and it took no less than twenty minutes before he was completely exhausted and sat slumped on a bench.

The trainer had talked about a high. Coyne felt nothing but low and inadequate looking at one of the other men pulling himself up on a chinning bar, issuing a kind of abbreviated Fu . . . every time his body was hauled up. Afterwards, Coyne saw him walking towards the Pec Deck, keeping his legs apart as though the exertion had forced a little accident in his track suit pants. Then he started using the Pec Deck on his neck.

Strange, Coyne thought, and secretly called him Neck Deck. That machine is meant for the chest, you thick fucking Neck Deck.

Coyne didn't last long. He gave it four weeks and felt nothing but intense claustrophobia each time he went there. It was clear that exercise in a confined space caused a delirium of sorts, along with an unexplained hatred for people he hardly knew. The same kind of irrational hatred he felt at school when he stared at the pronounced twin barrels at the back of O Ceallaigh's neck in front of him.

Always had a passionate desire to chop the side of his hand down on that neck for no reason.

Carmel tried to persuade him that it was only a matter of getting used to the place. You'll soon be grunting like the rest of them, she said, laughing hysterically.

I'm sorry, Pat, she said, trying to calm down. It's just the idea of you on the machines, grunting. Then she collapsed again, out of control. Breaking her shite laughing at nothing.

Coyne gave it up. It wasn't the exercise that got to him at all, but the other shapers. What made up his mind finally was the night he walked into the changing rooms, totally exhausted, and found none other than Neck Deck, carrying on with his exercise in the nude. The last few toe-touchers, with his hole staring up at everyone coming in the door. Coyne's timing was all wrong and he ended up having to sit in the sauna with him. Even having a nice conversation, talking about the new ferry, until some of the other lads started coming in and the place was suddenly packed out. Then it came, just as Moleshaver had forecast: some bastard farted.

I wouldn't put it past you, Neck Deck, you sly bollocks.

Oh Jesus, they all said, fleeing through the narrow door. The smell was like superglue at boiling point. If it had a colour, this was deep aquamarine with curling yellow streaks. The problem was that Coyne was the last out and so, inadvertently, became the culprit, stared at by all the others. It was the story of his life – always got away with the ones he did, always got blamed for the ones he didn't.

Coyne did make one more attempt to get fit. Cross-country running. At least he wouldn't have to put up with a pack of grunters with rubber buttocks. So he took the whole family with him out to the Phoenix Park for a picnic. The children could go to the zoo while he was doing a long distance around the fifteen acres.

Oh no, he said in the car. We forgot to bring Gran. Wasn't she meant to go back today.

What's that suppose to mean? Carmel huffed.

And Coyne was playing to the gallery again. Hoping his children were on his side at least. Turned round and told them that Gran Gogarty came from the zoo. She was let out on parole. Coyne had to go into the zoo and sign a document saying that he would be responsible for her.

Very funny, Carmel said. That's Garda humour, is it?

Coyne ran like a maniac around the Phoenix Park, staring down at the grass and the mud and chestnut leaves. Whenever he looked up he saw the Pope's Cross, stuck like an ugly big stake through the heart of Dublin, and the voice of the Pope echoing in his ears. People of Ireland – I loff you. Let us pray together for *piss*.

Coyne ran back to his family as though they were all he had. He joined them sitting on the grass near the Wellington spike eating sandwiches and apple boats. Little bars of Crunchy and KitKat. Zoo shrieks in the distance and a giant bottle of Fanta standing like a monument on the chequered green rug surrounded by white plastic beakers. He was thirsty as a dog. And Jennifer kept looking at his steaming forehead, tracing a line through the beads of sweat with her finger, saying: I like the smell of Dad.

You could never really be a hard man in Ireland anyway, because sooner or later somebody close to you would give the game away. Coyne would remember his own father and succumb to some hereditary softness, some underlying regret which tugged away at the heart, pulling the rug from underneath. You could act the brick all you liked until

81

somebody started singing 'Dirty Old Town'. Then you were fucked.

And you could not avoid a little self-irony too. Get a bell for that bike, and all that. Do you think I'm not a fool? Third Policeman stuff. You had to pre-empt derision and be aware of the vulnerability of your own country and its people. As a Garda, Coyne knew he was an open book, so he had to play it cool: eager but calm. Tough, but not outside the humour of the moment. Surfing somewhere between commitment and contempt.

The Rod Steiger–Gene Hackman school of authority, chewing the same piece of gum into eternity, didn't come off right in Ireland at all. Not enough heat. You could hardly wear those big, steel-rimmed reflector sun-glasses in the rain. And you couldn't stand with your legs apart because people would only be asking themselves if you had nappy rash or something. A truly hard man had a way of reflecting great anger, yet would still be ready to look a woman up and down. Don't fuck with me, chiselled into the frown. All it took was one more pestering fly to change the delicate balance. You had to be able to stop chewing suddenly, grimace, blink twice in rapid succession like a series of warning signals. One false move, pal.

A truly hard man turned his back on Ireland, buried his tragic past, slapped his fist and said something like: OK, any blood donors here? Do you like hospital food? They'll be reconstructing your face from old photographs. Coyne had developed his own brick qualities, like showing sudden curiosity for minute details. He could pretend he was highly interested in knowing where the underground drainage ran. Measure distances between blades of grass, between knuckles. He had a look that made people remember their prayers. Moved with slow precision, as though each blink was being recorded contemporaneously. Sweet suffering Jesus, hold me back.

But ultimately, the mask was flawed. The hard-man image would turn porous because he would remember his father, whom he had never really been able to get close to. Never managed to communicate with him or build up any real warmth until it was too late. When Coyne got married to Carmel, he finally became an equal, inviting his father to the christening of his son Jimmy. And shortly after that, just when they began to like each other, he died. Killed by his own bees. Every weekend, Coyne's father went out to check his beehives. Dressed with a square cage around his head, he was out there with his smoker calming the bees, taking out the frames, clipping the queen's wings. He had taught Coyne all about bees and chosen him to take over. But it was no way to get close to your father, with that lethal humming all around. And over the years, the bees had turned vicious through inbreeding.

The neighbours hated the bees even more than the Irish language. And every once in a while, when Coyne was a boy, there would be a scream from the garden as his mother or his sister, or one of the kids next door, ran wildly into the house with a tormented bee buzzing in their hair. Coyne was the one who would usually take the tea towel and crush the bee with a soft little crack, before it managed to get as far as the skull. Coyne remembered nights with bees all over the house, buzzing up and down the window frames. Bees coming alive again out of nowhere at night and flying madly with intoxicated light-fury around the naked bulb in the middle of the room.

And one Saturday morning, they got his father. Got under his protection. Stung him in the ear so that when he dropped the frame full of bees to stop the immediate pain with his hand, he inadvertently allowed more and more of them to get in. All over his neck. Under his arms. All the children had left. Only Coyne's mother was in the house at the time, and in the panic of their lonely marriage, they battled with bees, aggravating everything, running out into the street shouting, until one of the neighbours eventually came to help and brought him to the hospital.

At crucial moments Coyne was exposed to memory. And guilt. There was nothing you could do about that.

Carmel announced that she had been invited to Sitwell's studio. Sitwell had been urging her to come and join his workshops. He had been full of adulation for her work, telling her she had exceptional talent.

Pat, I've been asked to take part in a workshop, she said.

A what?

A workshop. You know, artists getting together and painting.

Ah, here we go again, Coyne muttered. What, like all painting each other, is that it?

It's just a few of us, she said, rubbing cream on herself. The art teacher is giving us a chance to use his studio. The ones with any talent.

Coyne looked her up and down. Once again she had turned herself into an artwork with white markings under her eyes. Two white blobs of cream clinging to her elbows waiting to be distributed. Against premature ageing, she had explained once. The elbows get older faster than any other part of the body.

Talent? Coyne questioned a little maliciously.

Don't look so surprised, Pat.

But he had reverted once again to his own fatalism, reading disaster into everything. He sat up reading *The Great Rivers of the World* and heard the noises coming from next door. Click, flush, mumble, bump. Then silence; the

84

echo of Coyne's own mute intransigence. While outside, the wind was pushing against the glass and shaking the life out of the trees.

Bum, bum, bum, Carmel said, staring up at the ceiling for a moment while she rubbed cream into her neck. Coyne looked at her with horror. What was this *bum, bum, bum* business all about, he wanted to know. She had the kids repeating it all the time around the house. Even Mrs Gogarty was cracking up laughing as though they were inventing some arcane gypsy language that Coyne wouldn't understand.

Bum, bum, bum, what? Coyne demanded.

Bum, bum, bum, nothing, she said. It's only what Mr Sitwell says all the time. He's got this real Anglo-Irish accent and keeps saying things like that. It doesn't mean anything. It's just like saying 'now' for no reason. Or you know when people are trying to think of something and they say, 'well – eh'. He just says '*bum, bum, bum*'.

Big fool.

Everybody laughs at him, Carmel went on. Do you want to know what he says at the end of each class? *Boom-she-boogie*. That's how everybody knows the time is up.

Boom-she-boogie, Coyne repeated, squinting at her.

Yeah. *Boom-she-boogie,* Carmel said once more in a Royal tone. Then she laughed and Coyne stared at the great green flow of the Amazon pulsing by silently through his hands.

Carmel arrived at Gordon Sitwell's house on Saturday morning, full of apprehension. Even going in through the gate, she hesitated, but then forced herself onwards, like a friend was pushing her in the back. Go on, what are you scared of. You're bursting with talent.

Darling, so glad you could make it, Sitwell gushed.

She found herself being led through the hallway, through a dining-room and into a large extension at the rear of the house.

Welcome to my studio, he said, ushering Carmel into a tall, spacious room which had sunlight streaming in through the skylights. Other people were busily painting away and hardly stopped to look up at Carmel, concentrating only on the slightly obese model, stretched out naked on a *chaise-longue* at the end of the room.

Natasha has kindly agreed to model for us today, Sitwell said. A medieval beauty.

Natasha smiled and shifted to contain the ache of immobility, setting off a chain reaction of movement along her body. She was a perfect subject, with lots of folds. Full of generous shadows and contours to work on. She seemed to be constructed in shimmering rings – double chin, neck, voluminous breasts as well as two or three stomachs, under which the pubic area seemed to disappear gracefully without any effort at modesty. Hard to say where it was under all those layers. Androgynous almost. Like Thelma and Derek rolled together into one big human waterbed of undulating flesh, legs and arms wobbling like buttermilk.

Would you like to set yourself up there, Sitwell urged. Have you done much life-drawing before?

No, she said. But I'll give it a go.

That's the spirit, he whispered. It's the greatest of all art forms. You'll see.

Carmel got herself ready in the most clumsy fashion, dropping things, clattering her easel around so that she drew some hostile glances from other artists. Hardly started working when a big blob of green paint shot out of a tube on to her knee. Tried to wipe it off with her hand at first, which only spread the paint around. She found a little cloth and rubbed at it, but it seemed to distribute it even further so that when Sitwell looked over at her, she appeared to be trying to conceal some intimate signal which had begun to spread around her knee and thigh like a green blush.

Boom-she-fucking-boogie.

Coyne was at home picking the debris out of the washing machine. Must have left a tissue in one of the pockets because all the clothes had white flecks of fluff attached to them. While the children ran around the house, he attempted to bring the washing from the kitchen out to the garden, getting distracted by other things all the time. Remembered that he still hadn't started building a swing for his kids. Read an old *Southside Advertiser* to see if anyone was selling any.

Neighbours then saw Mr Coyne running like a maniac out through the back door and into the garden, barking and growling like a cross between an Airedale terrier and a bloody inferno victim. A black and white cat on the back wall waited for a moment to see if this was for real then jumped down casually on the far side just before a colander clattered against the bricks. Coyne walked back into the house trying to straighten out the dent, and then answered a ring on the doorbell. A man stood behind a massive bunch of flowers and said there was no answer from No. 5. Could he accept them and pass them on later. So Coyne was left standing in the hallway with a bent colander and Mrs Gillespie's shaggin' bouquet, for Jaysussake.

Finally he managed to hang the clothes out on the revolving tree in the garden, stopping to examine the engineering design of Carmel's Wonderbra, like a frilly harness. Lucky that Mr Gillespie was out, because Coyne didn't want to be seen hanging out her tiny little string knickers.

There was nothing on TV except a programme on tropical fish, which Coyne decided to watch with Nuala sitting in his lap brushing his hair. He began to explain to her why the fish had such exotic colours. There were artists who dived down with a paint brush and a box of paints. It was a big job. They had to catch them in a net first and then give them their colours. It took years and years to get around to them all. And then they had to start again on the babies.

Jimmy looked up at the ceiling and Coyne smiled. But Nuala and Jennifer believed the story and wanted him to go on, so he went on to tell them that their mother was doing that kind of work, right at that very moment.

She's down under the sea painting baby fishes, he said, and after a while Coyne felt he was inside a big blue fish tank with his family, dozing away with a stream of fantastic bubbles going up from his mouth. Algae waving, surrounded by coral and the underwater plinking sounds of Nuala's constant snivelling in his ear as she combed his hair down to the front like a monk. Then Jimmy began to speak bubbles.

Dad, I think it's starting to rain.

Shit, he said, jumping up.

He ran out the back door once more, regretting the bad language, knowing that Jennifer would only repeat it to Mrs Gogarty. Do you know what Dad said today? Do you know that Dad once did a peepee in the sink? And Mrs Gogarty would believe anything because she was like the Stasi, or the KGB, with her omnipresent portrait commanding its place in the kitchen, the heart of the home, like a face that had third-degree burns.

He was too late. It was lashing already, so he simply lifted the whole clothes tree out of the ground by the roots and ran inside with it. Decided to erect it in the living-room, between two armchairs, so the children could play house underneath. And soon the windows began to steam up. He went to open a window and noticed that Mr Gillespie's car was back. At least the rain had done one good thing. It had prevented Gillespie from playing golf. Coyne ran out with the bunch of flowers, getting wet as he climbed over the wall just to get rid of the damn bouquet at last.

Through the front window next door he saw Mr Gillespie, playing pitch and putt on the living-room carpet. God's teeth. Am I seeing things, Coyne said to himself. And there followed a mime performance between the two men, as though neither of them could bear to make contact through language. It looked as though Coyne had suddenly contracted BSE and was dancing like a madman with a bouquet of flowers, warning Gillespie to give up this indoor golf lark immediately or else he'd stick that putter up his arse. Just you wait, Gillespie. I'll make a black banana sandwich out of your langer.

Flowers, he mouthed like a big fish outside in the rain. Flowers for your wife.

With a great deal of suspicion, Mr Gillespie finally came out like a man who had been caught in some deeply solitary, broad-daylight sexual perversion, with the golf club hidden behind his back and his mouth open in astonishment.

They're not from me, Coyne said, in case Gillespie got the wrong impression. You were out earlier when the van came.

Oh, Gillespie uttered.

Then Coyne disappeared back into his own aquarium. And when Carmel returned later on, she found them all asleep on the couch, except Jimmy, who was playing his computer games and producing sounds like a submarine. The clothes tree had fallen over on top of the TV.

Then there was a further tip-off from Fred. Apparently Fred had learned from a very good source that detectives

were now connecting Drummer with a butcher shop in
Sallynoggin. Fennellys had already come under suspicion
recently as a laundry operation.

From smack to sausages, Coyne remarked.

Tender loin chops to tender advances in the night-club,
Fred added.

So where's the connection?

Meat is murder, Fred proclaimed as he was slowly
opening a new packet of biscuits. There's more to that
butcher shop than black and white pudding, if you get my
drift.

Coyne waited to see if Fred would give him any more
details. But Fred just kept nodding and tapping a Gin-
gernut off the rim of his cup, as though he was some kind
of cult leader, preparing his flock for the big doomsday.
Coyne waiting for him to dip the biscuit as a signal for
collective suicide.

Remember the black plastic bag, Fred asked.

Yeah, Coyne said, trying to remain cool.

Brannigan's death hood?

Sure.

Looks like it came from that butcher shop. Forensics
found traces of animal blood and sawdust inside. They
only released that information to me the other day after a
lot of pressure. Check it out.

Coyne was off like a champagne cork. This was a real lead
for him to follow. He decided to investigate the butcher
shop under cover, as a family. Told Carmel he had found
a place where they could get cheap lamb chops. Lamb in
October? Brought the whole family with him as a kind of
smokescreen, so that he could ask some discreet questions.
Where was the lamb from? Wicklow, the owner said with

butcher's pride. And the beef all came from another farm near Trim, Co. Meath. We make our own sausages too.

And what do you do with your black plastic bags?

I'll take a half-pound of sausages, Carmel said.

Anything else I can get you, Madam?

And I know what goes into those sausages. Dirty smack money. Ecstasy sausages. Crack pudding.

Coyne found the right moment to ask if he could bring the kids up to the farm one day. Said he wanted to show them the sheep, and the pigsties. Where milk came from and all that. The butcher was only too glad draw a map. Two maps, stained with blood. So Coyne first drove up one Saturday morning, to a small farm near Roundwood. Carmel with her sketch pad, like she was some kind of scene of the crime expert gathering together all the geographical features on the location. Doing Identikit drawings. The suspect had brown eyes and a long nose. He was wearing a sheepskin coat and spoke with a Wicklow accent: Maaaah.

Coyne was going to be one of these thorough policemen, leaving no stone unturned. Kicked a few *sliotars* of sheep shite with the toe of his shoe. Eliminating them from his enquiries.

He found nothing at the farm near Trim either. Nothing but copious cow flops. Cows with their large faces and their little curly hairdos between the ears. Big grey tongues licking and clicking and a hollow sound echoing in their large round stomachs. Carmel did a cow's face that looked half human, smiling, with intelligent eyes. *La vache qui fucking rit.* A suspect with a bovine grin. Jennifer wanted to know why cows were so dirty and Coyne said it was the farmer who stuck all those bits on at the back. Flies were landing on cow dung one minute and on Nuala's face the next. And the highlight of the investigation was in the milking parlour when the Coyne family all stood behind a cow, watching the tail rise up and a stream of hot, green-brown liquid cascading on to the concrete. Splat. Splutter. Nuala screamed. Oh my God, stand back, Carmel exclaimed. And Coyne was amazed how a cow could chew, give milk and crap at the same time. Splash. Flop. It was like a whole pile of Telecom bills coming in through the letter box at once. Steam rising. Carmel blessing herself.

The family that prays together, stays together. The family that drinks together, stinks together. The family that laughs together at the sight of a cow's arse, will be blessed for ever in the eyes of the Lord. He was connecting the shite back to the arsehole all right. Make a note of that in your sketch pad, Carmel. Take a sample of that down to the Garda Technical Bureau for identification.

As an investigation, the whole thing was laughable. But Coyne had covered himself. Of course, there was more to the trip than watching grass turn to shite. Mystery man Coyne always had another reason for the outing up his sleeve. There was a place along the road to Trim called Echo Gate where he was told you could stand and hear your own echo perfectly. The most legendary echo that's existed since ancient Ireland. Since the Celtic Dawn. Where Fionn MacCumhaill once heard his own voice as clear as a modern tape recording and thought his soul had left him behind. All along the road, Coyne kept stopping the car and getting out, shouting over gates into the green fields, like an eejit. Hello. Hello. Hello yourself. But no echo. Nothing but dogs barking into infinity across the evening landscape, and the sun going down, stabbing through the clouds and casting long shadows, lighting up patches of raised land in the distance like a stage.

Carmel was laughing her head off. There's another gate. Try that one. Hello. Hey. Hey. Cattle stopped chewing for a moment to look up and see what the problem was. Until at last he found the right one and they all stood there shouting and howling and barking. The Coynes at the gate. Each voice clearly piercing the dusk. Then silence while they listened to their own echoes coming back from the monastic ruins on the far side of the valley like a strange, marooned family calling out to be rescued.

Carmel was always laughing. There was nothing to laugh at, but she would just suddenly crack up on the sofa. The only time she was serious was when she was painting. For the most indecipherable reasons, she would just go into stitches, holding her stomach, in tears. Jesus, Carmel, don't go into labour on me. And then she'd attempt to tell some story that would take for ever to finish because she'd break up on every second word. And in the end it wasn't even funny.

Coyne sometimes suspected that she was laughing at him, but agreed that it was just a paranoia he'd picked up as a boy. The paranoia of an islander. The same old fear of mockery in a small demographic pool with the rictus of derision on everybody's face.

He had come across an explanation for laughter once in one of his anthropological magazines. 'Laughter began with the apes and is first thought to have been used as a weapon of self-defence, long before it became recreational. Its effects were to suspend warfare and contrive a false surrender which offered a degree of superiority over other species.'

No wonder people in Ireland were laughing all the time.

But Carmel wasn't having any of it.

That was total rubbish, she responded. Why analyse fun? I'm only laughing because I can't help it, she said. And no matter how much Coyne tried to persuade her, she didn't want to understand the politics of fun.

If you stop to think about it, everything ceases to be funny, she concluded.

That's what I'm saying. There's a hidden agenda. *In risu veritas*, it says here. Every joke has its own truth.

Come on, Pat. It's just a laugh, for God's sake.

But there was more to it than that. And Coyne eventually realized that he had picked up the notion in the Aran Islands, where he was sent when he was fifteen, to brush up on his Irish. From the beginning, they called him Donkey-shite, and the way they pronounced it seemed like they wanted to say *Don Quixote* each time but ended up saying *Don Quix-shite* instead. After some time, when he started hunting rabbits with them, he realized that it was a form of inverse admiration. In Ireland, the insult was a truly intimate term of endearment in which you graced your friends with mock expressions of contempt. Only by hurling abuse could you allow people to enter your space and become your friend. If people ever stopped calling you Donkey-shite you had something to worry about. Politeness was a sign that somebody was about to violate your arse.

Maybe it was impossible to be close to anyone in Ireland without feeling suffocated. You could only have friends or enemies, nothing in between.

In the Aran Islands, Coyne felt like he had joined a noble race. As they allowed him to slit the rabbits open and throw the livers to the dogs, he knew he had become an equal. A hard man who drank his first pint and called them gobshites and puffing holes as good as he got.

There was always somebody laughing though. Animal laughter. Each time they caught a rabbit the islanders would yelp and laugh. Each time the rabbit escaped they would say: the bastard is laughin' at us now, hiding deep down in one of the fissures of the rock, with the sea crash-

94

ing against the base of the cliffs, and white balls of foam lifting up into the air across the Glasen Rocks. It was the edge of the world, where all other sound was obliterated by the violent thump of the waves and the wind humming like flutes across the openings in the rocks. The rim of the cliff luring Coyne to his death with a kind of vertiginous madness. And the dogs staring down into the gap in the rocks where the rabbit had disappeared. Tongues hanging out, whining with indignation. The lads poking their sticks down, but the rabbit safely out of reach, laughing his heart out, in Irish.

It was the same with the donkeys, roaming around the airstrip. They behaved a bit like a herd of wild mustangs, belonging to nobody and obeying no law but their own. By night, they stood in the middle of the road like solitary phantoms in the pitch black, trying to get into somebody's potato field. By day, they sniggered to themselves at the hoof damage left behind. And if you tried to catch them, they threw you off their backs and galloped away with their ears down, kicking out behind them and farting, stopping a hundred yards away to laugh.

On an island, there was always somebody laughing. Burglars, pimps, child abusers, dealers, beef barons. The Bank of Ireland was breaking its shite laughing. Cats. Dogs. Moleshaver Molloy, Mrs Gogarty, Chagall; all laughing themselves sick. These days, it was Drummer Cunningham who was doing all the laughing.

But we'll have the last laugh, Coyne vowed to his colleagues at the station one evening at the end of his shift. We'll have the last laugh. That's for sure.

Coyne made up his mind to take a look at Drummer's night-club. He needed to invent some excuse, however, so he got in touch with his friend Vinnie Foley. A little disingenuous, perhaps, but Vinnie was always ready for a binge with an old pal. They were sure to end up doing a trawl of the night-clubs, offering a perfect undercover approach. Foley never talked for long on the phone. Just gave the name of a pub and a time, like orders for a bombing campaign.

We're going to murder a few pints, he said.

They met in Conways. Foley had already planned out the whole night, like the old days. Let's do some damage, he kept repeating like the slogan of an underground army. Talked about women, past girl-friends, past drinking sessions. Quickly ran through some of the major events that they had experienced together, just to set the record straight, so they could carry on from where they had left off. And when Coyne tried to talk about a few things like the Amazon basin he found his friend looking at him as though he'd lost touch with the real world altogether.

Things are getting desperate, Foley complained. All my friends are happily married and talking about the Amazon.

I'd love to do it, Coyne said. I'd love to take an old beat-up ferry and sail down the Amazon. That's where it's at, Vinnie. Everywhere else is fucked.

You're reading too many nature magazines, Coyne.

Just put me down on a raft and let me go.

Look, why are we talking about rivers when we could be talking about women, Foley wanted to know.

Coyne was already drifting helplessly off course. He had lost the ability to communicate with other men. Beyond redemption.

Rivers are like women, he said.

And for once Foley stared at Coyne as though he was a prophet. At last he had come back to reality. His pronouncement had such depth and truth that it instantly made a new bond between them. As though men together drinking pints had a sworn duty towards glory and gloom.

Look at me, Foley said, as if to put himself forward as an example. I've been trying to stop the river for years. He described the women he had met in the past ten years. Couldn't count them all. I'm telling you, man, my career is a brilliant success, but my social life is a brilliant disaster. Rode the arse off them all and what have I got to show for it?

A smoking mickey, Coyne offered. But there was a suggestion of off-side because Vinnie Foley was being serious.

What I admire about you, Coyne, is how you can hang on to one woman, he said, as though he was referring to some extreme form of brand loyalty.

The conversation with Foley was always more like one-way traffic and it was clear he didn't really want to know anything about Coyne. It was like answering back to the TV. Foley just took over, rearranging the world in his own advertising vocabulary.

Carmel! She is beautiful, he said. That's all I can say. She's a fucking lady.

Ah, come on, Foley. You can't hold your drink any more.

I'm serious, Coyne. She is a real person. No question about it.

And Foley took a hold of Coyne's shirt to indicate that he meant every word he was saying. With the sincerity of a Toyota ad, he looked into Coyne's eyes, holding on to him in a fierce grip of white-knuckle friendship.

You are one lucky bastard, Coyne. Carmel and three lovely children.

Coyne was still indebted to Vinnie Foley for many things. He had got him a job at the harbour with Jack Tansey when they were growing up, selling mackerel and crabs and lobsters; working at the boats, hiring them out to people who came to the harbour for pleasure trips in the bay. Men who came to fish in groups. Families with all their children in lifejackets. Lovers sailing off to get shipwrecked on Dalkey Island.

Whenever Coyne and Vinnie wanted to get close, they would recall this time. They talked about the schoolteacher from Loreto Abbey who came down to swim at the harbour. All the lads working at the harbour knew Miss Larrissey's body intimately because Jack's shed had a small window at the end, through which they could watch women undress and perform a kind of Houdini act under the towel. The Irish striptease. Until the schoolteacher looked around one day and noticed a half-dozen faces crammed into that little window staring at her naked arse. And of course it was Coyne's face she remembered. And Coyne who had to get the lobsters for her the following evening, when she arrived down all dressed up with earrings and high heels and *Failte Romhat* written across her plunging neckline. Coyne who hauled the lobster storage box up from the water and sold her three of the biggest lobsters, knowing that they would soon blush and boil in the pot. And Coyne who forgot to tie the storage box properly so that the lid opened on the way down and all the remaining lobsters fell out into the harbour, splashing into the water one by one. Crawling helplessly backwards out to sea with rubber bands tied around their claws, defenceless and doomed.

They were quite drunk by the time they moved on to the night-clubs. But at last Coyne was back to his mission, sizing up the bouncers on the way in. Boneheads stinking of aftershave and with faces like hub-caps. Necks as thick as sewer pipes. Wearing tuxedos or double-breasted suits, like double glazing, making everybody feel honoured to be let in.

The Fountain! Coyne looked at the sign outside. Blue neon handwriting, with a small palm tree and a pathetic pink sprinkle of water pissing upwards and flashing on and off. Underneath, the words 'Nite Club'.

Inside, the methodical thud and the usual cast of frozen intellects that you found in any night-club. Stale basement air, laden with sweat, smoke and perfume. More men with big jackets and greased-back hair throwing deadly looks around as though they were going to mutilate all the women. And the women wore hunted expressions, dancing with packets of cigarettes and throwaway lighters in their hands as though the men were only after their cigarettes. Maybe they were all really nice, decent people at home, but the club brought out a cold killer instinct. Hot-pants and cold hands. *You Sexy Motherfucker – shakin' that ass, shakin' that ass.* One man allowing a young woman to lead him around the dance floor by his tie, turning him into some kind of farm animal out for the night. A couple dancing back to back like Balloo scratching himself on a tree trunk, and one guy on his own as though he was working out to a time trial on an invisible Pec Deck.

There was an oval-shaped bar with a bald barman and backless barmaids. Customers were perched on high stools and there was a fountain with green and occasionally pink water gushing upwards. At the end of the dance floor there were two elevated cages with railings, like raised corrals, in each of which a young woman did a kind of marathon breast-stroke in a silky miniskirt. Coloured spotlights flashing down on them and dry ice coming up under their legs.

Coyne approached the bar like a serious law enforcement

99

agent, ordering a bottle of wine, acting like he was Nick Nolte with a brain implant. Vinnie right behind him, already drawing up a short list from the dancers on the floor.

But you had to get all the talkin' off your chest first before you got to the shakin'. So Coyne and Vinnie had a further existential yak over a lousy bottle of wine, served by a waitress who refused to look at what she was doing. They stood facing each other, Coyne listening avidly to the healing power of his friend's proclamations.

I want you to know one thing, Foley said. We'll always be best mates.

Sure, Coyne agreed.

They had reached a level of friendship that could never be surpassed. It was like the old days. You couldn't go any higher. You couldn't become closer than they were at that moment, with Vinnie's arm around his shoulder.

No matter where I am in the world, you can count on me, Foley swore. No matter what happens, I'll be there.

The same goes for me, Coyne said after a moment's hesitation.

It was what Vinnie wanted to hear. Like a soul brother, he stared silently into Coyne's eyes for a long time as though he was close to tears. Tears of unbreakable friendship. Embracing him, then punching him in the chest.

You fucking bastard, Coyne.

Then he leaped on to the dance floor as though he was imitating a rooster recently aroused from his sleep. Elbows flapping to the music as he strutted Jaggeresque rings around the woman in fur-rimmed hot-pants. She was shakin' that ass alright. Coyne could see the bum-creases and all. Then he found his view blocked by a woman with a massive Georgian backside and conservatory who was slightly overdoing the hip movements, like she was making a point, doing a new Lillets ad. There was condensation running down the mirrors. Some total gobshite was doing air-guitar in the background with his head down like he was Rod Stewart or Aerosmith or something. And the dance floor was momentarily packed for *Let's talk about sex, baby*, as though it was a new national anthem, for a United Ireland. Exploratory talks that everybody could agree on.

Vinnie danced back over to the bar and told Coyne to come join them.

I'll say you're an accountant, he said, and dragged Coyne out on to the floor. The big Coyne come-back. But Coyne moved around a bit like a shaggin' knee-cap victim, lifting each leg alternately to see if it still worked, with the imprint of his inhaler clearly visible in his trouser pocket. Trying to look cool, noting details about the décor and the lights. Scanning every shadow in the place for suspicious signs.

At one point Vinnie came over and reminded Coyne how he had once saved his life. When they were out on the sea at night in one of Jack's boats, rowing across the smooth black water until they got to a cast of lobster pots. The plan was to steal a few lobsters and then call on two girls they knew who would cook them up. Food of love. The lights all along the shore like a necklace behind them. The lighthouse casting a flash across the surface and Coyne lifting one pot after another up to the boat. It was too dark out there to see into the pots, so Coyne had to stand up and hold each one up against the lights on the shore. Until he lost his balance and fell backwards, going all the way down into the deep black sea with the lobster pot strapped across his chest. Coyne would have drowned if Vinnie hadn't caught the rope just in time with his oar.

Started pulling the pot back up so that Coyne eventually surfaced again, coughing up mouthfuls of sea water.

Remember! I saved your life, Vinnie said as he danced a circle around Coyne, giving him a drunken kiss on the cheek before going back to dancing belly to belly with the fur-rimmed goddess of the sea. Coyne had the impression she had silver mackerel scales all over her body. As though they were on the floor of the ocean, surrounded by lobsters and waving seaweed.

Except that there wasn't a lobster in sight nowadays. Everywhere was overfished to bejaysus. Two or three hundred pots out waiting for the one poor unfortunate creature that was left, searching around for his mates. All emigrated. It was Armageddon for lobsters. The rest of his clan crammed into a glass holding centre in some bastard's sea-food restaurant. People coming in to look them in the eye and say: I'm going to eat you. Lobsters once had the whole bay to themselves. Now it was all over. And because Coyne was such a bad dancer, he found himself trying to talk to the woman with the conservatory at the rear, telling her about destruction, boring her to death with his endangered lobster statistics.

Don't tell me – you do the accounts for fishermen, she said, and looked at him as though she had detected the smell of mackerel coming from his crotch.

Coyne left the dance floor and sat alone at the bar, drunk, watching Vinnie Foley doing hip collisions with the mermaid. Some time later, Vinnie came over and said he was leaving. The woman with fur-rimmed hot-pants, smiling on his arm, with Vinnie's leather jacket thrown over her shoulders.

I'll be fine, Coyne insisted.

Give me a shout, Vinnie said, winking.

They were like warriors parting, locking arms and

vowing to reunite again in battle soon. Then Vinnie walked towards the exit and their friendship became suspended again. It would lie preserved in ice until the next time they met, who knows when. In a way Coyne was glad because he could now begin to search the place for anything that might be relevant to his investigation. He ordered another bottle of plonk and the waitress gave him a white plastic beaker as though he could not be trusted with a glass. Drank the best part of it until he suddenly saw a young woman he recognized on the far side of the bar.

I've seen that woman before, he thought, but where? He liked the way she looked. Dressed in the most provocative tight-fitting ribbed top that magnified every detail of her breasts. I'd eat broken glass out of your knickers, he muttered to himself in a drunken way.

It was only when the young woman spoke up and ordered an orange juice that Coyne's memory finally clicked into gear. It was Madonna on oysters and Guinness. Coyne was amazed to realize how close he had already come to the Cunningham gang.

He kept looking at her. Making mental notes. The real detective. He could teach Moleshaver a thing or two about the nature of crime detection. Wait and see, he repeated. Knocked back his beaker, grabbed the bottle and walked around casually to the other side of the oval counter.

Naomi, isn't it?

She looked up at him with a wasted expression. There seemed to be nothing behind the focus of her eyes but a series of interlinking empty rooms.

Do you remember, we met on the railway tracks, Coyne blurted. It was such a stupid thing to say. Blowing his cover right away. But she appeared to remember nothing. Just stared at him as though she had to pick him out of an identity parade of men in her memory. Coyne took the liberty of sitting down beside her, pouring the last of his wine into a plastic beaker for her. But she stared at that too as though all human gestures were alien to her.

What's your name, she asked suddenly, and Coyne was put on the spot, hesitating.

Vinnie, he said. Vinnie Foley.

But that was another mistake. Subconsciously he had always wanted to be like Vinnie. Now he was losing his cool altogether. Too drunk to be a cop.

Vinnie Foley, she repeated a number of times, then swivelled around as if to indicate that she had an announcement to make.

Well, listen carefully, Vinnie, she said, pointing at the door of a VIP lounge, with brown leather upholstery. You better not be sitting there when he comes back. That's all I'm saying.

Who?

Drummer, she said, speaking in such an exhausted tone of voice that it meant she was perfectly serious. Coyne felt rejected. Wanted to tell her how concerned he was for her. He could help her. He would look after her. Get her away from that gang.

Coyne had reached such a suicidal drunken pitch and was ready to have the show-down with the Drummer, right there and then in his night-club, vowing to protect her honour at all costs, when she suddenly showed him her wrists.

Look, she said, like a final warning, and Coyne stared down at the scars where she had allowed the hot blood to rush out. The taut, almost see-through skin draped over the thin blue rods of her arteries had been disfigured by a violent design. Gashes like melted wax. Healing over like white latex cloth which had been held to the flame. Coyne recoiled from the aesthetics of this mutilation, but also perceived it as an expression of intimacy. She was showing him where she had poured out her life into a blood-red bath. He took it personally. He was entertaining his emotions.

Do you need help? he asked.

She looked puzzled by that. And before she could even react, Coyne tore off a tiny piece of beermat and wrote out a telephone number. She refused to accept it in her hand, so he placed it in an empty beaker.

The man's name is Fred. He's a nightwatchman. He'll get in touch with me.

Moments later, Coyne was picked off the chair from behind by a large, beefy companion of Drummer. It was the Chief Accountant, pulling him up by the collar.

Are you giving trouble, mate?

And Coyne became instantly aggressive. Instead of leaving it alone and walking out, pretending that the whole thing was a mistake, he began to argue with Drummer's right-hand man. Trying to stand up for Madonna with the slashed wrists.

I'm having a conversation here, right.

Is this man hassling you? Chief asked her.

But Naomi didn't even look up, delivering Coyne up to his own fate.

Piss off and mind your own business, Coyne said, but there was a halting slur in his speech which lacked conviction. Perhaps he felt the security of Vinnie's companionship around him like a protective charm. Tried to shake the Chief's vice grip off his shoulders. Pushed him away with his elbow and tried to engage Madonna's eyes to show that she had a free choice to decide whether or not she wanted to talk to him. But Coyne was wasted. Couldn't even stand up properly, let alone fight back.

Out, Chief shouted, dragging Coyne away.

For a moment, Coyne felt it was quite funny to be hauled away like a limp statue, with his feet sliding along the floor behind him, and the dancers turning round to look at the cartoon simplicity with which he was being ejected from the club. The barman was already clearing away his beaker and wiping the counter. Naomi didn't look up. And outside, things were not quite so funny. The two bouncers took over from Chief, hauling Coyne up the cast-iron stairs on to the pavement with a punch in the ribs.

Before Coyne could retaliate or begin to speak out with righteous indignation at these men in tuxedos, he received a boot in the crotch. He didn't know where it came from, but the pain spread like a vicious stain right up through his stomach and stopped him from wanting anything. He doubled over obediently. Received a few more punches here and there, but they seemed only like minor pats on the back in comparison to the great purple ache in his groin. He sank down. Hand on the railings, face on the cool pavement, feeling the full ignominy of his expulsion.

Now fuck off home, he heard one of them shout through a cloud of sickness which had begun to churn around inside. His whole mind was white. Thought people in the street were looking at him, but could see nothing apart from the polished shoes of a bouncer, and the white socks, inches away from his eyes. He was vaguely aware of the men standing over him, folding their arms. His ears were whining with nausea. He dragged himself away by the railings, but stopped again, puking up all he had, holding the agony of his manhood in his hand.

Back in his humble Ford Escort, Coyne sat for a long time by the canal feeling huge anger. Then he went back to feeling stupid, knowing that it was his own fault. He felt self-pity. Felt there was no fair play left in the world and came full circle again with a growing fury that he had never dealt with before.

He drove around, knowing that he was too drunk. He was just the kind of man he would have been arresting if he was on duty. Drove past the night-club a number of times wishing he could do something, trying to find some way of getting back at the men who beat him before he went home and before sleep would rob him of all the resentment. He held an image of the girl in his mind. Felt he had suffered everything for her.

In a side-street he spotted Berti Cunningham's Range Rover, parked neatly under a street light. He knew the registration number by heart. He couldn't believe his luck. What if he just slashed the tyres. That would give them a taste of their own shite. That would teach them not to mess with Coyne.

He parked near a small laneway and waited for a while to survey the street. He had one concern, that a patrol car from Irishtown or Donnybrook might cruise past and one of the lads would recognize his car. They would stop and say hello, maybe. And he'd have to abandon the plan. When the street seemed quiet, he faced his car into the opening of the laneway, giving him direct access on to another street. Left the engine running and got out.

He walked up and down past the target car. When he was satisfied that there was nobody around, he first of all decided to urinate on the door of the Range Rover, looking around him all the time. A symbolic piss, transferring ownership to himself, like some common canine law where the property belonged to the individual who last urinated on it.

After that, Coyne had to act fast because it would all become very noisy and spectacular. He had no Stanley knife in the car. So he took the spare petrol can from the boot, along with the wheel brace. Went back along the pavement, calm as anything. Not a single nerve twitching. Broke the windscreen with one smack of the brace, setting off the agonized wail of the car alarm. There was no breeze and no danger of doing lateral damage to any other property. Precision bombing. Coyne threw the contents of the can on to the front seat and set the vehicle alight with one match. Coyne the car terrorist! Felt the air being sucked violently towards the flames from all around him. He didn't even need to look back and see it. Burn, you bastards. It was like 1916. Flames reflected in the Georgian windows all around the city.

That will teach them, he said to himself as he got back into the car with the adrenalin foaming around his brain. He raced down through the lane, crossed a main street and raced along another lane. Such intimate knowledge of the city enabled Coyne to put a considerable distance between himself and the scene of the fire. Within minutes he was driving back along Leeson Street just in time to see the men in suits bounding up the cast-iron steps of the Fountain, leaping out through the gate and lashing down the street like they just had a chilli pepper inserted up their hole. A positive indicator if ever there was one.

Coyne's Justice.

On the way home, Coyne found a hedgehog on the road. Jammed on the brakes and ran along the pavement as though he was possessed by some haunting guilt from which he needed to escape. Looked like he had been struck by some nauseating premonition. Drivers along the dual carriageway caught a glimpse of him bending down, picking a good spot along the granite wall to get sick on, it seemed. Christy Moore blasting out through the open door of the car as though it caused his stomach to turn.

Looked like he just puked up a ball of brown needles. Oh Lisdoonvarna.

Running after a fecking hedgehog, for Jesussake. What he intended to do was to catch it and bring it home to the children. They would be amazed to see a hedgehog in their garden in the morning. But there was a practical side too. He had been looking for a permanent and humane way of dealing with the snails who invaded his garden every year, preventing anything from growing. Liberation from snails. The hedgehog and the fight for Irish freedom, he thought as he took his coat from the car, gently picked up the heaving creature from the street and placed it into the boot. How was he to know that the Irish hedgehog carried twenty-six different kinds of fleas? Coyne was thinking story-book hedgehogs here.

By the time he got home, however, the hedgehog had disappeared. He searched the whole car, under the seats, everywhere. Coyne eventually figured out that it must have escaped through one of the holes where the rust had begun to eat away under the spare wheel in the boot. The night of the escaped hedgehog. He dreamed of missing hedgehogs. Felt a sense of immeasurable loss. Something deeper that he could hardly define. Something that could never be recovered. He'd lost far more than a hedgehog.

Carmel was going mad in the morning. Told him how she had been up half the night worrying. Nearly had to phone the Guards.

I was with Vinnie Foley, Coyne said, as though that was sufficient explanation in itself.

I should have known.

The children watched Coyne attempting to make porridge. They found a black rim all along his lips and Jennifer said there was a smell of petrol coming from his mouth. He stared back at them with cinder eyes, as red as Dracula's. Everything was too bright for him. They wouldn't eat the poisoned porridge, so he made a stab at the lumpy lava himself, gave them sugar puffs instead and returned to his crypt, where he slept all day.

In a coma of the undead, he was unable to tell whether he was dealing with dreams or reality. Occasionally he woke up in a panic and remembered the burning car. Saw for the first time with any clarity what he had done. He had broken through the thin membrane between good and evil, on to the criminal side of society. In a half-sleep, he understood the dangers of his borderland excursion, crossing into Drummer's world, perhaps never finding a way back. Sometimes saw himself back in the night-club, fighting, kicking the duvet from his bed with a great burst of unconscious violence. He heard Nuala banging a spoon against a toy wheelbarrow in the garden outside and dreamed she was hammering on the outside of his coffin. Voices came and went throughout the morning and afternoon, like muttering mourners. He was aware of Jennifer and Nuala's presence in the room at one point, whispering and giggling, but his eyelids were too heavy to open. From the kitchen he heard the cutlery being thrown back item by item into their separate compartments, like the bells of disapproval in the distance.

Drummer held a conference at his home in Sandymount. By lunch-time he had selected a team of seven men to comb the city for a guy named Vinnie Foley. He wanted the whole of Dublin to suffer until he found out who did his car. Hadn't even gone to see the damage himself because it would be too hurtful. Held on to his dignity and just allowed Chief to present him with a picture of the Fire Brigade hosing down the charred brown wreck of his Range

Rover hissing and tinkling, with smoke rising up over the streets like a Benetton poster. Took the news in silence, fists clenched, eyes staring into the distance like cigarette burns on the sofa.

All he did was question Naomi. Pinched one of her nipples in his fingers as if he was picking a cherry from a tree, until she squirmed with pain and gave him the name.

And what did you say to him? Drummer demanded.

Nothing. I swear, Berti. He just tried to chat me up.

I don't like you talking to people like that. Could be the law.

Let go of me, for fucksake. I swear to God, Berti, you're paranoid.

If I find out he's a cop, you're fucking dead, he said, finally releasing her nipple.

Berti Cunningham was the kind of guy with a high metabolic rate who would get up in the morning and think, who do I need to whack today? Now he had a real reason to feel he was under-achieving. He commanded such absolute allegiance that his gang of executive dickheads in suits hung around outside the downstairs luxury bathroom of his swanky home, waiting for instructions while Berti was inside, battling with a serious bowel blockage. It was just like the tribe of communal crappers, except that Berti was the only one who actually engaged in the ritual. The acrid stink imposed a sense of realism on to the proceedings.

Drummer even took his lunch into the bathroom with him, in the hope that it would shift his furious condition. Never ate enough fibre. He would start and end his day with fast food, and the more tense he was, the more he needed to eat. Even as a baby, his nappies used to smell like Big Macs.

I feel my allocation of mercy has run out this month. I want every mother's son in this city to scream until I find out. I'll knock long-lasting briquettes out of him, whoever did it.

The Cunningham gang spent the next three days extracting information by brute force from everybody they knew around the city. The Chief Accountant's trade mark was to hold a lighted cigarette butt up to a person's eye. Mick Cunningham preferred to let his boot do the talking while Berti had his own subtle techniques that would make his victims sing. He understood pain best of all and knew how to maximize the effects of sleep deprivation. They burst into a service garage at Dublin Bus and slapped some of the mechanics around, threatening them with spanners. At a snooker hall in the north of the city, the Chief Accountant tried to impale a man on a billiard cue. They even slapped Joe Perry around in an alleyway at one point, asking him out of desperation if he had anything against cars. A lot of people would have been cursing Coyne for the mayhem he had unleashed on the underworld.

The widespread investigation yielded nothing. Drummer's men-in-tights were flit-arsing around the city, cross-examining all kinds of innocent people, kicking rashers and eggs out of harmless junkies and coming up with fuck all. In the agony of his rage, Berti called on a second-rate, ageing dope dealer from Leitrim by the name of Noel Smyth who owed him some money from a long time back. They burst into his Ranelagh flat and slapped him around, going through all his possessions while Drummer stared silently out the window at a stained mattress dumped in the back yard.

You greasy fucking dopehead, Chief shouted. You still owe us some dosh.

Chill out, lads. What money?

There's a lot of interest due on that, Chief demanded.

I've no bread, lads. Take anything you want. You can

have Mick Jagger's underpants. Go on, take them. And Marianne Faithfull's Mars bar. Take the lot. Take Jimmy's roach too, that I shared with him in Marrakesh – there on the mantelpiece in the Woodstock ashtray.

Mick Cunningham started force-feeding him a bag of coke which they had come across. Chief looked through the CD collection and found *The Chieftains in China*.

The Chieftains in fucking China, he laughed. But Drummer wasn't amused. He continued to stare at the melancholy landscape of rainy back gardens, working everything out in his head. Didn't enjoy the idea of mindless violence. There had to be a purpose. He had to have the right man. So he told the lads to lay off Smyth. Allowed the Leitrim man to gather himself together, thank them for his life and shake his hand. Then they left again.

Carmel started going on these autumn painting workshops, organized by Mr Sitwell. Boom, boom. Off they went, drawing the halfpenny bridge, the Customs House, reflections in the canal. They did a whole series of harbour locations. Then they were off to Enniskerry to draw autumnal landscapes and mountains. Sitwell wearing a tweed jacket and a woolly scarf wrapped around his neck like one of the magnificent men in their flying machines. On top, he usually wore a navy sea captain's hat and he smoked a cheroot with a filter, leading his troupe of artists up the slopes of Wicklow. He was indiscriminate in his quest for beauty. Undeterred by flocks of sheep and fertilizer bags stuck in hedges, he trekked across the landscape like an explorer with a pack of converts carrying their easels and picnic baskets. All red in the face and sweating like cheese in a greenhouse, they stopped when Sitwell suddenly held out his arms, struck dumb by inspiration.

Splendid, he would say. Bum, bum, bum! But the words

were a mere insult to such a vision of magnificent creation. It was breathtaking. Stupendous. Sitwell would take a moment or two to reflect. The artists all humming in agreement, eagerly putting down their gear, before he spoke again.

This place has been touched by divine inspiration, ladies. It's got everything an artist could ever want in nature – a green patchwork of fields in the valley, a mountain slope of deciduous trees and a sky that was left behind by Michelangelo. The earth is on fire. An inferno of red and yellow shades, flaming along the hills and disappearing into an awesome darkness at the base of the valley.

He would get really exercised about light and darkness for a while. Puffing on his cheroot, pretending to draw a little sketch with it in the air. Then point out the awesome darkness again and say it was the key to genius, to be able to capture that absence of light at the end of the valley.

If you forgive me, ladies. But the artist's eye is drawn to that absence of light in the same way that a man is drawn to those intriguing, shadowy qualities in the cut of a woman's blouse.

Some of the women laughed or sniggered in complicity at his jokes. As though you were admitting you had had a mastectomy if you didn't join in. Some of them gave him more than he bargained for with a string of Wonderbra jokes. The valley of darkness. Twin peaks. Lift and separate. Schtoppem-floppen.

But everything settled down and his troupe was won over by the new purity of artistic invention. Everyone painting away quietly. A mixture of smells, ranging from Sitwell's cigar, his aftershave, along with the smell of cut hay, lingering in the air. In the distance, the crows arguing in the tops of the trees. At times an unseen car or a truck in the valley. And the landscape shifting with the angle of the sun, the shape of clouds, and the progress of sheep, swinging their jaws endlessly in a silent musical rhythm.

Coyne had left messages for Vinnie Foley. Wanted to warn him. Kept on phoning and speaking to these sweet advertising voices, telling him that Vinnie was not available. Or else he was at a presentation. And when Coyne hadn't heard from him a week later, he marched into the offices of Cordawl, O'Carroll, Beatty and fucking Banim to make sure he spoke to him. Yes, it was a matter of life and death, in a way. The woman at the reception greeted Coyne like she knew everything about him in advance.

Hi, she said, ushering him into an oak-panelled reception room, leaning over to show Coyne her lace bra. Blinking at him and gesturing towards a seat by the marble fireplace. There was a massive sculpture like a knotted penis by the window.

Have a look at the mags for a sec, she urged with a laconic smile as though everything had to be abbreviated into a sexual endearment. Vinnie will be with you in three shakes.

Three shakes of an archbishop's mickey.

Coyne was then brought upstairs by a chubby young woman wearing a big sweater and a ring in her nose. Took him by the elbow and led him into an open-plan office where people hung around talking in a sort of party atmosphere even though it was before lunch. The place was like a big crèche with a basketball net on the wall. A woman in black leather trousers was physically acting out the punchline of some anecdote, after which she turned and walked away with her arm in the air, waving without looking back, leaving two chuckling men behind her. In another part of the office, an old man with a crew cut started fencing a duel of rulers against a younger executive, while a woman with large pink horn-rimmed glasses was silently staring out the window, thinking up some new super-catchprase like 'Shaws, almost nationwide'. I mean what the fuck was almost nationwide – Dublin, Cork, Borris in Ossary?

All over the place, there were posters and silly messages – Vin, I want to share my last Rolo with you, Viv. Memo to Moll from Mike: cough up the Fisherman's Friend ad before the big storm. Memo to Fran from Dan: The Ancient Mariner wants the Fish Fingers poster by Friday. Alfie: the sex was great but the coffee was lousy. Everything paired, everything rhymed. Gary Larson humour had spread like a virus throughout the office and people spoke in cryptic one-liners which recalled the latest TV commercials. Somebody held up a three-day-old doughnut with yellowed cream and said: nothing added but time.

Coyne held them in contempt, even worse than artists or golfers, or even motorists. They thought they were all really clever and creative. But their language was just a series of semi-poetic, post-coital hints. They sounded like men on the make. Madame Bovary in leather. They were all living on an endless paradigm shift, like an infinite flat escalator at an airport.

Coyne, what are you doing here? Vinnie said. He was working on a Kerrygold presentation and was pressed for time.

I had to contact you, Coyne said, looking around, indicating that they needed privacy. But there was no such thing as privacy in an ad agency. It was all egalitarian. An open society with no secrets. And Vinnie thought Coyne had come to him with a marital problem.

Did you empty the tanks, Coyne? Vinnie asked, and Coyne looked startled. What tanks was he referring to?

No, I filled them, he replied.

So what's the problem?

Your life is in danger, Vinnie. I've come to warn you.

Foley laughed as though his friend was reading out a script for a new insurance commercial. Coyne explained that he had spoken to a girl by the name of Naomi who was linked to the crime world, but Vinnie took him by the arm and led him back towards the stairs again.

Relax, Coyne. You're sleep-walking.

I'm serious, Vinnie. These heavies at the club will come after you.

Why? What have I done?

I'm sorry, Vinnie. It was all a big mistake, but I gave her your name. Just for the crack. Then this situation developed. Vinnie, you better not stay at home for a few days. Stay somewhere else for a while.

Vinnie thought the whole thing was a practical joke. Felt his privacy had been invaded. He was ten minutes away from making an all-important presentation to Kerrygold and his brain was like rancid butter.

Jesus, Coyne, you don't even look like me.

Carmel was complaining about a terrible smell in the car. A really evil stink of something rotten. It was so bad that Mrs Gogarty had been forced to anoint the vehicle with Lancôme.

Carmel didn't drive the car very often. But when she did, it was a spectacle. She never hit anything, but the sight of her leaning forward, driving in a high gear and turning her whole body around to look behind, was enough to make Coyne nervous. He didn't have to witness her driving, of course.

Except on that one occasion, when she picked up one of those luminous yellow Garda cones. Somehow she had chosen to park in a restricted area, thinking that she was immune from the law, and while reversing out, managed to run over and lift up one of the plastic bollards on the fender without hearing the crunch. There she was, driving across Dublin, people waving at her from bus stops and Carmel thinking they were all being terrible friendly or terribly hostile that day. Thought the man in the blue Mercedes was making a pass at her, so Mrs Gogarty beside her kept telling her to ignore him – the dirty scoundrel. Three young children in the back of the car and all. And what had to happen of course was that a squad car from the Clontarf district eventually flagged her down. And she explained that she was married to Garda Pat Coyne from Irishtown, so the news went around double quick – Coyne's missus dragged a No-Parking cone all the way from Black-rock to Clontarf.

The journey was undertaken on those rare occasions when Carmel's mother felt the need to go back across to the Northside to visit old friends, look at the old house and chat with the neighbours. A journey of triumph. Behaving like a returned lottery winner. With the Brown Thomas walk, and the scent of Lancôme marching ten paces ahead of her. I'm living in Dun Laoghaire now, near my daughter Carmel. It's nice over there. Very convenient. But Mrs Gogarty still could not help being curious about her origins and the place she had lived in for so long with her husband. Couldn't help noticing the improve-ments around the neighbourhood – a new porch here, a new fence there, an attic converted, and the fact that a certain Mr Donore had finally died so that his pigeons weren't a nuisance any more. She could not resist the secret feeling of envy, knowing she had betrayed her real friends and was therefore banished for ever across the city to the Southside and a life of imagined superiority.

The tea was better on the Northside, she had to admit

on the way home. Back into exile, where her only friends were Carmel and the kids, and another widowed lady by the name of Bronwyn Heron. Brownwind, as Coyne called her. And maybe the perfume was wearing off on the way back over the toll-bridge, because Carmel and her mother both agreed that there was a foul smell in the car. Mrs Gogarty of course thought it was the smell of her son-in-law, the way she held her nose up and looked around the car. They had to drive with the windows open. Such a vicious stench that Mrs Gogarty insisted on dousing the whole vehicle with Lancôme as though it was holy water.

So much that nobody could smell a thing after that. Coyne gathered it must have been the hedgehog. May have left behind a few little trophies in the boot before escaping. Found nothing when he examined the boot, however, except three little black marbles. And now he had to drive around the shagging place in what smelled like a beauty salon on wheels. Pong all over his uniform. Such a slagging he got from the lads.

The trouble was that Coyne was seriously indebted to Mrs Gogarty. Mrs Gocart, as he sometimes called her, had given them the deposit for the house. Otherwise they'd still be renting. When her husband died, the life insurance, along with a very good offer on her house in Drumcondra, enabled Mrs Gocart to set up a nice little empire on the Southside. Bought her own house, put down a substantial deposit on Pat and Carmel's house nearby, as well as retaining more than enough money in the bank to live comfortably for the rest of her days, yacking to Carmel over tea and spelling things out in letters so that the kids couldn't hear.

Coyne was compromised by the deal. She owned him. The clothes the children wore were practically all bought by her. And still Coyne never had any money. Carmel had gone into debt just to buy curtains and fittings, just to keep up with her mother's image of her daughter's lifestyle. And because of Mrs Gogarty's constant presence, Coyne's own mother refused to come over to the house any more. She'd rather sit on her own watching TV than have a posh conversation with Mrs Gocart. Instead, Carmel and the children went to visit Mrs Coyne once in a while. Coyne's mother never tried the self-appointed role of special adviser to the new family, telling Carmel that Coyne shouldn't be seen coming and going from the house in his uniform.

You don't want the neighbours knowing what he does.

Wait till they needed him next, that's all Coyne would say. It was all right to look down on a Garda and call him a pig and a redneck and all that. Until the time came when you needed him. Coyne to the rescue. Like the time he had to get a ladder and climb up into a bedroom on the estate, because a three-year-old boy had locked his mother into the bathroom and Coyne found the bedroom destroyed, lipstick marks on the walls, jewellery all over the place, like a break-in. It was all fine until Madam Gocart needed to have her hedge cut back. It was all right to laugh until the next little domestic crisis turned up and Coyne would be called in to fix a hoover, or just explain that the trip switch had gone on the fuse board. Where would you be without Coyne?

In fact he had a reputation for his eco-friendly inventions. Carmel had once told him that the only ecological disaster to get upset about was the toast burning. So he had come up with some great domestic innovations. Like the wooden clothes peg he had screwed up against the kitchen window to hold the rubber gloves. And the wooden tray he invented with spare door handles at both ends.

But as usual, Coyne took his inventor status too far. Like the time he gathered his whole family around the kitchen table, asking them all if they could find a way of standing a raw egg up. And everyone kept trying it and laughing at their own inadequacy, Coyne watching them with his arms folded and a smirk of absolute wisdom on his face, until they all said they were giving up and Coyne just simply took the egg and cracked it on to the table so that it stood on its head. Ah but that was cheating. We all could have done that, Mrs Gogarty said.

Then why didn't you do it, Coyne said, full of triumphant glee, while Carmel started cleaning up the mess and muttering that he was getting a bit too silly.

Mrs Gogarty was beginning to get on Pat Coyne's nerves. Sitting around the house all the time, always giving advice, indoctrinating the kids and holding Carmel under a spell of moral superiority.

I always pick the number seven, Mrs Gogarty was saying to the children one evening before Coyne went out to work on the late shift. He was in his uniform, reading the paper. He looked up and saw Mrs Gogarty filling in the Lotto numbers.

Seven or any number that has a seven in it, she said. Like seven, fourteen, twenty-one, twenty-seven and so forth. If I run out of numbers then I pick a number and add seven to it.

Coyne gazed in amazement at this new Gogarty rationale. Could not concentrate on his newspaper any more.

Is seven your favourite number, Gran? Jennifer asked.

Seven was the number on my hall door when I was a little girl like you.

Coyne threw his eyes up to the ceiling.

I like seven too, Nuala said.

It's my lucky number, Mrs Gogarty continued, and Coyne was ready to contest this new arithmetic ritual. She went on about seventh heaven, and the seven-year itch and all the other superstitions that revolved around the number. Some say you get seven years bad luck if you crack a mirror.

What about Seven-Up, Coyne burst in. And Seven Brides for Seven Brothers.

Absolutely, Mrs Gogarty argued back with great venom. For your information, Pat Coyne, the number seven happens to be the most vital number in the human cycle. The basis of all mathematics.

007, Secret agent James Bond.

Ignore it if you like. But seven is the number of goodness, she said. Seven is kindness, righteousness, love of God.

Yeah, like seven shades of shite, Coyne concluded as he got up to leave the kitchen. He was having the last laugh and Mrs Gogarty looked like she had swallowed seven barrels of Seven Seas cod liver oil.

In the squad car with McGuinness, Coyne's patience was ready to snap. All he needed was one little trigger, some small incident to set the fuse.

At a set of traffic lights they pulled up beside a red BMW which McGuinness began to admire.

Nice machine, he said.

Heap of shite, Coyne returned. He had been going on a serious ticketing binge recently, as though he was conducting a personal crusade against the private car. He had taken Fred's words to heart. Cars had the effect of alienating him.

What are you talking about, McGuinness insisted. That's a work of art, that car. Beautiful.

Wouldn't be seen dead in it, Coyne said, and before McGuinness could say another word they noticed that the driver of the BMW seemed very young. With a shaven head and a bomber jacket. It was none other than Joe Perry.

Bejaysus! It's fucking hatchet-man.

Coyne had had enough of these joyriders hooring through the streets of Dublin like it was Los Angeles or someplace. He would teach them. There will be one less car on the streets tonight.

We'll see who's laughing now.

Take it easy, Pat, McGuinness kept saying. We're not meant to give chase.

The BMW shot off and Coyne was pleased to get a chance to prove what the squad car was made of. They caught up with the BMW again on its way out towards the power station. Chased it all the way, in through a number of side-streets, doing handbrake turns outside front windows. Coyne felt a crisis dose of adrenalin rushing into his already boiling bloodstream. Nothing came close to the roar of engines, the squeal of the tyres and the wailing siren, howling like yobbos through people's dreams. Coyne and Perry communicating through burning rubber.

You should be back in your pram, Perry.

Where's your L plate, Garda?

Go back to your toy cars, Perry, you little sparrowfart.

You thick Garda gobshite. You couldn't drive a fucking wheelchair.

Life seemed to accelerate here. It was touch and go as Coyne put the squad car up on two wheels, falling back with a thump and a jerk, leaping forward again with new determination like a super-horse.

Jesus, McGuinness prayed, and then phoned for a back-up vehicle. He was all white in the face. This is going too far. Don't do a Mr Suicide on me, Pat.

But Coyne had saved time with the wheely and saw an opportunity to trap the stolen vehicle this time. He was thinking ahead, trying to corner Perry in a dead end as though everything else in life had suddenly become irrelevant.

McGuinness was putting his foot down on an imaginary brake pedal, trying to persuade him it wasn't worth it. Coyne laughed: You've got nothing to worry about, mate. I've got a wife and three kids. Which didn't sound very reassuring, because Coyne raced up through the gears again, and McGuinness felt he was suddenly changing from golf to Russian Roulette. Mice to men. McGuinness saw an image of the great floodlit golf course in the sky.

A small crowd of youths had gathered to watch and McGuinness said it was all a set-up. They had been drawn on to some kind of race-track, for a laugh. We're doing exactly what they want us to do, he said. But the idea of being laughed at urged Coyne on even further. There was no way that Perry's new BMW was going to get out of the trap. He was was in a duel, racing at his opponent with McGuinness fast forwarding through his prayers.

Hail Mary – fucking hell, Amen he said, but Coyne had no religion left, just an icy devotion to victory in this contest of wills.

The headlights of both cars had picked each other out in a high-speed stare. Coyne was racing straight at death. Who will blink first and run back to the safety of life? Coyne experienced the manic passion of his choice. Kept his nerve, even had time to look right into Perry's eyes before swerving away at the last moment, just as the tail of the squad car was clipped by a searing screech of metal. He lost control and could do nothing to stop the squad car going into a spin, tumbling over on its roof three times before it crashed into a wall. Nobody was hurt, but the steam of defeat hissed from the engine while the red BMW raced on, laughing. By the time Coyne and McGuinness got out, a small group of boys and children stood around the overturned wreck.

All right now. Stand back, Coyne said.

Moleshaver was crapping himself, of course. By the end of the shift, Coyne had to face him in his office again. Red West Cork ears flapping with incomprehension.

Mr Suicide is absolutely correct. It's a complete fucking write-off, Molloy was saying.

Molloy was even trying to be dignified about this. Trying to cling to the Garda ethic of standing by your own. But that ethic was eroding each time Molloy looked down at the caption underneath the wrecked squad car in the morning paper. Midnight duel. Gardai and joy-riders in deadly show-down at the Pidgeon House.

You must have paid off Saint Christopher, that's all I can say.

I had him cornered, Coyne offered. It's that bastard Perry again.

But that just sent Molloy into paroxysms of rage. He was like a kettle that somebody forgot to switch off in 1922, boiling off all its water and going into the initial stages of melt-down. The hair flap lifting off his head with the steam.

Look, I've had head office on to me about this already. You're like a crazy shorthorn. Worse than any joy-rider. This is the last warning.

Moleshaver had no bloody idea. He was locked into his own tiny universe. Part of the problem of this city, just pretending to enforce the law without any concept of where society was going. Moleshaver, you're as thick as the rest of them, you dense briquette brain.

But Coyne was thinking about more global issues. He was thinking about the whole nature of society and predicting the decline of the car culture.

There are too many cars on the road, he said.

What? Molloy stood back as though he'd just been called a horse's bollocks.

There should be no such thing as private cars, Coyne insisted. There's too much privacy. It's the dogs of illusion. The wheels of destruction.

Molloy had difficulty breathing. But instead of finding his rage, he was completely baffled by this outburst of sociological wisdom and could think of no response except a disintegrating cough and splutter.

You need your fucking head examined, Coyne.

Carmel and Coyne had been invited to a dinner party by some of her new artistic companions. All that Saturday she had been going on about art, so that Coyne was half threatening not to go with her. He hated dinner parties anyway. All that empty talk. Watching people buttering water biscuits and pecking at cheese and de-seeding grapes like an assembly line.

In the kitchen, while Carmel was feeding the children, she seemed to be struck at one moment by a vision. Looking out through the back window, she saw some kind of apparition, like the Blessed Sacrament exposing itself to her outside in the back garden. Coyne was getting worried about her.

Isn't the light really amazing, she said. So strange. So mystical.

Coyne half got up from his seat to see what she was on about.

That's what all these artists and film makers are coming to Ireland for. It's the quality of the light. The Irish skies. So atmospheric. So magical.

Magical my arse, Coyne said. He got up from his seat again and gazed out the window properly.

What light? he said.

Can't you see the sky. The sunset illuminating the walls. It's like cande-light. Like one of those ancient oil lanterns in the sky somewhere.

That's the floodlights, Coyne remarked. He had never heard her talking like this before. It was most probably the light from the football field at the back of the houses, he explained. On Wednesdays and Saturdays, he could hear the anguished shouts and roars of men's voices. You'd think they were killing each other. Re-enacting Vinegar Hill on a floodlit battlefield. Agony and torture echoing through canyons of semi-Ds. Pass the ball – Aaargh. You Saxon foes. Croppy, croppy, croppy. Maybe the Battle of the Boyne – Billy, Billy, Billy. Then the unified roar whenever there was a goal, followed by deadly, lingering silence when everybody was gone home again.

You're as blind as a bat, Pat. That's the reflection of the sunlight.

It's the lights from the football field you're looking at.

Carmel ignored him. Went upstairs to have a bath and get ready for the dinner party. Jennifer and Nuala went up with her. Jennifer playing shop with all the bottles of talcum powder and conditioner and hair spray, while Nuala was washing Carmel's knees with a sponge.

Will you wash my back, love, Carmel said, and Nuala dipped the sponge down deep to get lots of bubbles and soap.

Were you painting fishes, Mammy, she asked, and Carmel looked up smiling.

No, lovey. Why?

Dad says you go down under the sea with the colours.

Did he say that, really?

He said you have to paint the little baby fishes.

Well, don't mind him, love. He's only joking.

The dinner party was everything that Coyne had predicted. Lipstick marks on wineglasses. People talking shite. Coyne ended up sitting beside a hypochondriac by the name of Mary Donoghue, talking about homeopathy and rebirthing in every detail.

What line of business are you in yourself? she eventually asked, and Carmel on the far side of the table tried to pass Coyne off as a barrister.

Law, she said. But that backfired because Coyne overdid the legal terminology. Without prejudice, this soup is really excellent.

Would have been better off just to say you were in the Force. Except that somebody would be thick enough to pursue it and say: what force? Star Trek? Oh, a Garda; that must be a fascinating job these days. Or else they would ask him how much more they could drink, taking into account that they'd already had two gin and tonics and four glasses of wine approximately. And every time he tried to make conversation, he would say something stupid, something nobody understood. Like something about the environment. People looked at him like he had a slice of lemon up his nose.

Coyne could see that Carmel was drinking like a fish. She had the capacity of a water biscuit and he knew by the volume of her laughter that she was well on the way to getting plastered. By the end of the dinner she was arse-holes, talking about the healing power of art.

I just think people have become blind to beauty, she announced. Beauty can heal us.

Sweet Jesus, Mary and Joseph and the donkey. Where's my inhaler?

There's beauty all around us that we don't see. Every object has its own healing personality.

Then Carmel picked up some lettuce. Look at this leaf of lettuce, she said. Everybody takes it for granted.

Thanks a lot, the host, Deirdre, said with a smile.

But Carmel was talking aesthetics here, holding up the leaf of lettuce like she was starting a new religious cult.

Will you just eat it and shut up, Coyne interrupted.

But Carmel was hurt. Threw him a dirty look across the table and prepared to get her own back. Heat-transferring currents making their way across the table.

Excuse my husband, she said. He doesn't know a thing about culture. He's a complete philistine.

Coyne shrugged his shoulders. Other couples sometimes slagged each other too, as long as it didn't go too far. He saw Carmel knock back her wine and look at him in defiance.

When it comes to aesthetics, zilch, she said. Forget it. It's like showing a Goya to a goat.

Well, at least I can make up my mind about lettuce.

Silence followed. Everyone looked at Carmel, then at Coyne, to see who was going to back down. Deirdre cleared the air a little by saying she took it as a compliment to her salad. But then Coyne felt he needed to put the record straight – people took art far too seriously – while Carmel argued back from the opposite end of the table saying that people had become immune to it. Somebody joked about goat's cheese and Mary Donoghue tried to change the subject back to vitamin supplements. They were all too eager to brush everything under the carpet. There was a point to be made here, Coyne felt. People were afraid to say it.

Why is everybody getting so worked up about art these days? There's too much bloody art, if you ask me. We're all going to suffocate in culture.

Coyne talked far too fast. Tried to cram all his ideas into one argument and make it sound prophetic. He said that culture was the next form of totalitarianism. Look at MTV. The beat goes on like a dripping tap. It's war on the senses. Forget the cold war, this is the fun war.

Everyone stopped eating. He didn't know if they were interested in what he was saying, or completely dumbstruck. Or were they going to start laughing?

Listen to him, Carmel said. Mr Philosophy.

The host tried to force more wine on everyone and Coyne blocked his glass with his hand, like a karate blow. Carmel was the only person to hold out her glass, as Coyne stared in horror.

It's called civilization, Pat. In case you never heard of it.

Well, we need a bit less civilization, if you ask me. Like, we've got to stop interfering with nature. Art is pollution.

Carmel laughed out loud. Do you hear him? That's complete and utter bullshit, Pat Coyne. Culture is part of human nature. It's art for art's sake.

Art for fucksake, is more like it.

An awkward silence descended over the table. Coyne and Carmel stared at each other as the host went to get the water biscuits. Carmel reached a pitch of fury and hurled the piece of lettuce across the table at Coyne. But then she could no longer hold on to her anger and started laughing at him. She was hysterical. Absolutely skuttered, pointing at him and breaking her heart laughing until Coyne announced that they were going home.

It was true. On the way home in the car there was a terrible smell. And it wasn't Lancôme either. They had to drive with all the windows open. Carmel was still laughing, trying to sing the Cranberries song – *did you have to let it linger?*

Coyne was furious. Then he eventually had to pull up suddenly and let Carmel out to get sick. It started with a giant hiccup. Then came the unmistakable splash on the pavement. Puking with her fancy underwear on. Stomach heaving. Coyne holding on to her from behind.

Come on, Carmel. Pull yourself together.

But she was starting to sing again and a new stream of gazpacho lyrics came rushing forward like the first gush of water through the spout of a rusty roadside pump. He gave her tissues. Wiped her face. Pulled matted hair away from her mouth and asked if she was all right now. He never said a word about the vomit on his shoes. Such a gentleman. And she flung her arms around him and said she was sorry. Drivers thought they were snogging in the street in answer to some spontaneous passion. Love sick. Carmel's lips all slack. Eyes drained of sight. Spittle shining on her white cleavage and the legs collapsing from underneath her so that Coyne had to drag her back into the car like he was abducting her.

She had to keep her head out the window until they got home, the stench was so bad in the car. And then it dawned on Coyne at last. Christ. He was driving around with a dead hedgehog.

During the night Vinnie Foley paid the price for ignoring Coyne's warning. Returning home to his Ballsbridge apartment after the clubs, looking forward to a night alone in his own bed, a car pulled up beside him. The window rolled down and a man casually called his name, to which

Vinnie automatically responded with a smile. He was living in the positive reality of the TV ad, where everything turns out right and where he was immune from the real world. He was buying the right cars, eating the right chocolate bars and using the right deodorant.

In spite of all that, two guys in bomber jackets just got out and slapped him around. Vinnie didn't even have time to look at their faces. Received a few crunch kicks that made him regret the last half-dozen sexual encounters as he dropped to the pavement moaning. He issued a long-drawn-out whine that sounded like an old door hinge. One of them gave him a going over with a rustic fence post from the boot and Vinnie was ready to do a deal with them. Anything so that his punishment squad would finally leave him alone and drive away again. He was spitting blood on the pavement and cursing Coyne.

I swear, I had nothing to do with it.

Who's your mate then? Chief wanted to know.

I don't know who he is. I just met him that night.

Vinnie suffered a few more blows of the fence post and surrendered all.

Coyne, he said. His name is Coyne.

Come again, Chief urged.

Coyne. He's a Garda at Irishtown. Garda Pat Coyne.

Sunday morning, Coyne's house was like a mortuary. Carmel had such a hangover that she was crying all the time. Stayed in bed with the curtains closed, moaning like a dirge. I am stretched on your grave. Children silent as in church.

Coyne gave them all crunchies and set them up with jigsaws. Got them started and told them he was thinking up a big story for them, about ships and treasure while he slipped out quietly and began searching through the car with a handkerchief tied over his face. He searched all around the boot, under the seat, in the engine. Finally, he took off the side panel on the driver's side and had to jump back from the assault of the stench. He got his torch out and found the creature at the bottom, trying to get out through the tiny air vent, a victim of his own ideals.

Leaning over the vicious fumes, Coyne could see the shape of the hedgehog lit up by the beam of his torch, like a corpse at the bottom of an elevator shaft. The needles gleaming with rage. Screaming thirst and starvation. He felt the hair standing up on his back. Heard Carmel upstairs getting sick again, with her head leaning over the stainless-steel bowl, spitting as if she was paying back all the kisses of her life until there was nothing left but a dry, velvety mouth. With a long set of pliers Coyne reached down into the narrow cavity and pinched at the needles, dislodged the dead animal and dragged it up slowly: a spiky brown bag of rotting entrails, dripping from the nose. Big black drops splashed on the driveway as he carried it over to the side of the garden.

With both hands clamped around the pliers, face held as far back as he could, he brought it to a place beside the new tamarisk bush where he quickly dug a hole. Then he rolled the hedgehog over so that it fell down into its grave, feet up. Settled the clay back again, stamped his foot and then stood back in shock. All three of the children were at the window, staring out at the burial.

Drummer treated the news about Garda Coyne with extreme respect. Didn't like it at all. The fact that he was dealing with a cop gave him a sinister feeling. He could not work out whether the arson attack on his car was some kind of new departure, some official Special Branch action designed to flush him out, or whether this Coyne character was some kind of maverick. He hated the possibility of being drawn into a trap, having to fight an all-out war with the Gardai. He preferred to keep them at a distance.

Of course, somebody was going to have to pay for burning the Range Rover. Though he had already bought himself a brand-new, spiffing red Nissan Pajero, and the insurance would soon cough up for the damage. He wanted to find the most suitable way of getting his revenge. He would not be rushed into anything. This was delicate.

Whack the fucker, his brother Mick urged.

He'll do it again, Chief added.

But Drummer was uneasy about killing a Garda. All hell would break loose if you did that.

They'd be on to us like flies on horse's shite, he said absently, because he was no fool, and would not just lash out indiscriminately. He was a quick-thinking individual, but also had the capacity to give a measured and calm response. That's why Drummer was still in business so long. In fact, the flies usually had to pay landing fees.

At the same time he knew that this new menace had to be dealt with. On a cold November morning they were walking along Sandymount Strand discussing the matter without fear of being overheard. The Rottweilers were bounding way out near the water's edge raising flocks of gannets and seagulls into the air, forcing them to fly off and settle again at the far end of the strand. The tide had retreated away from the city like a lover. A man digging for lugworm left a trail of gashes behind him along the smooth surface of the sand, giving it the appearance of an unmade bed. In the distance, one of the Pigeon House stacks was smoking.

The fucker has to cough up, Chief insisted.

Give him an offer he can't understand, said Mick.

Drummer had no intention of letting Coyne off the hook.

He stepped on little spiral mounds of sand. Red and brown shore cockroaches fled. His Nike runners left wet prints where they sank into the moist surface and slowly dried up again as he moved on. A DART train drew a line along the rim of the city, clattering far behind them from the edge of civilization.

The guy must have a wife and kids, Drummer said, looking out to another thin blue line ahead of him where the sea met the sky. The dogs came back briefly seeking encouragement before they ran away again to chase more birds.

His missus, Mick echoed.

Drummer stopped walking. Sat down on his heels for a moment to pick up a shell. Examined it for a while like a natural scientist. Then stood up again, tossing the shell like a coin in his hand. Heads or tails.

Everybody has a vulnerable side, he said. You can find a man's flaws in his wife.

Carmel's paintings were everywhere: on the landing, in the hallway and in the living-room. Every square inch of wall space was occupied by her work as though it would soon obscure the real world altogether. Another painting of Mrs Gogarty hung outside the bathroom door looking like she had severe eczema. And when Carmel could not paint Coyne, she decided to begin a replica of their wedding photograph, transcribing their marriage on to a voodoo canvas which changed every day according to the way they spoke to each other. Work in progress, she called it. She kept talking about an exhibition that Sitwell was organizing for her and wanted Coyne to help her select the best paintings. But Coyne came to a road block at the mere notion of praise. He was so shocked by the accuracy she had achieved in her art that he feared and despised it. The paintings of the harbour were so vivid that they exposed him to the memory of working with Vinnie Foley as a boy. He was afraid to compliment her, afraid of being positive in case it might backfire on him like some islandman's curse.

Coyne went to visit Vinnie in hospital, where he lay bandaged up like a pharaoh's mummy. He brought grapes and Lucozade as though it would repair their friendship. If there were peaks and troughs in every kind of relationship, this was the lowest they had ever reached. This was beyond salvaging.

What the hell did you do, Coyne?

Vinnie could hardly speak without triggering off some pain or discomfort somewhere. Even the sight of Coyne's pathetic grapes on the little bedside locker was enough to make him weep.

Don't worry. They'll pay for this, Coyne said.

Get well cards hung on a line at the back of Vinnie's bed. Most of them had come from his colleagues in the advertising world, from another country it seemed almost, the country of health and fun where life was being lived to the full. Coyne glanced through some greeting cards on the locker. Ready to donate my DNA for you, love Viv. Survive, Tom. Nurse on call, any time any place, Gillian. At work, his desk had been turned into a shrine with flowers and speedy recovery messages. The switchboard was jammed with calls.

Coyne asked some questions about the attack, but Vinnie wouldn't go into it. He had already told the Gardai all he knew. And he had about as much faith in the Gardai as he had in the concept of loyalty.

You fucked me up, Coyne. Vinnie spoke on a great wave of self-pity. I should never have had anything to do with you.

I'll get them, Coyne vowed.

They'll get you, you mean. I had to give them your name, Vinnie said.

Coyne remained silent. Just stared at Vinnie while a great cloud of fear and emptiness came across him. Everyone was deserting him. Coyne would soon be alone in the world. An orphan with nowhere to go and nobody he could talk to any more. Looked like a man on a sinking ship, not knowing how to say goodbye.

What could I do, Coyne? I had to. They were going to kill me.

Inevitably, Coyne had to explain to the children what happened to the hedgehog. They were asking so many questions that he could not side-step it any longer. Brought them out and had them all standing around the front garden while he placed a wooden cross on the grave. They said a prayer and he allowed them to pick a posthumous name: Here lies Robert. Robert, the hunger-striking hedgehog. They hung a black flag up and held a minute's silence, and afterwards the children asked lots more questions like: how many spikes has a hedghog? How long does it take for a hedgehog to die without food and water? Or, why didn't he just go into hibernation? Would it be better to die of starvation or thirst? Would you rather be nearly drowned or nearly saved?

Nuala subsequently locked herself into the bathroom and refused to come out. While Carmel was off on one of her art excursions, Coyne spent an hour gently coaxing Nuala to pull the little brass bolt back, only to find that she had gone on a dirty protest all over the walls and the floor. She had smeared herself and the tiles and stared at him when he came in as though he would admonish her. But Coyne wasn't angry because he understood the nauseating smell which clung to the air like a sweet, pungent self-accusation. Just said they'd have to clean this up quickly before Mrs Gogarty came, changed her clothes and then went downstairs to give her biscuits and milk and read her stories from books so that she'd forget.

Coyne felt sorry for his kids. With a hurt love in his eyes, he began to embrace them with a kind of dangerous and exuberant affection. He covered them with a paternal cloak which they craved and feared simultaneously. He wanted to bind his family together against all threats from the outside so that he almost suffocated them with love and warmth, like an overheated room. The smell in the car had been replaced by a strong whiff of detergent and he began to drive them all over the place, up to the mountains, out to Newgrange. Sometimes he came back from his shift bringing home presents for them and flowers for Carmel. He would hug everyone, not even wait to have his dinner and just say: come on, let's go, taking them all off for chips again, or ice-cream. Carmel would have to drop what she was doing and just go with the sheer passion of the moment, get into the car with the children already in their pyjamas. He would mindlessly fill them up with Fanta and crisps and park on the hill overlooking Dublin Bay so they could look down over the world and see a million sparkling lights below them like the reflection of infinite stars in a black pool. Howth glittering in the distance like the sequined arm of a tango dancer stretched out along the sofa. Coyne re-invented the world. With the smell of crisps and alcohol on his breath he turned it into a city under the sea, giving them fables and great new mythologies of strong, honourable men on horseback and beautiful women who could put whole armies under their spell with a song. With his stories, everything could be put right in the little republic of Coynes.

Ultimately, however, that spell of elation and hope was followed by an equally ardent phase of despair in which Coyne returned to the genius of gloom. He abandoned the car. Told his family that they would walk everywhere from now on. Began to warn them about imminent disaster again and went on endlessly about things like the ecology and global warming and biodiversity, which nobody understood except Jennifer and Nuala, because they were spellbound by the fatalistic tone in his voice. He made European cereal growing sound like a wicked-witch story. Told them about featherless chickens being held hostage for life in battery chicken farms. Had them all scared out of their wits of the Colorado beatle, so they would no longer eat potatoes in any shape or form, not even chips. And at night they began to dream of giant unstoppable bugs, the size of Alsatians – immune to all pesticides, until Carmel came and sprayed her special Christian Dior twenty-four-hour protection all over the bedrooms so they would calm down and go to sleep.

Have you nothing better to do than to terrify the living daylights out of your own children, she accused.

I'm informing them about the world.

Well, go and inform somebody else, she said, because the kids had already begun to hoard their sweets, thinking there was another famine coming.

Invaded by doom and paranoia, Coyne visited his mother on the outskirts of the city and decided to put in a proper three-levered mortice lock in the front door this time. Checked the security arrangements all over the house again, got rid of all the stale bread and took his mother out shopping. With her arm on his he walked through the nearest shopping centre at a shockingly slow pace. Her handbag dangling loosely from her arm with '*Go on – snatch me*' written all over it. Coyne daring every young passerby to come within a yard of her. Even allowed her to walk around some of the shops alone, keeping an eye on her from a distance, ready to leap over trolleys, hurl himself down the escalator, crash through all kinds of news-stands and flower arrangements and absolutely clobber the living shite out of the assailant who should attempt to take her handbag. Pat the protector.

It was around this time, too, that Coyne discovered his son Jimmy was being bullied at school and felt it was a direct affront to himself. Thrown back on his own memory of school, Coyne flew into an instant rage and vowed to deal with the bullies for ever.

I know which shoes belong to which face, Jimmy claimed, and after Coyne first admired his son's powers of observation, he wanted to know why Jimmy would be standing at the wall, memorizing all the other boys' shoes.

I just know the shoes that kick, that's all, Jimmy said, already regretting that he had brought the subject up, because he was developing other ways of counteracting the bullies, through humour. Carmel said he should let Jimmy fight his own battles, but Coyne was going to do something about this and the following afternoon, in uniform, he collected Jimmy from school and sat in the car waiting until one of the Fitzmaurice brothers came out through the gate. Jimmy tried to talk his father out of it; not knowing that there was an ancient battle to be fought here and ancient debts to be repaid. Coyne was dealing with all the bullies in history.

A few boys stood outside the school gates, chopping the air, kicking each other's schoolbags, when Gabriel Fitzmaurice eventually came out. Coyne was amazed that such a fat, red-faced little punk could strike fear into his son. But he understood the dynamics of terror and school-yard sectarianism. He was determined to resolve it and told

Jimmy to wait in the car while he got out, adjusted his cap and stood blocking the schoolboy's path, the way he would one day block Berti Cunningham's path.

Hold it right there, Coyne said, and the schoolboy stood back. Jimmy in the back of the car with his head down.

Are you Gabriel Fitzmaurice?

Yes.

We've had a complaint about you. You've been bullying some of the other pupils in the school.

The boy's mouth was open, denying everything until he eventually burst out in a wail of self-pity and tears.

We're going to let you off with a warning this time. But the next time we'll arrest you. And what's more, I'll twist your ear around a hundred and fifty times and then let it go – whizz, have you got that? Fitz-whizz. Now move along.

But it was no triumph. Ridiculous. Just kid's stuff. And on the way home, Jimmy was completely silent. Coyne felt it was like being with his own father. Three generations of taciturn Coynes.

Then came the letter from the bank. Carmel had gone bananas on the oil paints, so they had to go and see the manager, Mr Killmurphy – Mr Killjoy, as they called him. It wasn't the first letter either.

Carmel went to the meeting with him and they walked through Dun Laoghaire, on the sunny side of the street. Coyne blinded by the sun reflecting off the bonnet of a car. Wintry breeze piercing through his shirt.

They were brought up the stairs, along a corridor to a room at the back of the building and invited to sit down. Killjoy glared at the Coyne file on his desk. A small barred window behind him had not been washed in years. Encrusted with dusty grey rain marks. Because nobody ever needed to look out there. There was no view. Only a granite wall with glass and razor wire on the top.

We're going to have to add this overdraft to the existing loan, Killjoy said.

Carmel tried to explain that she had become an artist. Her art teacher said that she would soon be in a position to sell her paintings. That would solve everything and Coyne thought it was a stroke of genius. Fair juice to you, Carmel.

Let's get this in order first, will we. Killjoy smiled. You'll just have to learn to budget a little better. You'll have to stop shopping in Brown Thomas.

Coyne looked at the plastic Brown Thomas bag beside Carmel. It wasn't even hers. It was Mrs Gogarty who had been out shopping, for fucksake.

The bank manager did a sort of cavalry imitation on the calculator with his fingers. He was trying to look grave and sincere, like he was just about to tell Carmel she had breast cancer. Carmel and Pat still trying to look respectable and nice. We like you, Mr Killmurphy. You're a decent man.

Who's in charge of the finances? Killmurphy asked, so Carmel and Pat looked at each other.

Look, you've got to run your home like a business. This feckless spending has to stop. You've got to have a balance sheet – your income has to match your expenditure, simple as that. And if you can't afford Brown Thomas, then you'll just have to go to Dunnes Stores like everybody else.

Coyne saw that Carmel had tears of artistic rejection in her eyes.

You've no right to say that to her, he said.

Mr Coyne, I have every right to keep the bank's finances in order. If you can't control your spending, then I'm afraid I've got to do it.

Coyne sat forward, furious and helpless at the same time. As though he was going to put his fist through the bank manager's face. You bastard, Killjoy, you made her cry. But Carmel put her hand on Coyne's arm to restrain him.

Killjoy watched Carmel take out a tissue. He was trying to show compassion and understanding. But he wouldn't give you the steam off his piss. He had as much regard for human feelings as a dead badger's back passage.

We all have to shrink our expectations, he said gently, nodding his head like a social worker.

I'll shrink your goolies, pal, is what Coyne wanted to say to him. But ultimately, it was all bark and no bite. Carmel was blowing her nose quietly and her eyes were red. She was entertaining her emotions. As a last resort, Coyne pulled out his inhaler, as though he was suddenly short of air. Appealing for mercy with his little blue sympathy pipe.

It was no use. Killjoy didn't flinch. His brain was in formaldehyde. He had turned them into criminals, turfed out of the Garden of Eden. He drew up the new repayment schedule and pushed the contract towards them like a confession. Sign here – unless you'd rather go for suicide counselling. The bank offers a very attractive package whereby you can solve the whole problem with no strain on your domestic budget. Why not avail yourselves of our friendly advice? Take a long walk off the short pier, Coyne.

And Killjoy had a recent sun-tan, the bastard. Off roasting his arse in Gran Canaria or some place. Brown hands, immaculate pink shirt-sleeves and grey suit. It's a wonder you wouldn't clean that fuckin' window some day and let a bit of sunlight into your office. Coyne stared at the confession and Killjoy handed him his own special blue fountain pen. What – you want me to kill myself with this shaggin' pen?

Carmel had decided she was taking over control of the finances from now on. Nothing new in that, except that she had become more price conscious than ever before. She would budget like Michelangelo. Art before food. Yellow-pack, no-name brands all the way, even if she wouldn't stoop so low as Dunnes Stores.

On Saturday morning, Coyne was making none of the shopping decisions. His role from now on was to do nothing but push the trolley, like a horse and cart, waiting for the click of the tongue so as to move on. Leaning forward over the handle, pushing with his elbows, while Carmel was rushing around with the list, and the children were chasing each other through the aisles. In the background, the omnipresent sound of Phil Bleeding Collins, or Chris De Shagging Burgh, or somebody else that would happen to be Princess tacky-heart Di's favourite too. Shoppers high on emotion. Interrupted every now and again by the voice over the loudspeakers calling for assistance. 'Staff call!' 'Spillage!'

Occasionally, Coyne abandoned the trolley to investigate certain items. Wanted to take part in the new fiscal rectitude. Had his own views on economy.

Look at the feckin' price of that, he said, picking out a jar of marmalade and turning around to Carmel, only to find that she had moved on and he was suddenly speaking to a startled old woman wearing a sort of pastel-green turban on her head. Found himself apologizing and putting the jar back sheepishly. And because he hadn't realized that Carmel had gone ahead with the trolley, he then started pushing the old woman's trolley away by mistake.

That's not yours, the woman squealed in horror as though he was a madman. A crazed supermarket fiend.

I beg your pardon.

Carmel sniggering as always. Shoppers mistaking her effort to contain the laughter for some kind of neuralgia or facial paralysis. And Coyne back to leaning on his own trolley, drifting through the aisles after his family; arse imperviously stuck out behind him as though nobody could see him. As though people in supermarkets were blind.

And who should they see at the check-out only Mr Killjoy, of all people. As though he had been following them to see if they were acting on his advice. Not at all; they were spending like bedamned as soon as he, Killjoy, turned his back. Coyne tried to shield the trolley from view; like a shoplifter, hiding the bottle of wine with a family-sized packet of cornflakes. But he had made eye contact with his basilisk-eyed bank manager who greeted him with a minimal smile like he was giving him a last warning: I said Dunnes Stores, Coyne.

And look at all the junk that Killjoy had in his trolley. No way he was sticking to the Marietta biscuits. And there was Nora Killjoy walking along beside him like she was his colostomy bag or something. Fellatio face. Skin like a crumpled brown envelope, you'd think she rubbed herself down with French polish every morning. And him trying to look forever young beside her, in a yellow and blue Battenberg jumper. I hope you get coronary thrombosis, hardening of the arteries, angina, the lot. I hope they give you a pig's heart, you bastard. Killjoy – the Wank of Ireland.

Late on a Friday afternoon, Chief drove the new Pajero slowly along the street. Even though they were travelling at walking pace, there was a new sense of purpose. Mick Cunningham was sitting in the passenger seat while Drummer sat in the back. They were watching Carmel Coyne walking along the pavement with a black portfolio under her arm. It was tied together with a red ribbon.

Looks like a big Valentine card to me, Chief remarked.

More like a Mass card, Mick laughed. She's going to a funeral.

She was, in fact, going to see Gordon Sitwell at his house. He had promised to look over her paintings and help her make a selection for an exhibition.

That's a portfolio, you ignorant pack of dickheads, Drummer finally informed his gang. She's into art.

The men examined her in a new light. A walking work of art. They tried to remember the names of famous artists, as though they were having an impromptu table quiz in the car. Michelangelo. Van Gogh. Vermicelli.

That's pasta, you prick, Chief said. It's Vermeer.

Picasso!

Pick your own asso, mate.

But Drummer didn't like the idea of his men acting out Beavis and Butthead while they were out on a reconnaissance job. So they all shut up and watched. Carmel walked up to a red-bricked house and rang the bell. Chief pulled up across the street and they waited until Sitwell came out and let her in.

Hang on. Is she plugging your man here? Chief asked. They fell silent again until Mick had an idea that it would be a good thing for Berti to get his portrait done.

It might be a good way of getting paid back for the burned-out car, Drummer was thinking quietly to himself.

Do you reckon she's any good at dancing? he wanted to know.

Chief was puzzled. Turned around and looked at the shadow of a grin widening on Drummer's face, trying to read his mind.

You mean Irish dancing. Diddli-eye stuff, Chief answered with a big laugh.

Brilliant. Extraordinary. *Shama-Lama-ding-dong*, is what Sitwell thought of Carmel's paintings, smacking his lips as though they could be consumed. He talked about her

146

harbours with all the emotional slither of an emigrant returning to his birthplace after years abroad. Her work was so evocative that he was frequently moved to tears of artistic joy and wanted to hug his protégée. Carmel found him gazing at her body to see if it matched the undiscovered genius of her art. He was falling over himself as they poured over canals and forests and halfpenny bridges, churning up intense excitement.

You will be discovered very soon, Carmel, he said with a tremor.

Then he changed gear and started moving around Carmel as though she had suddenly been covered in a silver web. Stared closely at her hair, her eyes, her face – standing back and squinting as though he was struck by a new creative ailment that would kill him if he didn't instantly take to the brush.

Shhssssssh . . . he said. Don't say a word.

He pushed her gently backwards and forced her to sit down under the fading autumn sunset coming through the skylight, standing back to follow an aura of pale light around her with his outstretched hand. Feeling her face and hair and body from a distance with his brush, narrowing his eyes and inhaling deeply.

Shsshhh . . . It's the light, he said. An occasion of sheer benediction. One must seize the moment.

Carmel was pinned down in the chair while Sitwell ran back and forward, getting a new canvas ready, mixing paints and occasionally coming towards her to arrange her hands, one lying over the other, like a Royal portrait.

Sheer benediction, he repeated. The illumination is unique.

He brushed vehemently at the new canvas and Carmel was unable to move. The light was fading fast and Sitwell worked in a race against time before they were both almost in darkness, unable to see each other across the fog of inspiration.

Coyne decided it was time for action. From now on he was taking a more holistic view of things. Society could only be brought back from the brink of insanity by direct intervention. Before going to work that evening he made up his mind to start taking the shite back to the arsehole in a more general sense, with the duty sheet in one hand and the flame thrower in the other.

He would start with Killjoy, the bank manager. Somebody needed to fix the man for all seasons with his pink shirts and his year-round sun-tan. He should be squashed into a sunbed and frazzled like a burned sausage sandwich. Coyne first contemplated a little surgical strike on the bank itself; but the staff there were all a pack of smiling fish heads and the person he needed to get was Killjoy.

So Coyne planned a little job on his home in Killiney – Dublin's Beverly Hills. Cruised by the house in the early evening just after dark and waited until he saw the Killjoys leaving for the weekend. A little autumn break in the west of Ireland perhaps. Dinner out in Bunratty Castle, stuffing yourselves with duck and pheasant, like chieftains before the Flight of the Earls was even thought of. Then up to the Cliffs of Moher to buy the postcard of a dog lying across the donkey's back smoking a pipe. Maybe out to Lahinch for a round of fucking golf, what?

Killjoy's house was a dead easy target. Wide open. No need to disturb the alarm. All Coyne had to do was walk right in through the side gate of this delightfully detached residence overlooking Dublin Bay. Where the fuck did you get the planning permission to build an eyesore like this, Killjoy? And everything so neat and tidy. All the garden tools neatly stacked in the little wooden shed. Hose rolled up perfectly. And the garden furniture all beautifully arranged on the patio.

Coyne casually opened the tin of bitumen and began to pour it across the Liscanor slates. Coyne, the patio terrorist, strikes his first blow, turning the thick tar out over the pristine white deck-chairs. Over the beautifully pointed granite barbecue in the shape of a miniature Norman castle. Over the replicated Burren rockery. Lovely thick black blood dripping all over the crazy paving half-way down the garden until it ran out and Coyne was so pleased with his work that he regretted he hadn't brought a camera. Now there's a nice little surprise for you, Killjoy, when you come-back from your dirty weekend. That'll teach you not to insult people in your office.

When the light had disappeared, Sitwell put on a small lamp beside Carmel. Another one had already been lit over his easel, shining down on the nascent masterpiece like a beam of inspiration. It was warm in the studio and Carmel had taken off her jacket. She was leaning back now across the *chaise-longue* offering herself to art by holding forward a naked shoulder and a naked arm, looking out with a natural expression of self-awareness. She was no longer shy because she was communicating her body to an enlightened public. Nor did she pout or try and look vampish, but rather understated her own sexual presence by looking confidently out across the room, not so much at Sitwell, who had become the intermediary, but at the people who would file past her in a gallery and say: there is a woman at ease with herself.

It would have been difficult to establish the precise chronology of events that afternoon, but it seemed that Carmel was now obeying each decision that Sitwell made on canvas. He had begun with her face and her hair and the vague outlines of her body reclining along the seat. But as he worked silently, it became clear that he was crafting an image of Carmel with less and less clothes on. She fully understood this creative progression and responded by discreetly removing her shoes, her dress, her underwear until she lay back in the pose of a classical nude, liberated by each brushstroke, a thin scarf draped across her stomach.

Sitwell waved his brush about with excitement. Came forward for a moment and said he needed to get a more precise idea of scale and take some rough optical measurements. He closed one eye and held the brush up vertically. Then stood over Carmel holding the brush across her body like a spirit level. Took in all the details of her skin, the little folds in her elbows, the shadows under her arms, the slight burr of goose-pimples along her hip and the hint of natural gravity in her breasts. Her chest and stomach were moving in and out on each breath like the sea, and one of her legs was half crossed over the other so that her pubic hair looked like fine, dark-brown seaweed, swept into a cleft by a receding wave.

Sitwell felt his subject was beginning to make the subtle, indefinable leap from the earthly world into the imagination. One more delicate touch and he could elevate her from life into art. He churned up some light-blue paint on his pallet and drew a line beginning at her shoulder and continuing down along her arm. He covered her thighs and her breasts with light-blue markings that made her look like a bedouin queen.

Coyne called around to Fred for a cup of tea before going on duty. It occurred to him to tell Fred about everything that had happened, but he decided not to. The news of Drummer's car burning had been greeted by the Special Branch as though they were a pack of sniggering schoolboys. They put it down to some gangland feud. Some reprisal for a drug deal that had gone wrong. Coyne decided to keep the real facts under his hat, only informing Fred on a need-to-know basis so as not to incriminate his mentor.

Fred was about to have something to eat and brought out his lunch box.

Blasted chicken legs again, he complained. You'd swear they were breeding chickens with ten legs.

Have some of mine, Coyne offered, going out to his car and coming back in with his own lunch. He had gone off food. Eating had become one of his lesser priorities. Fred loved Carmel's sandwiches and said each one was a masterpiece.

She's up to something, Coyne said.

What?

There's something going on. I know it.

Who, Carmel?

The whole art workshop thing is just a front for something else. It's art for fucksake. I know it.

But Fred would not believe him. Said it was all just in his imagination. He would never allow himself to think for one instant that Carmel was like that. She's got a heart of gold.

She's messing, Coyne insisted.

You'll have to talk to her.

I'll do more than talk to her. I'll kill the bastard, whoever he is. I swear. Either that or I'll kill myself.

Ah now relax, Pat, Fred said, offering him a drumstick. Here, have one of these.

When Carmel had almost reached home, walking along a tree-lined avenue, the Nissan Pajero pulled up beside her. She thought somebody was looking for directions when they rolled down the window. She stopped and got ready to help, but in that same instant two men jumped out from the back and grabbed her round the waist. One of them held a gloved hand over her mouth. She could smell leather.

The portfolio dropped out of her hand as though it had suddenly become too heavy to hold. She tried to scream, but managed only a tiny squeak. She was powerless. Within seconds she had been bundled into the car and was being driven away from her home again. She thought of her children and her husband Pat. A man wearing a suit spoke in a very polite tone, holding a gun to one of her knees, telling her not to make a fuss. The other man slowly released his hand from her mouth and she was in such a state of shock, she could do nothing but stare at the metal mouth making the print of a capital O on her skin.

Drummer untied the red bow of her portfolio as though he was undoing a dressing-gown. With a glance at Carmel, he seemed to ask for permission to take a look at the paintings. Examined them with great respect and awe.

They're brilliant, he said. You're very talented.

Where are you taking me?

Are you any good at dancing, Drummer asked.

Back in the squad car, Coyne decided go and investigate Sitwell for himself. Found his red-bricked house in Black-rock and rang on the doorbell. There was nobody in, so he began to keep the house under surveillance, getting to the source of the problem at last. They were a long distance off their beat and McGuinness became apprehensive.

What are we doing here, Pat?

Just need to check out something. Won't take long.

But McGuinness was very agitated.

Come on, Pat. This is over the top. You can't just watch somebody's house like this?

I need to verify something, Coyne replied. Wait.

By then, they could see the shape of a stout man coming down the street towards them. It was Gordon Sitwell. The man with the artistic touch. Coyne got out of the car and met Sitwell just as he reached the gate.

Are you the owner of this property? he asked.

Yes, I am, Garda. What's the matter?

Coyne wanted to tell him straight out to keep his visual arts mickey out of other people's marriages. But he kept his cool and looked like a concerned Garda.

We have reason to believe that there may be an intruder on the premises, Coyne revealed. We have been keeping your house under surveillance for the past twenty minutes.

Good God.

If you'll allow me to accompany you into the house Mr . . .

Sitwell. Gordon Sitwell.

Mr Sitwell, Coyne said in a whisper. Perhaps you'd better let me have the key. For your own protection. I would like to satisfy myself that the house is safe.

Sitwell thanked him and Coyne opened the front door of the house, signalling to Sitwell to stay outside for the moment. Walked into the iniquitous mansion with his torch shining ahead of him, lighting up the interior art world which he had held under suspicion for so long. He soon found the extension at the side of the house where Sitwell had his workshop.

Even as Coyne shone the torch into the studio, he felt the nauseating shift of betrayal rise through his body like a fever. He saw the little podium and the props used by the models. Then like a kick in the stomach, the beam of his torch fell across a painting on the easel. It was Carmel,

153

reclining on a gold green *chaise-longue* with nothing on except a loose *crêpe de Chine* shawl draped over one of her breasts and along her stomach. She was absolutely naked otherwise and her auburn triangle seemed to be darker than he'd ever seen it before. Her nipples redder. Her skin pink and glowing, like it was after a hot bath. The painter had given her a slightly masculine nose. But they were Carmel's eyes. No fucking mistake about that, Coyne thought.

He stood over the painting, admiring her with a helpless feeling of betrayal. He had never known her to look so beautiful, as though seeing her through another man's eyes was like a critical revelation. Here, pinned on to Sitwell's canvas, she was stunning. For the first time in his life he could watch her like a voyeur, without having to make conversation. He loved the blue markings along her body with a flood of passionate jealousy. Beside her stood an Irish harp. In the grassy background landscape, a round tower.

The Pajero drove through the Phoenix Park, pulling off the main artery on to a side-road towards a more remote area of the fifteen acres. It progressed slowly, then stopped at a quiet intersection close to a stand of trees. In the distance, the orange glow of the city had discoloured the sky, steam from the Guinness brewery adding a touch of grey. The headlights of cars continued to pass up and down along the main road through the park, and it struck Carmel how far away civilization could be, even if she was staring straight at it, only three hundred yards away. The only thing that separated her and those people in their cars were some trees.

The doors of the Pajero opened and she was pulled out. There was nothing rough about the way they were handling her, which increased the sense of fear. It might only make things worse if she started screaming now. Nobody would hear anything out here.

Chief took her by the arm and walked her a few paces towards the trees so that she stood directly in the beams of the Pajero. Light shining through her legs, giving her a luminous appearance. She felt cold and could only think the worst. Maybe she should try and run.

Drummer put some music on the tape deck in the car. Irish music. A reel ripping through the night air with fiddle and accordion, flute and bodhran, belting the living daylights out of a simple melody. Suddenly it felt very homely in the park, and Drummer looked at Carmel as though he expected her to know what he wanted her to do.

Go on, dance, he ordered with a hint of impatience. Waving the gun at her legs.

Give us Riverdance, Chief added.

She stared at the three men and slowly began to obey. Made an attempt to hop and kick out her legs. Kept her arms stiffly by her sides. Her hair bouncing off her head. But in doing this, she realized that her knees were so weak with terror that she was ready to collapse. She danced like a marionette, with rubbery legs and rigid upper body. Stopping and starting again to show that her heart wasn't in it.

A h-aon, do, tri agus h'aon, do, tri . . . one of them shouted. But there was nothing fluid about her movement. It was the worst humiliation she had ever felt. The dance of fear. The dance of servility and introversion. Of chastity and repressed liberty. They watched her with great amusement for a few minutes, then got back into the car and drove away. Before the Pajero had gone very far, however, it stopped and reversed all the way back to where she stood on the grass, petrified. The door opened and her portfolio came flying out, landing at her feet.

If you talk to the Gardai about this, we'll come back and kill you, Chief shouted.

The Pajero disappeared and she stood for a long time, crying and staring at the leaves which had begun to blow across her portfolio.

Coyne could not look at the painting any more. He switched the torch off and made his way back outside. He wanted to say nothing, go straight home and talk to Carmel. But when he emerged from the house he found Sitwell standing on the granite step with his arms folded, anxious to see what the Garda had to report.

Mona Lisa lost her clothes, Coyne said.

I beg your pardon?

You're a painter of some sort, aren't you? Coyne asked, indicating that the danger of intruders had passed.

Yes I am, actually, Sitwell was proud to announce. I teach night classes at the VEC – Painting for Pleasure.

Well, there's too much pleasure and not enough clothes, if you ask my opinion. Coyne pointed back into the house. There's too much nudity in this painting business.

What are you suggesting, Garda?

Boom-she-boogie. That's what. You're nothing but a fucking piss-artist, Mr Sitwell. Coyne knew that he had broken through the barrier again. He'd lost his cool. Sitwell gazed back with enlarged eyes, neck throbbing with indignation.

This is outrageous, he said. Get off my property.

Coyne watched Sitwell getting worked up, moving towards him, as if to whoosh Coyne down the path off the premises. And Coyne just couldn't allow himself to be expelled like this, so he put out his hand to stop Sitwell. Coyne had lost all respect for his own uniform.

You couldn't paint shite in a basket, he delivered as a final blow.

There was hardly any physical contact at all. It was more like a rapid gust of wind between them giving Sitwell enormous problems with his own centre of gravity. His body lost its sense of balance, as though he was being sucked back into a vacuum behind him. In a slightly ungainly fashion he began to flap his arms backwards to try and regain his upright integrity, while attempting to cross his legs at the same time. What the fuck? Coyne thought, as he observed this strange acrobatic performance. But then he understood what Sitwell was attempting to do. There was a low box hedge running along the path and Sitwell looked like he had decided it was a good idea to sit down on its flat, perfectly sculpted surface. Be seated, Mr Sitwell. Still flapping and already looking comfortable with his legs crossed, he lowered himself down on the green wall, which supported him for a moment, but then gave way with a multiple crack of little twigs. It sounded more like the rip of an involuntary fart as the hedge parted to allow his weight to take its natural course. Sitwell disappeared and his legs went up in the air. Feet with slip-on shoes sticking up out of the wrecked hedge.

Coyne could not stay on duty that night. He drove the squad car straight back to the station and said he felt ill. Drove home and found that Carmel wasn't home yet. Mrs Gogarty gave him a dirty look as though she was going to accuse him of being a cat killer or of some other asocial misdeed. Said she was mildly worried that Carmel wasn't back, but didn't want their mutual concern to lead to anything closer than that.

157

As soon as she left, Coyne began to search through stacks of Carmel's sketches to see if he could find anything incriminating. There they were; a half-dozen drawings of nude men. Sitwell, no doubt. Large as life and bollock naked, grinning back with his lascivious half-shut eyes. Well, Coyne admitted, it was the head of Sitwell all right, but the body a hulk, with massive pectorals and brawny arms. It was Sitwell with superhuman genitals. Not the fat specimen of a man he had just knocked over the hedge.

Coyne paced up and down the kitchen. Every now and again he went back to take a look at the paintings, just to keep his sense of betrayal at its peak. Just to gaze at the sheer obscenity of Sitwell's oversized genitals, allowing himself to descend into a deep depression.

When Carmel eventually returned home she walked into the kitchen to find Coyne standing there in his uniform, with his arms folded. She looked pale, dropped her portfolio on the floor and sat down, exhausted. Before she could say a word, she met a tirade of accusations.

I need to have a word with you, he said, talking to her like a child.

What?

I have reason to believe you are fooling around, Carmel.

Carmel placed her chin in her hands and gave Coyne a look of weary disbelief, followed by a sort of laconic half-laugh.

I don't think I heard that, she said.

Is it true? Are you messing?

Pat, what is wrong with you? she said, looking at the male nudes spread out on the kitchen table. Are you going to take me down to the station for questioning or what?

It's true, isn't it. All this art business is just a cover-up. Isn't that so? You're up to something.

158

Jesus, I don't deserve this, she sighed. You've got this all wrong, Pat.

If it's true, Carmel, I swear I'll kill myself. If you don't stop all this painting for pleasure, I'm serious, it's the end. I'll do myself in.

Carmel's head sank down. Her shoulders began to shudder and it took Coyne a moment to realize that she was crying, not laughing. He looked at her quite helplessly. Then went over and sat beside her, taking her hand. She was shaking. Tears rolling down her face as she looked up.

These men attacked me in the street, she finally said. Three men just jumped on me and took me away in a car.

Coyne put his arm around her, as if to offer some belated protection. He felt miserable. Could not believe how cruel he was to accuse her.

Where? What happened?

I couldn't scream for help or anything, she explained. They just drove me to the Phoenix Park. I thought they were going to do something. Jesus, I was really scared, Pat.

She burst into tears again and he pulled her close. His face wet on one side from contact with hers.

Are you all right, Carmel? What did they do, love?

They got me to do Irish dancing. They made me get out and told me to do Riverdance. It was horrible, Pat. Right in the middle of the Phoenix Park, near the Pope's Cross. They told me not to go to the Guards.

What did they look like? Coyne wanted to know. Did you get the registration?

No, she said. One of them was big and fat, with braces, and a shaved head. And a young guy with a baseball cap. I've never been so afraid in all my life.

Coyne held her in a fierce grip of remorse.

You're all right now, he said, pushing the male nudes away with his elbow.

From then on it was war. He would have to deal with the Drummer direct. Back on duty the following night, the whole city looked like it was going to commit suicide. Saturday night mayhem. Coyne and McGuinness came across a teenager who had died from a drug overdose. They went to a flat where the occupants were so stoned, they were trying to pretend the victim had merely dozed off, when it was clear that he was as dead as a mouse with a hatchet in the back. Then they came across an old man, staggering in the middle of the road outside the New Jury's hotel with a limp hand held out, just in case some motorist might accidentally stop, or money came falling out of the sky. So blind drunk, the hoor couldn't even see a coin in his hand. Reeling all over the street with the cars dodging him left and right, as though it was some kind of rugby international in which everybody denied they had the ball. Until he did a late tackle and half attempted to grab a Saab by the aerial, spun around like a whizzing turnstile and fell down flat on his back, blood pumping from the back of his head, like a broken jug.

What was going on? Coyne no longer understood the logic of ordinary life. Where he had once been reassured by his role in protecting the nation from itself, he now felt subjected to a new wave of cynicism. Somebody sprinting across the toll-bridge with a car stereo. Some students banging like shite on the door of the Hare Krishna Temple, saying they had a message for Harry. A bunch of girls waiting for the Nightlink bus, singing their heads off and screeching *I want you back for good*. Some gobshite *extraordinaire* trying conduct a moral campaign against prostitutes, and a bunch of kids trying to make a horse swim across the canal like it was the wild west, with the animal's head out of the water, grinning with fear.

Coyne went ballistic. He spewed Exocet lyrics, effing and blinding as he drove the squad car around the city. In his head there emerged a new obsession with the idea of operating outside the law like a real extremist. Where Coyne had once derived his sense of belonging from his uniform, he now felt it to be the principal barrier in his internecine war with Cunningham. From now on Coyne felt he would have to operate outside the nation.

Later on that night, they got a call to a house in Ballsbridge where somebody had committed suicide. Walked around to the back of a semi-detached house and found a man hanging from one of the trees. The bright security lights shone down, giving him a gaunt, agonized appearance, swinging on the axis of the rope, head leaning to one side and the feet searching for solid ground. His beige trousers soiled with a spreading stain around the crotch. Self-murder.

Jesus, Coyne said, involuntarily taking his cap off. But in the same instant, just as McGuinness was about to say a brief prayer, the deceased man suddenly spoke up.

Jesus, Billy, it's the Guards.

Coyne and McGuinness jumped back. It was only then that Coyne realized there were other young men in the garden too, standing behind a video camera on a tripod. Another seemed to have his face covered in blood.

What the hell is going on here, Coyne shouted.

Get down from there, McGuinness said to the dead man, lifting a step-ladder that was lying on the grass.

He's OK, one of the men behind the camera said. He's in no danger. He's got a harness around his neck. We're just making a film.

Well, you can't be doing this kind of thing in the middle

of the night, Coyne announced. We've had a complaint from the neighbours.

This is obscene, McGuinness echoed.

Coyne took a moment to put the scene into perspective. With a nickname like Garda Suicide, he felt he had been picked out specially for derision. Was this some kind of practical joke? Were these people trying to give him a message?

What are we going to do, Coyne roared. Start dancing around like we're in some shaggin' margarine ad? Come on, get him down out of there.

The step-ladder was placed under the dead man's feet and he rejoined the world the way he had left. Found his footing on the top step, slipped the rope over his head and descended the ladder like a ghost helped back to life. Coyne's attention was then drawn to the man who appeared to have shot himself, with half his head blown off. Blood spilling from his mouth and a gun hanging loosely in his hand.

What's wrong with him, Coyne demanded.

That's just a wig, the director explained, showing the flap on the man's skull, a bit like what Moleshaver had on his head. You see there's a built-in hinge and it just explodes.

Do you have a licence for that firearm?

It's decommissioned.

Coyne took possession of the gun. Said he would have to confiscate the weapon and have it examined. Told them to put an end to these antics. Couldn't understand the logic of these aesthetics. Did they not think there was enough of this kind of thing happening around the city?

It's the only sub-culture left, the director said.

Snuff movies, Coyne muttered to McGuinness. But the whole incident seemed to have a depressing effect on him.

He turned back to the director and raised his voice again, menacingly. Do you want us to charge you with disturbing the peace?

And wasting Garda time, McGuinness added.

Gordon Sitwell went to Irishtown Garda station and lodged a complaint against Coyne. Said he had been attacked. Verbally abused and assaulted on his own doorstep. When Coyne arrived for work next evening, he could see by the look on Larry McGuinness's face that something was wrong. Before he could find out anything, Superintendent Molloy said he wanted to see Coyne in his office. Moleshaver could hardly wait for Coyne to close the door before he hissed at him in a kind of half-scream, half-whisper about a serious breach of Garda rules.

What the hell were you doing at that man's home in Blackrock, Coyne?

I was investigating a suspected burglary, Coyne replied.

Investigating your arse, you were. It's way off your beat. And I don't see it on the duty report. We've had a serious complaint from a gentleman by the name of Sitwell. Said he was assaulted outside his own home by a Garda with a description that bears a remarkable resemblance to you.

Coyne feigned a sort of puzzled expression. As though the gentleman in question must be out of his mind to make such an outrageous complaint. He stared at Molloy and got the impression that the mole on his face was flashing on and off in warning, like a little pilot light. Do not exceed recommended temperatures.

He's a crank, Frank, Coyne tried to say.

I'm near disbelief, Moleshaver uttered with a shake of the head. You better have a good explanation for this. I don't know what you have against this man, but you can tell it to the enquiry. In the meantime, you've left me with no option but to suspend you from your duties until further notice.

Somebody else had already replaced Coyne on the beat in the squad car. And Superintendent Molloy was strangely dignified about the whole thing to demonstrate that it had gone out of his hands.

This man Sitwell is pressing charges, Moleshaver added in an official tone, shifting documents on his desk. Suspension without pay, that is.

I need protection, Coyne suddenly said.

Moleshaver was dumb-struck.

I need protection for my wife and family. She was abducted by Drummer and his gang. They assaulted her and threatened her.

Don't start entertaining your emotions, Coyne. What's that got to do with this?

She needs Garda protection. Her life has come under threat from the Cunningham gang.

Molloy smiled to indicate how ridiculous this request was. He looked at Coyne as though he had gone soft in the head. Living in some kind of fantasy.

Look, if you need protection for your wife, then you go home and protect her. Is there something going on between you and the Drummer gang?

No way. Coyne hesitated. They just abducted her and took her to the Phoenix Park. Subjected her to inhuman and degrading treatment.

Like what? Molloy demanded. The story had become too far-fetched and he was already picking up the phone and dialling a number, as though Coyne didn't matter any more.

They made her perform Riverdance. She needs protection, Frank. Who knows what they might do next.

You can tell that to the enquiry, Molloy finally said in

the hope of dismissing Coyne out of his office. He didn't want to listen to any more extracts from Coyne's imagination. He was too busy.

But . . .

Stop looking for sympathy, Coyne. You know where you can find sympathy, he said, holding his hand over the phone. In the fucking dictionary, between shite and syphilis. You're suspended.

On the way home again, Coyne called in to Fred and explained the whole Sitwell situation to him.

It was all the art stuff that got to me. I went out to investigate his house and what do I find, a nude painting of my wife. I'm telling you. A nude painting of Carmel, he has. Then he has the nerve to report me, the bastard.

You'll have to talk to her, Fred advised. Just tell her the whole story. She'll sort it out. Maybe she can get him to withdraw the charges.

There's going to be an enquiry.

Fred thought long and hard. Drawing inspiration from the soggy brown corpse of a marshmallow he was pulling up from his tea.

I've never heard of a door closing without another one opening at the same time, he said.

Coyne tried to work that one out. As far as he was concerned, there were too many doors opening and closing. It was all too much like a revolving door for his liking.

It's an exit I'm looking for, he said in despair.

Ah, now take it easy, Pat. Don't be talking like that. Explain the situation to Carmel. She'll go and sort this Sitwell fellow out for you.

By the way, Fred said, changing the subject. That girl was on the phone looking for you.

Who?

Naomi, the one you told me about. Hangs around with Drummer. Said she was looking for Vinnie Foley. That's a pal of yours, isn't it?

Sure. He's my friend.

Fred got up from his seat and went over to Coyne, placing his hand on his shoulder. He stood staring at the yard outside the dusty blinds. One of the arc lights was shaking on a pole in the breeze, throwing unstable shadows around the parked trucks. Making them look like they were beginning to reverse slowly.

You'll have the last laugh, Fred said after a while. The doors are beginning to open. Go home and talk to Carmel.

But Coyne could not go home. He drove back through the city aimlessly, merging with the lights of night-time traffic, drifting around slowly in his own car as though he was still driving the squad car. For once he had changed out of his uniform at the station, but he was still vigilantly looking at people on the pavement, taking in all the tiny details. He was still a cop, and the fact that he had been suspended had not yet sunk in. He stopped at a pub and drank aimlessly, one pint after another. Moved on to another pub and drank till closing time, then bought a small bottle of whiskey and went back to the car. He couldn't face the questioning from Carmel, so he parked by the river for a while to consider his position. Drinking down the whiskey, he watched the lights on the far side reflected on the red-brown water, until he became mesmerized by the flow and felt the river had stopped and he was travelling back up into the city.

His life was finished. He would be dismissed from the Guards and have to take up some job as nightwatchman, like Fred. There was no future for him. He would be a disaster in the eyes of his children. He threw the empty bottle into the river and contemplated going in after it himself, driving straight over the edge. It seemed like a perfect ending. He had always had that passion for endings.

Instead he drove back into the city, feeling a new anger growing. He wasn't finished yet. If was going to be hounded out of the Guards, then maybe he should go out with a bang and make one big, final, heroic act. Something that might even save the day and make the whole Sitwell thing look like a plastic bag in the wind; one of those tattered bags stuck in the trees. He would show the bastards what it was all about. Coyne would be remembered as the man who took on the Drummer. This was the showdown he was waiting for.

Coyne stopped at a petrol station, one with an all-night shop, where he bought an assortment of odd items. A bizzare shopping list. Sun-glasses, packets of steak, chewing gum, pliers, screwdriver, a holdall bag, as well as a T-shirt and one of those baseball caps. All the things he needed on his final mission. Driven by a new mood of optimism and complete fearlessness, he placed them in the boot, all except the items of clothing, which he put on. He needed a new image to go with his make-or-break role. Wearing red sun-glasses and baseball cap, along with a brand-new T-shirt with Madonna staring lasciviously at an angle out from his chest, he drove up towards Leeson Street and parked in a quiet street close to the Fountain night-club. He calmly peeled back the wrapper on a piece of chewing gum, allowed it to fold over neatly in his mouth and got out of the car. He was chewing vigorously as he walked towards the club.

Drummer was having a slight problem with the builder, Brendan Barry. All the work that had been done on

167

renovating the club had not been paid for. Builder Brendan was coming to the club every night hassling Drummer about some kind of instalment plan. But Drummer never liked to part with cash and was trying to encourage the builder to invest in the night-club business. He was buying champagne and telling him he could have shares in the Fountain instead of payment.

Look at the place, Bren. You'd be doing the right thing, investing.

I need the money, Builder Brendan kept saying.

Don't worry so much about money, Drummer said, pouring out more champagne. We have different ways of settling our bills.

He looked away towards the dance floor where Naomi was dancing in one of the elevated corrals. She was wearing a short blue skirt and a belly top that was hardly more than a bra. She had retreated into her own internal world, rocking herself like a baby.

Builder Brendan had a face like a dartboard. Looked like he was into sailing, wearing a blue blazer with gold buttons and a matching red, pock-marked face. He had the mentality of a mechanical digger but he also had all the attributes of respectability that Berti Cunningham admired. Lived in a white mansion in the foothills of the Dublin Mountains that had a Doric porch and a tennis court out at the back. Drummer wanted him as a silent partner. Some true redneck gobshite who was as clean as the Pope's underpants and would keep his mouth shut at the right time.

Let me guess, Drummer said at one point. You do a bit of sailing.

But Builder Brendan said he was more into flying. Looked up as though he'd spotted a Cessna tracing across the ceiling of the night-club. Said he already had hundreds of flying hours behind him.

When you're up there, man, it's like holding Sharon Stone by the hips, he said. From behind.

Into the aeronautics, are we?

I'm just waiting for the day when I get a young one up there for a bit of in-flight service at two thousand feet over Glendalough, the builder bragged.

I think I've got somebody in mind for that, Drummer said, looking away towards Naomi again.

Coyne entered the Fountain by stealth, linking up with a group at the door, shifting around, hopping a little on one foot, and blending in with the real clubbers as though he couldn't wait to get inside and start dancing his head off. Are you buzzing, they all kept saying to each other. The usual bouncers in tuxedos were standing outside, and Coyne recognized the men who had beaten him up. He felt quite drunk and didn't care. But he was only interested in getting past them so that he could hit his real target. The disguise was perfect and he was sluiced through the entrance with the flow of the crowd.

The dance floor inside was packed. A spawning mass of arms and legs shifting and jerking to a never-ending beat. At first it looked like a heaving jar of tadpoles, bursting to live and give life again. *Get your rocks off, Honey, get your rocks off* . . . Flashes of coloured lightning illuminating individuals for one or two seconds at a time in a thunderstorm. What was it in music that caused such democratic epilepsy? Some electrical interference with the human pulse that made the nervous system jump. Coyne jittered through the crowd, manoeuvring his way towards the far corner of the dance floor from where he could see the whole night-club virtually. Through the shifting mass he could catch glimpses of Naomi at the bar. She was there with Drummer and some of the other men, dressed in a provocative skirt. Coyne couldn't take his eyes off her. The shape of her nipples was printed out through the little belly top and her legs beamed mercilessly at him like a flashing WIN sign in an amusement arcade.

Drummer was introducing her to Builder Brendan at that moment, letting them shake hands and get to know each other. He was like a matchmaker, a one-man dating service.

Have you ever been up in a small plane, he asked her. He explained that Builder Brendan with the red neck and the Pope's underpants and the stupid, South Country grin on his face, was an expert in the air.

She gave Drummer a forced smile. The dual meaning of his words was not lost on her. She read them like a threat, looking the builder up and down with a mixture of contempt and nausea. Pass the bucket.

Naomi would love a trip, Bren. All around Wicklow. Show her the round tower.

But Naomi was happier to stay on the ground. She said she had a lifelong problem with altitude. Anything higher than the third floor was tricky, unless it was something injected. So Drummer put his arm around her and promised he'd provide her with a parachute. Then he squeezed her in his vice grip to give her a subtle, sub-verbal message. You're a natural air hostess. Then he dragged Builder Brendan out on the dance floor and set them both afloat among the sea of dancers. The perfect couple. Builder Brendan in his navy blazer with a little flap at the back that looked a bit like a cat door when he put his hands in his pockets. And Naomi with a belly button that swivelled and swung like a hypnotist's watch.

The builder was already drunk on the champagne. His

sense of rhythm wasn't bad, but he moved as though he was lifting breeze blocks in his arms. His feet were stuck in concrete. Arse like a swinging sandbag. And it was only when he tried to introduce the aeronautics theme into dancing that he really took off, flying around her in a drunken figure of eight, arms stretched out like a fucking cement mixer that had been converted into a glider.

Coyne watched all this from a discreet distance. He waited a while until he saw Cunningham and Chief retreating to the VIP lounge. And when he spotted the builder futt-futting around her again with his tie flung back over his shoulder in the wind, Coyne decided his moment had arrived. It was time for action.

He took off his baseball cap and danced over towards them. Stood before Naomi and took off his sun-glasses. She seemed to recognize him through a myopic stare.

Let's go, he commanded, taking her by the hand.

He began to pull her away and she said something that he didn't hear. She didn't offer any resistance. It was only the builder who thought of putting up a struggle, trying to hold on to Naomi by the shoulders. But Coyne turned back quite lazily, bringing the builder down to earth with a neat punch in the stomach. He doubled over and swayed back into the crowd vowing horrific ramifications. Everyone looked on in amazement as though they were watching a trailer from a movie. Coyne pulling her towards the exit. Naomi tottering on her high platform shoes behind him.

Outside, the pack of Neck Decks were only concerned with people getting in and seemed to ignore those who were leaving. Coyne did it with great chivalry, escorting her out silently on his arm, but then, when he saw a look of suspicion in one of the bouncers' eyes, he began to push her up the cast-iron stairs towards the street. Somewhere close to the top, she lost one of her shoes and it fell all the way back down into the den of dickheads below, just as they started to come up the stairs after him.

Where do you think you're going, mister?

Coyne managed to get her out on to the pavement. Fuck the shoe, he thought. The men were bounding up the steps, holding the hand rail in one hand and their chicken curries in the other, keeping the jackets tucked in neatly around the stomach to maintain their dignity. Coyne had time to notice their dickie bows and the dainty buckles on one of the men's shoes. Then whack! Just as Coyne was getting ready to say he was a Garda from the Special Branch, taking this girl away for her own safety, he realized there was no point and simply stuck the boot into the first groin that came up the steps, followed by a smart crack of the fist on the nose. He felt his hand had turned into a packet of sausages with the impact. Tit for tat. It had the desired effect of sending the bouncer back into the arms of his companion and both of them crumbled down the steps under their own weight as though it was all choreo-graphed in advance. The first man laying his cheek softly against the railing, loosening his dickie bow and moaning to his friend to go after Coyne.

But Coyne was half-way around the block by then, pulling the limping beauty behind him. He got to his car and bundled her inside. Left the lights off as he drove away, just in case they might get his number plate. He had struck deep at the heart of Dublin's crime empire.

Coyne drove around in circles. Now that Naomi was in the car with him, he had no idea what he should say or do. He was drunk, and as the tension of the escape wore off, he tried to think of his next move. Stopped the car by the canal and left the engine running. Asked her where she lived, but she gave a cynical grin to indicate that it would be suicidal. The first place Cunningham's men would go looking. Coyne had got her out of a potentially nasty situation at two thousand feet over Glendalough. She was expecting him to take her somewhere interesting. Her legs were stretched out in the car, recently rescued written all over them.

You're in trouble, he said, talking like a priest. You're entertaining some very bad company.

Yeah, she said with laconic resignation. What a creep? Wanted to teach me flying, for fucksake.

Not him, the Drummer.

What about him? she asked suspiciously.

You know he's killed somebody. Murder, Naomi. That's what.

You're a cop, aren't you, she said, looking him in the eyes. I knew it.

Coyne gave a little affected laugh.

What makes you think that? I work in advertising. I'm only trying to help you out of this mess, Naomi. You're a nice girl. You shouldn't be hanging around with those guys.

In fact, he sounded just like an archbishop. Really in touch, like. There she was, with her legs all over his car and he was starting to speak like a concerned parent. Giving her a load of paternal advice that she didn't want to hear.

If you're a cop, then I'm dead, she said.

Don't worry, I'll take care of you. You need treatment. I can help you.

Chief and two of the bouncers who could recognize Coyne got into the Pajero and drove around the area searching in the alleyways, checking all the side-streets. Mick went out on foot while Drummer stayed behind in the night-club

173

trying to calm Builder Brendan down a bit. He was more interested than ever in making sure that the builder was enjoying himself and saw the potential of a neat little sex scandal which he could hold over him. Gave him some explanation about a jealous former boy-friend. Got two of the silky girls down from the elevated corrals and asked them to dance with him instead. Drummer ordered lots more champagne and persuaded the builder he was still having the time of his life. That plane trip over Wicklow was still on schedule, with a new cabin crew.

Coyne left the engine running. He felt uneasy by the canal. It was too close to the night-club scene and he should have driven away to some other part of the city. But where? He had no game plan. Thought of driving up to Fred's lock-up compound. That was the safest thing to do. Fred would have some things to say.

What do you do for a living? Coyne asked.

I'm a dancer, she said. I dance people to death.

Come on, Naomi. I'm trying to help you. Where are your parents?

Fuck my parents. They should have used a fucking condom, she said. Now look at the result.

You need them, Coyne argued. They're the people you can turn to.

Like fuck. Are you trying to rescue me or something, Vinnie?

I'm on your side, that's all, he said.

Coyne was just about to drive off again. He had finally decided to take her to Fred. Perhaps she would start drinking tea and eating lots of Mikado biscuits. See the light of justice and tell the whole truth about Drummer and his gang. It was worth a try. There was nowhere else.

But in that moment, Naomi began to embrace him.

Threw her long bare arms around him and kissed his cheek. Coyne froze. Looked all around him as though the people of Dublin were watching him, even though the street was silent and empty, with nothing stirring except a few leaves being blown along the canal bank walk. She rubbed the back of his neck with her fingers and he felt a warm, erotic shiver. He denied it and began to push her gently back into her seat.

Look, you must be cold, he said, reaching into the back for a jacket, which he placed around her shoulders. He was treating her like a daughter again. And she stared out at the canal silently. Disappointed.

You're married, aren't you?

She leaned forward and picked up a child's furry rabbit from the floor of the car. Played with it in her hands as though it was one that she had owned not long ago as a small girl. Her childhood flooded back, and for a moment she was like Coyne's daughter, grown by almost twenty years in the space of one night.

You need protection, Coyne tried again. I can get you protection. Trust me.

Protection, she said, puzzled. You're married and you're a cop.

She sat looking at the soft toy in her hand. Tickled it under the chin as if it was her baby. Held it to her chest and then started crying. The sudden exposure to such family warmth had overwhelmed her. She opened the car door, threw off Coyne's jacket and stepped outside, running away along the street.

Wait, he shouted.

He took the jacket and followed her, leaving the doors of the car open. It was sure to attract attention. So he ran back and switched the engine off and closed the doors. Then went to where Naomi had stopped in the mouth of a small alleyway, back against the wall, staring up at the yellow street light through her watery eyes. All around her, the junk which people had thrown out into the lane. He reached her and put the jacket back around her shoulders again, trying to take her hand and coax her back to the car.

Let's go and see Fred, he said. He's a good pal of mine. He'll help.

Love me, Vinnie, she pleaded, throwing her arms around him once more. I swear I want to go clean. I'll get off junk. I'll go for treatment. I'll do anything for you, if you love me. Just once, Vinnie. Go on.

She looked different in that laneway, in a jaundiced twilight, with an upturned couch and an old electric cooker dumped a few feet away from her. Coyne had been asking her to make a choice and realized that she had been so whipped by authority, so subservient to the demands of her addiction, that he would have to employ a more commanding tone. For her own sake, he would have to drag her forcibly back to the car. But when he took her arm and allowed the soft, milky flesh to enter his imagination, his conviction slipped.

Coyne was drunk and did what Vinnie Foley would do in this moment; took hold of her hands and kissed the mutilated wrists, to which she responded by looking into his eyes as though they were in a suicide pact together. Their faces were green, almost, under the yellow light, and he was struck by a great spontaneous urge to fuck her brains out. He was being honest about his desire. More than ever before, with the graffiti and the scorch marks of old fires along the walls of the lane, where men pissed on their way home from the pubs and where cats howled their tortured songs at night, he wanted to follow his instinct. In the gap between her top and her skirt, he watched her navel moving in and out gently on her breath. He placed his mouth on hers and pushed himself up against her so that he was no longer sure how tall she was. As he began to examine her body with his hands, each part of her took on such an immense significance that she seemed to be completely out of proportion with any other earthly or material measurement.

For once, Coyne did not ask questions. Under this gold-grey reality of the yellow street light, his mind stopped triggering off a running commentary to his audience. Her eyes and her mouth looked black, with a wet, liquorice tongue and sweet liquorice breath. His lobster-blue lips sucked her nipple as if it was a dark-green cough drop. Even her knickers looked black when she pulled them down and stepped out of them like she would step out of a *currach*, holding on to his arm. She placed them in the pocket of his jacket for safe keeping and he held one of her legs, the one with no shoe on, by the knee underneath. His feet crunched on broken glass and he pushed her against the wall with such ferocity that he was in danger of breaking her bones. He was doing it now. What he had never fully been able to imagine. Unprotected. Unforeseen. Irreversible. He had become Vinnie Foley. He was sailing down the Amazon. The fact that he was striking at the Cunninghams increased the intensity of his desire and he squeezed her slender jaw in his hand to extract a contorted expression of pain on her face. The Pajero passed right by them.

You should have told me that's what you meant by treatment, Naomi said afterwards when they got back into the car. Coyne wanted to tell her all about himself but couldn't risk such a compromise. He would never let her go again, he vowed to himself. He wanted to bring her back to where she lived and repeat the whole thing, but she suddenly had an idea. She was starving and wanted chips, so he drove off to find a chipper on Baggot Street and got out while she sat in the car with her feet up on the dashboard, inhaling the glory of her recent sexual encounter with a Garda, knowing that she would never be the same again. When he came out, however, carrying two bags of chips, she had disappeared.

Chief and the bouncers returned to the night-club. Mick was already back there talking to his brother. Chief was worried, saying the girl could no longer be trusted. Something should be done with her, he was suggesting. But Drummer was far more relaxed about the whole situation. They underestimated his power over women. He knew exactly how to deal with Naomi. And besides, there was no point in making a fuss right there and then. He didn't want Builder Brendan with the red-brick face to get the impression that something was going wrong. He had plans for him and had invited him back to his house in Sandymount for a private party.

Coyne threw the chips into the canal where the rats would swim out in due course and claim the salvage rights. Sat in the car waiting to see if she'd come-back. Then it was his turn to cruise around like a returned emigrant and search for her like a distant first love in his memory. He should have gone home and stored it in the vaults of his mind, but he drove back to the laneway and stopped to look at the place where they had stood together, staring at this love shrine of casual sex. He was soon filled with such longing and fury that he decided to move straight on to the real mission. He had planned to target Cunningham's house that night and the self-destructive aftermath of sex with Naomi forced him into action.

As Coyne drove out to Sandymount, he began to think about Carmel too, feeling a new guilt which could only be avenged by war and attrition. He ripped the luminous green statue of Our Lady from the dashboard of the car and put it in his pocket. He had already spent long enough surveying the house to know that there were two dogs at the back waiting for Drummer to come back and feed them. The house seemed impenetrable. There was an alarm and wire meshes on the back windows. In any case the two ugly-looking Rottweilers in the back garden went into hysterics as soon as Coyne glanced over the wall with a Man United holdall bag under his arm. They snarled and barked as though they hadn't been fed in months. There was a sign saying: 'dog bites first, then asks questions later'. Rottweiler number one was consistently showing his dentures to Coyne, while Rottweiler number two kept turning around and coming back again. Like a man in a stetson hat renewing the pleasure of seeing himself in the mirror, the dogs kept running back and then attacking all over again from the beginning, as though they wanted to relive the darkest experience of their lives, the first sight of Coyne's face coming over the back wall. Imagine the neighbours having to put up with the barking and the pungent stink coming at them from the next garden, like a burning hamburger, Coyne thought. Not to mention the sight of Berti Cunningham every now and again in his jock strap feeding them scraps of his kebab and petting them like he was St Francis of Assisi or something.

Coyne had come prepared. He threw them a piece of meat: nice fillet steak for you, lads. They ignored it at first because they were just too angry and disgusted. Who the fuck do you think we are? Mind you, we'd settle for the prime hindquarters of a live Garda through a seven-foot concrete wall with razor wire on top, they seemed to be saying. But eventually the glistening red piece of fillet steak became too tempting, flashing at them like a neon sign in the grass, so that each dog was inspired by subliminal jealousy at the thought of the other dog getting it. Even if it wasn't Garda loin chop, one of them just inhaled it between barks, before you could say succulent.

Coyne had his gloves on. From the bag under his arm he took out some more pieces of mildly tranquillizing meat, giving the less fortunate of the two Rottweilers the chance to get his own bit as well. Very soon the barking stopped and the dogs dropped down where they were standing. Lie down, ye dogs of illusion.

Quickly Coyne took the opportunity to snip the razor wire and climb across the wall. He had to negotiate his way among the landmines of dogshite all over the lawn until he got to the back door of the house. It was locked. But then he found the patio door unlocked so that he could walk straight in. Berti hadn't even switched on the alarm. Or maybe he didn't have an alarm, just put the box on the wall like everyone else. Probably thought he was immune to crime. And what about all this neighbourhood watch? Some neighbours you have, Berti.

Coyne's first concern was to find some evidence which would put Berti behind bars. Even though the house had been searched in vain many times before by the Guards, Coyne tried to locate secret lockers.

The twin reception room was furnished with a white Louis XIV sideboard and a white piano, for God's sake, with Richard Clayderman open on the stand to show the level of refinement in the Cunningham home. There were two suites, a leather one and a pristine white one on which there were two long brown stains. Coyne worked them out to be the fake tan stains left behind by one of Berti's women. As though everything in the man's life was fake.

Coyne threw a few cushions around. Ripped the leather sofa in order to stick his hand right down and feel for hardware. He searched the whole room and came up with nothing more than a few Bryan fucking Adams CDs. Whitney dentures Houston, and the fucking 'Woman's Heart' album. Berti, you sad bastard, there's more musical taste in a donkey's fart. If ever the courts needed evidence of a complete bone-brain moron, here it was.

Coyne took a quick blast of his inhaler, holding it up in this strangely tacky and elegant palace like a symbol of demonic vengeance. He had decided that gathering evidence was too much trouble at this late stage and resolved to deliver justice right into the heart of Drummer Cunningham's home. There was no point in acting like gentlemen any more, Coyne thought as he pushed the Waterford glass cabinet over until it rocked and fell into the room like an office block collapsing into the street. There was glass everywhere and Coyne thought the noise would have been heard right across the street. The dogs outside had heard it and he was taken by surprise when they were up again so soon, barking like never before, knowing how easily they had been duped. They could see Coyne inside the house, smiling at them, kicking over the TV set, which fizzled as it imploded. No more MTV, for you, Berti Butthead.

On the way home, Drummer decided to call into Abrakebabra for some kebabs for the dogs. Brendan Barry and the two silky girls on either side of him were in the back of the Pajero, while Mick and Chief were stopped right behind them in the Chief's Mazda 626. What a service! Drummer offered his creditors only the best of everything. They would even phone his wife in Stepaside for him and tell her he was detained at an official function. And food too. Drummer came out carrying a bag of kebabs, offering them around.

Anybody want some of this dogfood? he asked, placing them on the dashboard, where they steamed up the windscreen.

Coyne wandered around Drummer's house, ate a chocolate chip cookie in the kitchen and found the study full of Berti's law books. The constitution. The one and only *Bunreacht na hEireann*. But what did Cunningham care about Ireland or the Irish people. He was only interested in his own rights and what was in the constitution for him. He had other books on case history since the foundation of the state. Extradition law, the lot. Jesus, the guy knew more about the law than a Supreme Court judge. No wonder he was impossible to pin down. The latest government white paper on legal reform lay open on a small Victorian desk. A notepad beside it on which Coyne hastily wrote his guiding slogan – The law is an asshole.

Coyne went upstairs and took a small petrol can from his bag, placing it on the landing. He laughed when he saw the master bedroom and thought Mrs Gogarty would appreciate the pink, two-inch-deep, furry carpet, heaving with house mites. Pink bedside lamps held up by brass snakes coming out of the wall. Brass bed posts for Drummer to tie up his women, and mirrored wardrobes so he could watch his own arse as though he was in a porn movie.

Outside the dogs continued barking again and Coyne stared down at them, knowing that his escape out the back was blocked off. He felt he had already spent too much time in the house and intended to leave again, giving his enemy a slightly religious message to reflect on. Took out the luminous Virgin Mary that Mrs Gogarty had once stuck on to the dashboard of the car and placed her in Berti's bed, tucking her in under the duvet. In bed with Madonna. Sleeping with the BVM – the immaculate contraception.

Coyne heard the car outside. Then the voices coming towards the house, followed by the key in the hall door. He was trapped, and it was too late to start pouring petrol.

Drummer Cunningham came in and dropped the keys of the car on the hall stand, ushering Brendan Barry and the two silky girls inside. Mick Cunningham was there too and they stood in the hall for a moment where Coyne could see them from the landing. Berti with his blond hair; short on the sides and long at the back like some kind of helmet. Whenever he moved his head, the helmet of hair moved with it. Any minute, all hell would break loose, and Coyne took the decommissioned gun from the Man United bag. He had kept possession of it instead of handing it in, initially with the intention of threatening Mr Sitwell. Now he stood in Cunningham's home with a useless weapon. It was all he had.

Ah fuck, he heard Berti shout downstairs. The bastards. We've been done.

Drummer came rushing back out into the hallway, just as Coyne ran down the stairs, pointing the gun straight at his head.

OK, hold it right there, Coyne shouted, stopping half-way down.

Just give me a reason to paint your brains all over that wall, Cunningham. Come on.

But Berti kept his cool and said nothing. A lot of things could go wrong, so he just stared at Coyne, memorizing his face. Brendan Barry was the first to put his arms up in the air. You could say what you liked, but no amount of aeronautics with the silky girls was worth having to look straight at the foreskin of a gun. There was peace at any price written all over his Stepaside façade. The Pope's underpants were not so pristine perhaps.

Get down on the floor, all of you, Coyne shouted, and when they obeyed him he was amazed at the power of the weapon.

You won't get away with this, Chief said. We'll get your wife and kids.

Like fuck you will, Coyne said more quietly. If you go near her again, I'll come and kill you all. I'll do the same as I did to your car, Drummer. I'll burn down your house and your club and everything you own. Nobody will even remember who you were.

Let's rush him, Mick Cunningham whispered.

Go ahead, Coyne shouted in response. If you want to increase the number of holes in your arse?

Coyne roared so loud that it echoed all over the house. Drummer Cunningham held his brother back and nodded reassuringly to the builder.

Relax! Nobody's moving.

Go on, lie down and put your arms out over your head, Coyne commanded. He remembered that the gun was useless and began shaking, eyes wide like a possessed man who was capable of anything. Then he walked down the stairs, took the key-ring from the hall table and made his way to the front door.

We'll get you, Chief said in a burst of injured pride. This is not the end.

Make my day, you gobshite, Coyne said as he retreated towards the door, pointing the trembling gun at the mass of bodies on the floor of the hallway. He laughed in a state of self-induced shock as he opened the door, slammed it shut and locked them inside.

Coyne could heard the shouts coming from inside the house as he ran.

Get the dogs, Drummer roared as Coyne fled past the cars in the driveway, out on to the pavement. He threw the keys into a nearby hedge. Then sprinted back towards his car, parked around the corner in the next street. He was only half-way there, however, when the dogs came shooting out of Drummer's house with the full velocity of diarrhoea. The hounds of illusion, ready to rip Coyne's arse into shreds for playing such a dirty trick on them with the meat.

There was a lot of shouting going on. The neighbourhood watch had finally been brought into action. Lights went on everywhere and residents looked out through their bedroom windows at the cold street outside. Mick Cunningham was running down the drive with a hammer in his hand, ready to use it as a mace and make a bloody pudding of Coyne's head. But Chief held him back, waiting for Drummer to come out with the gun.

In the meantime, Drummer had been upstairs, ripped a firearm from the mattress in the bedroom and found the Virgin Mary sticking out from under the bedclothes. It freaked the shite out of him all right, like seeing his own mother in the bed, holding her teeth in her hand. He also saw the petrol can sitting on the landing. But he put his fears on hold and was already hurling himself down the stairs again carrying the gun in one hand and the mobile phone in the other.

Get the Pajero out, he shouted, throwing the phone to his brother. We're going after this cunt until he bleeds.

Then he ran down the street after the dogs in the hope that they would catch up with Coyne and drag him back like some unfortunate Jock-of-the-Bushveld victim. Drummer Cunningham unleashed his hydrochloric invective across the prim hedges as he ran. You'll die with fish hooks in your eyes. Rats crawling up your arsehole. Don't worry, Naomi is going to dance for you, my friend.

He was a hurt man, with one hell of a bee sting in the crotch. So sore that he stopped, out of breath, just a hundred yards short of the corner, whistled at the dogs to come back and steadied himself in order to take aim. Bewildered neighbours withdrew their faces again in case his indiscriminate wrath might turn on them instead. It wouldn't be vomit on the hedges this time. Or empty Strongbow flagons on the lawns. It would be more than slashed tyres and broken windows from now on. They jumped back from their windows as if they had seen lightning with the naked eye – some of them hiding behind sofas, like they were going to be watching the TV with their backsides from now on.

A shot whipped through the street, hitting nothing but the trunk of a hawthorn sapling. The dogs kept on running after Coyne. And Berti sprinted down the pavement after them, his body passing along the hedges at a steady elevation and his legs fast-forwarding in multiple small steps underneath him. He was holding the gun across his balls, helmet of hair lifting up at the back, nose flaring, and his thin, minimalist lips puckered into a raging arsehole as he ran. A late-night pedestrian stopped to look at this extraordinary athlete.

Coyne had taken the corner faster than he intended. Mr Suicide was right. He had lost his footing along the kerb and fallen down. Now there was a huge pain in his chest as he got up again. He could feel the asthma attack coming and thought he was crawling out of his own nightmare, unable to move. The whole idea of fear came to him like a charge of lucidity, a great rush of mental energy in the face of death.

He managed to get up and half run or limp away towards his car. His knee screaming with new pain. He had dropped the decommissioned gun on the pavement. But the more immediate concern was the sight of the dogs hooring around the corner after him, so that his legs felt like Pedigree Chum by the time he reached his car. He was in a palsy of terror. Like a rabbit in the headlights, he was overcome by a powerful weakness as he fiddled with the key and watched the Rottweilers' eyes and teeth lurching towards him in great bounds along the street. Finally he opened the door and only just slammed it shut again behind him as the dogs leaped up on to the side window, paws scratching the paintwork, saliva all over the glass.

Piss off, you savages. Go back and give your owner a blow job.

Then Berti came belting around the corner with a face on him that would do for a haemorrhoid in a medical journal. Saw the dogs trying to mount the little Escort and ran across the street towards them.

Coyne's chest was killing him. Don't fail me now, Vlad, he muttered, as he took out the inhaler like a gun, preparing for a final shoot-out. He puffed and kept trying to start the car, or start his lungs, whichever of them would stop coughing their shaggin' rings up first. Felt he was trying to pull fuel in through a tiny pin-hole. Face turning blue with the effort, and wishing he could just pass out like the prey of a grizzly bear and let Cunningham do what he had to do. Rip Coyne's entire face off with a downward strike of his paw. At least he didn't have his back to the enemy.

As Berti ran towards him, Coyne could see the gun in his hand. Their eyes met, white with rage, just as the car

187

started and surged forward like an unexpected ejaculation. He heard the crack of bones against the fender, along with the involuntary wail as the Drummer was lifted into the air. His legs were all floppy, as though he was practising Irish dancing horizontally on the bonnet. Face sliding along the windscreen for a moment in some bizarre attempt to kiss Coyne goodbye before he disappeared. The force of the acceleration felt like a hand pressing into the small of Coyne's back. Back to the future. The car shot forward so fast that the dogs were left barking at an empty parking place, until they saw their owner sitting on his arse in the street, feeling his legs, repeating the registration number over and over as though it was going to kill the pain.

Coyne woke up in the car and tried to piece together his last movements. It was almost dawn and the light was coming up over the sea. He had parked at the harbour and now found himself looking out over the water at full tide. His head was in a vice; massive hands were gripping the side of his neck and it seemed as though he was carrying a dead hedgehog in his stomach. He was like Major Tom, lost in space. The record he had played for his kids, ever since Jimmy was small, was now Coyne's own reality. He had told them endless stories so that they believed Major Tom was still adrift in space, floating into infinity, arriving at an unending succession of planets, searching for ways to get back home to earth. The planet of laughs. The planet of bad memories. The planet of sudden holes in the ground and the planet of colours. Jennifer and Nuala wanted him back to tell them more planets and explain things like infinity. He had a great one in his head about the planet of friends and enemies.

The events of the night paraded around his head in a procession of detached and incomprehensible images. He got out and stood on the pier, staring into the water. There was a slight breeze blowing from the shore and he felt the absurd urge to go fishing. He listened to the sounds of the harbour and caught the smells of seaweed, oil, paint, tar and the fish skeletons dumped at the end of the pier. In the pocket of his jacket he felt Naomi's knickers in his hand. A souvenir or a trophy which he had been given inadvertently, recalling the overwhelming meeting of their bodies. Holding this frail proof in his hand at first light, he noticed that they were not black. The details of her body evoked by the sight of her wine-red knickers would be buried in his memory like a hidden icon. He put the tiny garment up to his face and inhaled deeply before throwing it out on to the water, where it floated on the surface, as though Naomi was dancing and swaying her hips, swimming languorously on her back. He longed for her with such a sad, guilty desire that he wanted to join her and die. There was nobody around and Coyne could easily have plucked one of the boats from the moorings and rowed out, like Major Tom of the sea. All the islands he would get to. He would drift across the ocean beds, banqueting in the realm of lobsters, swimming with shoals of mackerel, talking to men with fins and lidless eyes as he passed through their extraordinary underwater kingdoms. Some stories he would get out of that. It would take months to tell them all. It would be an epic voyage. Coyne of the sea.

He turned his back and walked up the hill, away from the harbour. There was a great fury in the way his feet marched forward. He had never experienced this level of emptiness before, as though he had lost everything now, his friend Vinnie Foley, his wife, his family. Coyne had become an individual. A grown-up. Abandoned. An islandman, with a blue glimmer of dawn in the sky at the end of the street, increasing the panic in his soul. He began to notice dogshite everywhere. He had had hangovers before, but this one beat them all. This was revisionist. The dogs of illusion had been let out during the night and left their columns everywhere along the pavement. Dirty big craps of every denomination. Chalky versions, fossilized on granite kerbstones. Some trodden on already and carried on along the pavement like a piece of abstract art. It was like the aftermath of a war. Faeces clinging to his brain. Every shade of shite, from black to brown, littered all over like battle debris under the street lights. With great revulsion, his intellect became unstuck with guilt.

He kept walking uphill. As long as he was moving, there was a feeling of going somewhere, until he reached higher ground and saw that the dawn sky over Bray Head had turned blue. He turned back in shock and remembered suddenly that he had still not begun building the swing for his kids. He was hit by a great swell of love and self-loathing. He wanted to be with Carmel and his kids again, feel their chubby arms, hold their dimpled hands or pretend to bite their toes. Tell them of his great adventures under the sea. He was going to start building the swing for them at last.

Drummer and Chief caught up with Naomi in the early hours of the morning at her flat. After Drummer went to hospital to get his fractured arm seen to, he found her at home, fretting and crying. With one arm in a sling, he slapped her around a bit with his good arm, saying that he had no mercy left in him at all any more.

You didn't put up much fuckin' resistance, he shouted at her, but she swore she had been abducted and made her escape as soon as she could. Explained that she had tricked him into buying chips and then slipped away.

Drummer looked deep into her eyes. He engaged in a little foreplay with a kitchen knife, just enough to hurt her and make her see the colour of her own blood again. But he needed her for a dance of revenge with Coyne and let her go at last, when she was pale with fear.

I wouldn't trust her any more, Chief whispered.

But Drummer was clearheaded. Prepared a little fix for her. Knew that all he needed in order to get her absolute allegiance was to find a vein in which he could deliver the full force of his chemical cocktail.

I want this done right, he said, cleaning a spot on her outstretched arm with a swab of gin. I want to get this fucker myself. He'll be coughing up his goolies. I want to see the wax shooting out of his ears. Then I want to see him dying, slowly. Psychedelic, like.

He's probably got Garda protection by now, Chief warned.

Didn't fuckin' help Brannigan very much, did it?

The weather had turned very cold overnight, and by afternoon, when Coyne got up, the children stood around outside with their scarves and their hats on, pretending to puff smoke while he measured the garden. It was an odd time of the year to start erecting a swing, but Coyne set about the task like a farewell act – ordering the cast-iron frame, and the concrete blocks, and the bolts. It was going to be a decent swing, not like those useless contraptions he saw in the DIY Centre, with a hollow frame that lost balance and hopped up each time somebody swung out. It became a major project which absorbed him completely, spending hours in the garden hacking back the hedges in order to clear enough space. Standing back to look and imagine it when it was finished. Holding an image of his smiling and excited kids in his head all the time.

He thought of it as an essential last-minute deed before Drummer Cunningham would come and eliminate him. As long as they left him enough time for that. If it was the last thing he would do, he would see Nuala swinging back and forth, with one sock up and one sock down. But he was not giving them any clues and kept them guessing.

It's a big secret, he said to them. Not even Carmel knew.

Carmel was worried about other things. She was still reeling from the shock of her abduction. Felt she should have reported the attack to the Gardai, for the record. But Coyne said he had dealt with it at the highest level already.

I'd hate to think they knew where I lived, she said.

You can put that out of your head, he assured her. The lads are on to them. The Super even asked me if I wanted protection, but I said it wasn't necessary. Nothing will happen.

Are you sure?

I'll protect you, love, Coyne said with a big smile.

That evening he went to the Garda club for a drink. He had the longing to be with his colleagues in the Force. McGuinness came to meet him, along with some of the other members. He also needed to be out of the house so that he could pretend for the time being that he was still at work. He hadn't told Carmel anything about the suspension.

At the Garda club, Coyne was excited. Talked as though he hadn't seen them in months. Telling them about things he had read, people who had survived mauling by lions and Bengal tigers.

The Elixir of Prey, he announced, holding them spellbound with the facts while he drank back his pint.

This guy was mauled on the ice by a polar bear, Coyne went on. Said it was like an orgasm. Stronger than anything he'd ever experienced before in his life. His companion managed to shoot the bear just in time.

Was the polar bear wearing a condom? That's what I want to know, one of them asked.

I'm not messing, Coyne insisted. They did a big survey on people close to death. They all said it was a sexual experience.

Would you fuck off, Coyne.

You mean to tell me that dying is the same as riding? somebody questioned sceptically.

They were laughing at him. Coyne ignored them, trying to drive his point home. They were chuckling away like the rabbits on the Aran Islands, but they would soon see that he was right all along. Laughing out of uneasy acknowledgement, they were. Reflecting on the times when they were most recently lying with their partners, heaving and struggling in a furious sexual contest, bucking in the throes of death. Recalling the encounters when they expired on a wave of pleasure, edging closer and closer to the moment when the soul parts company with the body.

No shit, lads, Coyne continued. They're not denying it frightened the shite out of them. These people knew they were fucked. They were staring death in the face. They were half-way to heaven. But after they were rescued, they said it was like a climax. There's a close link between sex and death, that's all I'm saying. Same snowfall of endorphins.

I'm dying in your arms tonight, one of the men started singing.

Coyne took it as a signal that somebody understood him at last. Sex is a form of epilepsy, he said, bursting forth with all his anarchic thoughts about men who had been tricked into death and thrown from helicopters at three feet. Bank clerks who felt an orgasm of fear during an armed raid. Victims of failed assassination plots who recalled the smell of the beast in their nostrils. And then there were the sexual proclivities that involved suffocation. The last ejaculation of a hanged man. Until they stared at Coyne like a new Freud, or Fromm, informing them that they underwent a death rehearsal each time they made love.

Think about it, Coyne said. But they had all begun to laugh again. The whole country was laughing at him and Coyne got up to go to the bar with his pint. McGuinness was the only disciple to follow him, keeping the faith where other men had lost their way.

Sheep shaggin' is probably all they know about, Coyne muttered.

But McGuinness wanted to talk to him about other things. The forthcoming enquiry. What he was going to do in his spare time. And there was another matter that troubled him about Coyne.

Pat, can I ask you something. What did you do with the gun?

Coyne looked at him and hesitated. Drank down an enormous gulp of his pint and ordered a new one with a nod.

The gun you confiscated. Molloy has been asking about it.

Coyne was drunk again. Walking back towards his car he stumbled across none other than Joe Perry. Hatchet-man Perry. The small-time criminal who had caused Coyne so much trouble with the post office job and the joy-riding incident. Perry had just hopped across the gate of a building site through which he had taken a short cut and was unfortunate enough to run straight into his worst enemy. Coyne caught him and pushed him up against the hoarding.

You little sparrowfart, Perry, he said.

I done nothing, Garda.

You little bastard. If I catch you near any cars again, I'll put your lights out. Do you hear me? Keep away from cars.

And Perry was even more surprised when Coyne let him go and walked away, turning back only to give him a last warning over his shoulder.

Stick to public transport, Perry. You hear.

Next thing, Coyne's mother got broken into. He immediately thought it was a reprisal. His world was falling apart, bit by bit.

She's had a mild stroke, Carmel said. It was the neighbours that found her. She's been taken to Tallaght.

Bastards, Coyne shouted, as though they had been waiting for the moment when he was off guard. He drove straight out to the hospital. His chest was tight and he took a blast of the inhaler. He rasped and coughed as he ran across the car-park, spitting out a priceless golden globule on to the tarmac, where it seemed to bounce forward before coming to rest. Bastards, bastards, bastards, he kept repeating.

The nurses said his mother would be fine. She'd only had a very mild stroke and was as tough as old boots, they assured him. But his anger had already changed to remorse. He sat beside her and looked out the window at the tops of trees. Staring through a fine drizzle he realized that he had let his own mother down in the end.

He drove down to the local Garda station to speak to the lads before going up to the house. No fingerprints had been found, apparently. But they were following a definite line of enquiry all the same. Of course, it wasn't the Cunninghams, but Coyne felt he had lost the whole battle. The intruders had removed the entire back door, including the door frame. All those security measures that Coyne had taken had been less than useless. It was only a joke. And all they had stolen was her television set. All she ever did in the last few years was watch the *Late Late Show.* Tele and Mass. Mass and Tele. And then they came and almost killed her for it. At least she was safe now in hospital.

Coyne stood in his old home and tried not to get worked up. He left again and didn't even put the back door up again. Left it open with the breeze blowing the wet garden debris right on to the floor of the kitchen. Spiders, wasps, all the creatures of Ireland could come in now. It was all after the fact. His mother would probably move straight to a nursing home from there. They were welcome to take whatever they wanted. There was nothing left of his home, only a gaunt set of memories. Rapacious cats could come in and wander around the whole house. There was nothing to protect.

While Carmel was selecting paintings for her exhibition, Coyne started digging away passionately in the garden on Friday morning, making dirty big holes in the lawn without anyone having any idea what they were for. Four black gashes in the little patch of green, so that even Mr Gillespie from next door took a furtive look out the bedroom window. Must have thought Coyne was erecting another one of those white pagodas that they had in number fifteen. The whole nation was in suspense. The final act in Coyne's life.

He was digging to beat the clock, trying to get the project finished before the rain came, before the kids came home from school, before the Cunninghams arrived to execute him. Carmel inside with her mother, trying to choose between two identical harbours. Spot the difference kind of thing. She couldn't ask Pat because he would say nothing. In the end, every artist had to manufacture his or her own confidence, Sitwell always said. You couldn't rely on other people. You had to be your own supporter.

And then they saw Coyne with a steel arm crossing the front window. The leg of a giant steel spider maybe. Holy Mary, Mother of God, Mrs Gogarty exclaimed. So they ran out to see Coyne struggling to get a big metal frame over the side gate of the house. Scraping half the pebble-dash off the side wall and not saying a word, just puffing like a set of *uileann* pipes on the run from a pack of greyhounds.

He ignored them completely, and when he shoved the frame into the four holes in the back garden, Mrs Gogarty and Carmel were standing at the kitchen window like com-mentators in a press gallery, reporting silently on every little development. Chuckling and arguing among them-selves as to what it could be.

Looks a bit like a gallows to me, said Mrs Gogarty.

Coyne laboured all afternoon with the swing, missing one deadline after another. First it rained. Then the kids all came home from school and saw him trying to bolt down the steel frame and having no luck at all, cursing and blasting because he discovered the bolts were too small.

It was too late on Friday afternoon to replace the bolts. The kids were already getting excited about the swing, begging to be given the first go, until Coyne drove them all inside and he sat in the kitchen like a condemned man, jumping up at every knock on the door. The milkman came like a cool assassin to collect the money, so he told the kids to say they would pay next week, which he had already said for three weeks running. Next week: no problem. A milkman's mercy, smiling a sinister reprieve. Nobody knew if Coyne would even be there next week.

Coyne stayed awake all night, thinking he would die leaving behind an unfinished swing. First thing on Saturday morning, he drove around to the DIY centre to see if he could get some bigger bolts, only to find that he had to buy a set of eight bolts plus a set of steel brackets, all in a pre-wrapped packet. The man in a mauve uniform and a teak Rustin's Wood Dye suntan shrugged his shoulders and Coyne went bananas again. Wanted to wreck the shop, spill chemicals all over the floor, rip big holes in bags of cement, maybe even pour adhesive all over the new tools. What kind of a fucking DIY centre is this, when you can't even buy a few bolts, Coyne raged. Next thing they'll be selling you a shaggin' barbecue or a wheelbarrow every time you want a few posi-drive screws. Special offer: get this power drill free with every six-inch nail.

And the amount of DIY dickheads hanging around on Saturday morning was unbelievable. People all over the place couldn't stop the urge to improve things. Can't you just leave the world alone, you pack of demented dipsticks? Nothing better to do than to start taking apart your sad little semis. Guys deciding to build shelves every Saturday morning of the year until they had drilled an almighty hole in one of their plasterboard walls. Women looking at new wooden toilet seats with adulterous glints. A man wobbling a saw in his hand like a diviner, as if that was going to tell him something. Some absolute wanker asking one of the men in mauve how you put up the self-assembly pagoda, while his family sat down inside one that was already assembled to see if they'd all fit. And what about the attic stairs with the picture of a woman half-way up like Dracula's bride smiling and handing a mug of coffee to a terrified man trapped in the attic with his hammer. Maybe he had just put his foot through the bedroom ceiling, the fucking eejit.

In the end, Coyne decided to rip open the packet and put the bolts he wanted in his pocket. Bought a 60-watt screw-in light bulb instead. God knows, he had bought enough stuff off these guys before. What about all the tar he bought for Killjoy's patio?

Then he lashed back home to screw the bolts on to the concrete blocks he had already sunk in the garden holes. While the rain held off, he mixed the cement and poured it across the blocks, then covered it with sheets of plastic. Nuala doing everything in miniature somewhere else in the garden, mixing mud with a spoon.

In the afternoon, he gave Carmel a lift into town to her art exhibition. The kids all piled into the back seat, separated from their parents by a massive black portfolio with its red ribbon, all wrapped up in anoraks and woollen hats, fighting among themselves behind this opaque membrane of their mother's art. Coyne couldn't see through the rearview mirror, so he was unable to confirm the constant feeling that the car was being followed.

He pulled up in Merrion Square, where Carmel had arranged to meet Sitwell. Coyne was going to have to play this one very cool, so as not to be recognized. Quite possible too that he would simply get the urge to step out of the car and knock flying shite out of Sitwell as soon as he laid eyes on him. But there was something else to think about when they both saw the rows of paintings hanging along the railings of Merrion Square. So this was the gallery. For amateurs and enthusiasts who drew nice pictures of Irish life with no rubbish in the streets, no puke and no poverty. Trinity College without the kids holding out the empty Coke cups. People who drew the faces of Joyce and Beckett five hundred times a week. Liffey paintings with the severed heads of Swift and Wilde floating along the water. Halfpenny bridges with pink, candy-floss skies. Where was the statue of Daniel O Connell with the white wig of seagull shite?

Is this what you call an exhibition, he said maliciously.

Carmel and Coyne exchanged a look. He could see the moment of naked disappointment in her eyes. He was ready to say to her that she was much better than this. This is beneath you, Carmel. Your stuff is too good for here. But she misread the silent allegiance in his eyes for hostility and got out of the car, dragging her portfolio out violently after her. She kissed the children goodbye and stood waiting on the cold, windy corner, within a stone's throw of the National Gallery, assailed by an inward shock of deep artistic defeat.

Coyne drove away, but he stopped again at the traffic lights, where they all looked back at her for what seemed like the last time. He was struck by an overwhelming pity. She was exposed to the wind of betrayal, on the coldest corner in Dublin, in her black coat and her blue scarf, waiting for the gobshite who had duped her into thinking he was going to offer her a future in the arts. Coyne saw Carmel the way he had once seen her waiting for him long ago when he was late for a date. He was stunned by her spontaneous anger. Her sense of independence. He secretly admired her from this distance until she saw him and all the kids staring at her and waved them away. Get lost and stop embarrassing me. Because Sitwell came sauntering along the pavement with his arms out, wearing a sheepskin coat.

Darling, he said.

But Carmel wouldn't allow herself to be kissed or welcomed. Showed resentment.

You call this an exhibition?

It's the best start you'll get, Carmel. Cheer up, for Godsake. You'll be discovered here. Merrion Square. Many a true artist has had their humble beginnings here and gone on to great things. Wait till you see.

And then he put his arm around her and led her to a small space along the railings where she was to put up her precious work. If Coyne had not already driven off, she would have asked him to take her away immediately. But then she decided to make a go of it. Hung up some of her paintings, refusing to speak a word to Sitwell or any of the other artists. Frozen with fury, waiting to be discovered.

There was no point in going home because the cement around the swing had not dried yet. So Coyne decided to take his children for a walk around town. Showed them Trinity College with its cobbled courtyard and its green railings. The railings of exclusion, he called them. Stood outside the gates holding their hands and staring at the Saturday afternoon traffic crossing College Green.

Some day there will be no traffic at all here, he told them. No cars or buses or anything. Just a big square with fountains and benches. Wait till you see.

Then he brought them to the zoo. Got them all chips and cheerfull cartons of orange juice with twisted straws. He was happy to be in public places. Drove through the streets, looking at the wind pushing people along the pavements. There was always wind in Dublin, hurling everything with contempt along the street – plastic bags, cans, dead umbrellas. He saw trees beyond garden walls where all the leaves had been blown off and some of the red apples still remained.

At the zoo, they would be protected by crowds. And Coyne felt like a real father again, talking to them about all the different animals and how cruel it was to keep them behind bars. Explained to them what it was like for each animal to be in its natural habitat. Spoke to them like David Attenborough. Told them how leopards teach their children to taunt lions so that they would learn to run faster. Told them about the owls who eat the eyes of mice, like sweets. Watched the motionless crocodile for twenty minutes, and finally announced that all nature had been turned into a zoo.

When they came to the elephant enclosure, he began another speech. Here we have a great example of the African elephant, he said. In his native habitat, he feeds on grass and leaves, eating up to . . .

He stopped abruptly. Reading straight off the information plaque, he suddenly found something wrong.

Hang on a minute. The elephant's tusks are made of ivory.

Coyne gave a sort of manic laugh and looked at the other people all around him. Sleepy families trudging around, exhibiting their ill-fitting teeth and their little domestic whines and squabbles to the animals. Another chance for the zoo's inhabitants to see some typical families of greasy-head Hibernians on a Saturday afternoon outing.

The elephant's tusks are made of ivory – Jimmy, tell me what's wrong with that.

I don't know, Dad.

The elephant's tusks are not made of ivory, Coyne said with great indignation. The elephant's tusks are ivory. It's the other way around. Ivory is taken from elephants' tusks. That's outrageous.

It was the final straw. The ultimate insult life could throw at him. Robbing this great animal of his dignity, even if the elephant didn't look like he cared very much.

The elephant's tusks are made of ivory. I've never heard such bullshit.

He had a duty to inform the superior race of Irish families around him and shouted his message out a few more times like a possessed idealist, just like his own father would have done on the subject of Ireland and the Civil War, and the Irish language. Until Coyne realized that his children got distinctly embarrassed and dragged him away, followed by the shocked gaze of the small crowd, who must have looked on him as a dangerous, unbalanced psychopath. Far more deadly than any of the docile animals in their cages.

In the background, two men were leaning on the rail of the seal enclosure, watching him.

Carmel's humiliation reached a pitch. Her feet hurt with the cold. She might as well have been barefoot on the concrete pavement. Other artists had all worn boots, double pairs of socks, long johns, double tights. Not a soul had come even to look at her work. She was in a bad spot, she told herself. If only she were up closer to the National Gallery, people would already be buying her stuff. But the likelihood was that her precious paintings would end up in grotty B&Bs, along with the pictures of stallions in the moonlight, tall ships on raging seas and toddlers in pyjamas with tears in their eyes. Paintings that people didn't bother screwing into the wall because nobody would steal them. Thatched cottages and country roads, bought by the dozen for approved, dirty-weekend guest houses. It was all like a fucking Bank of Ireland calendar.

Nobody was interested in looking at her art. Nobody except Drummer Cunningham. He was there, strolling among the general public, wearing sun-glasses, looking as though he was a very keen art collector with his arm in a sling. He didn't come too close, however. Stopped at a selection of dog paintings some distance away. He was bewildered by art. Took a great interest in the little puppy drawings as though they tugged at his heart.

Sitwell dropped around to check on her. What was he expecting? Big-lip Sylvester Stallone to come along and rescue her with his testosterone talk: I'll take every last god-damn one of these things. I love 'em. Got any more, honey? Sitwell even had the audacity to ask her to come for a drink later on, to celebrate.

Celebrate what?

Your first exhibition, dear.

You must be joking, she said.

And one of the women next to her heard this rebuff and began to talk to her as soon as Sitwell disappeared again.

I've been here two hours and nobody's discovered me yet, Carmel said.

The only people who'll discover you here is the St Vincent de Paul, or Focus Point. Your stuff is too good, that's why. You shouldn't be in outdoor galleries, the woman felt.

Thanks, Carmel said.

Just rubbish around here, really. It's like background music.

Carmel had a quick look at her neighbour's paintings and, sure enough, it was nothing but cottages with a grey curl of smoke rising away from the chimney. Lots of nude women with harps and round towers in the background. The woman admitted she was only there for the money.

I don't even paint these myself, she said. Any thick eejit could do them. I'd never bring my own stuff here.

And the two of them conspired to find ways in which

they could get a place in a joint exhibition, maybe. The woman had some addresses. And perhaps because of the cold, the two of them started laughing and giggling, watching Sitwell throwing his arms around himself to keep out the wind, chatting up more women with weather talk. Winking at one of his old girl-friends and turning to one of them who had just tried to tickle him and saying: you devil woman.

Carmel collected her paintings from the railing, put them back in her portfolio and left without even saying goodbye to Sitwell. *Boom-she-boogie.* She was happy walking away and in many ways it felt like a new start. She had made a new friend. And with a stack of gallery contacts in her diary, she got on the bus back out to Dun Laoghaire. When Sitwell came back later on to check on his most gifted protégée, he was surprised and disappointed that she could have left so suddenly without saying adieu.

Sugar puffs, he said.

When she got home there was a car waiting across the road with a man sitting inside. She got a fright when somebody called her name, but it turned out to be Coyne's colleague, Larry McGuinness.

Can I talk to you for a moment, he said, so she brought him inside and offered him a cup of tea.

It's Pat, McGuinness said nervously. I'm a bit concerned about him, you know, since he got suspended.

Suspended? Why? He never told me anything.

Maybe I shouldn't be telling you this. I don't want to interfere, like.

That's all right, Carmel said.

I was just a bit worried about him. I'm trying to get him to play a bit of golf.

Carmel stood in the living-room with McGuinness. It

was like the schoolteacher coming to the house to talk about a problem child.

Has this got something to do with the abduction, she asked. But McGuinness was equally stunned.

What abduction?

The men who took me up to the Phoenix Park.

What men?

So Carmel had to explain the whole thing to him until McGuinness became nervous and thought Coyne would arrive back any moment and find them having a secret meeting about him. Afraid that he might have to reveal everything, he left before Carmel could ask any more questions. Told her he would have a word with Superintendent Molloy about the whole thing. Assured her that there was nothing to worry about. But Molloy was showing no interest in the matter. He was up to his neck in work and wasn't in a mood to deal with any more trouble from Coyne. What he was interested in was another round of golf. Suggested they might try Straffan again some weekend.

It wasn't till late that night that Carmel got a chance to speak to Coyne about the whole thing. He was standing at the bedroom window in his boxer shorts, barricaded behind his folded arms, looking out with great disdain at the golfer next door. He asked her if she had sold any paintings. She shook her head and seemed very quiet until she finally asked him about the suspension, dragging it out of him like a sexual secret.

You must have done something to get suspended, she said, when he tried to get out of it with a minimal explanation.

Somebody lodged a complaint against me, that's all, he said.

There was a pause and Carmel sat up on the bed looking at him, waiting for the story to emerge in its own time. He would have to tell her in the end. And suddenly he had a great urge to give her bad news. The worse the better.

I'm in the right, Carmel. I was just checking a suspected break-in when the owner came back. Claims I assaulted him where, in actual fact, he just fell over himself.

How can he just fall over?

He tried to push me off the premises and I just reacted and he fell over his own shaggin' hedge.

Carmel laughed in disbelief. As though the whole thing was too childish to belong to the real world of Gardai. Her reaction seemed so flippant that Coyne felt he needed to shock with more information. The bridge of truth.

It was your art teacher, if you want to know.

What? Gordon Sitwell?

Yes.

I don't believe it, Pat. Why didn't you tell me? Carmel's eyes were wide open. Coyne was expecting her to go mad and start punching him around the head.

You pushed him over the hedge, she said. There was no burglary. You went to his house because of me.

He's going to make trouble, Carmel.

That little box hedge in the front garden? You threw him over it. That's deadly, Pat. What made you do it?

He had become a hero. He had demonstrated his desire to defend her at all costs. She began to laugh her head off and Coyne wanted to know what was so funny. He was about to tell her about the painting he had found of her. Couldn't understand how she had suddenly converted to his side and wanted a full description of Sitwell's legs up in the air. And when she had finally got the whole incident out of him, she got up and went over to embrace him.

207

Shag me, Pat, she said. I want you to shag me, right now.

Coyne stood back as if he was being assaulted. She had broken through the shield of melancholia and hailed him like a hero in his own bedroom. Coyne leaned awkwardly against the window, unable to reverse any further, staring down at her kneeling below him, pulling his boxer shorts down. She found his testicles, like precious copper artefacts rediscovered after a millennium in the bog, hidden on the retreat from some battle. Celtic spirals on his scrotum. Monastic messages along his penis recording sacred, mythological moments long ago. He almost fell over at one point, spancelled by his own shorts.

But then Coyne pulled back from her. Pulled his shorts up again and moved away. She was left kneeling like she was Bernadette of Lourdes or somebody in her knickers. Looking up at him in shock. Rejected.

What's wrong?

Nothing, he said. It's just all this . . .

Forget about it, she said, trying to reassure him. I'll sort out that fool Sitwell. God's clown, that's who he is. He'll withdraw his complaint. Wait till you see.

Carmel jumped up again and went over to the wardrobe. She found one of Coyne's Garda caps and put it on. Stood in the room with her breasts standing to attention. Bangarda Carmel Coyne in her cap and her white underwear, posing for him again like a pin-up.

You won't be needing this for a while, will you? she said provocatively.

Coyne seemed to be uneasy with her antics. Something was holding him back. He just turned and stared out the window again.

Look, will you stop worrying about Sitwell. I'll sort him out for you.

It's not that, Coyne finally said. It's other things. Things that I can't put right again. Things nobody can put right again.

Is there something you want to tell me?

She went over and sat down on the bed again, knees up, waiting for Coyne to speak. But he wasn't able to say anything. He wanted to be honest with her and tell her everything. All about Naomi, all about Drummer, the whole lot. But he stood silently at the window as if words had not been invented for what he needed to say. The gap between his mind and the simplest methods of communication was too large.

There are things I can never talk about, he said. Things I regret too much that I can't even speak about them.

Like what? What are you saying, Pat? Is there something else you haven't told me?

Coyne looked at the floor. He remained silent, as though language had betrayed him. Carmel waited and waited, looking at his eyes, encouraging him to reveal whatever it was that was on his mind, showing great patience with him. She feared what he was going to tell her. She scanned all the bad news that she had ever imagined. Betrayal was undoubtedly the worst. She hoped it wasn't that. She hoped it wasn't him being unfaithful, because that was the worst.

I can't speak, he said at last. I never learned to talk. I never learned to say what was on my mind. It was my father. We never really spoke to each other.

Carmel kept listening to him. She saw that he was struggling with words. Sitting on the bed, she rested her chin on her knees and gave Coyne all the time in the world. She was relieved, and took off her Garda cap again.

I never got to know my father, he said. He was always very distant. Things like that you can never put right.

You don't say much about him, do you, she said.

He didn't recognize me in the street. Just passed me by.

Maybe he didn't see you, Pat.

I was coming home from school one time and I met him, but he didn't recognize me.

What do you mean?

I was standing at one of these news-vendors on O Connell Street, looking at the papers and the magazines, you know. He came right up beside me. I didn't see him approaching. I just looked up and saw him, because I recognized his voice asking for the *Evening Press*. I knew it was his hand holding out the money. It was his briefcase, so I smiled up at him and waited for him to see me.

Coyne searched deep in the lonely memory of his Dublin schooldays to come up with the right words for this day. It was Dublin lonely. Unlike the loneliness of a foreign land, it was more private, more exclusive. As a boy, Coyne walked home from his city centre school alone, past Parnell, the Gresham, the Savoy, and Daniel O Connell, past the news-vendors with their lurid racks of crime books, daggers and stilettos. Press-ah-Heral', somebody was always shouting. And Coyne remembered how, one day, the familiar voice of his father spoke softly in his Cork accent beside him. He was seeing him for the first time as an ordinary person, an ordinary Irishman in Dublin. Beard. Glasses. The briefcase with its flask, morning paper, comb and a book on the bombing of Dresden. Or was it the new book on bee keeping. That was Sean Coyne's life. A private person – an idealist.

I was literally as close as you are now, Coyne recalled. I said, Dad, it's me, Pat. But he didn't hear me.

He was about to tug his father gently at the sleeve. I'm here. It's me. But then what? What would they have said to each other after that? They would have spoken in Irish, forced to go home together on the train, stared at by everyone. Father and son: the last silent survivors of the Irish language war.

He saw his father hand over the money. Knew each vein. Knew each knuckle and the white tufts of hair between them. Admired him like nobody else, and wished there could be a truce for a day so they could laugh and just be like ordinary Dubliners. Wished, above all other people in the world, he could talk to his own father like a friend. The vendor folded over the newspaper and accepted the money in his blackened hand. Coyne smiled and waited to be noticed, but then watched his father walking away – newspaper under his arm, not very tall, limping a little from polio as a child, merging with the ordinary people of Dublin.

I just stood there watching him until he disappeared in the crowd.

You never told me this before, Carmel said.

I should have run after him, he said.

There was a long silence and Carmel came over to him. She put her arm around him, his only friend. Kissed the side of his face. Rubbed the back of his neck and said nothing for a moment, just to let him know that she understood him. Everything would be fine in the republic of Coynes.

I still wish I could run after him. I'd talk to him now. I'd have things to say to him now, he said.

She knew that he had tears in his eyes, but was too proud to let her see them. Tried to turn away again, towards the nocturnal golfer outside in the moonlight. She continued to kiss his face and his chest so that he felt the warm healing sirocco of her breath on his skin. Carmel was the only person who would stand by him. He was not alone.

Come on. Lie down, she said, drawing him away from the window, and pushing him towards the bed.

She switched off the light so that only the moon shone across the bedroom, turning his body blue. At intervals of twenty seconds or so, the neat smack of the golf club was heard outside lifting the plastic golf ball, followed by the echo of a hollow click against the back wall. She kneeled beside him on the bed and kissed him silently all over his chest. There was no need to speak any more, because they had finished with language. They had reached the intimacy of islanders where nothing needed to be said. She threw herself across him like a surf and made love. Gave him such a complete understanding of drowning and submission that he thought he had sunk down into a deep, blue underwater room where he heard nothing except that violent kiss of the golf club and the plastic ball, and the pleading response against the concrete. Coyne reached the floor of the sea and heard the last of the sounds outside, confirmed some time later by the Gillespies' back door closing, and a few more indoor sounds, like water running, a drawer being shut, muttering, an elbow accidentally punched against the wall and a flick of the light switch, followed by the utter silence. It was the end of language.

During the night, Coyne woke up in a terrible panic. It was 3:33 and his body snapped up into a sitting position, like a bear trap. He was ready, listening out for tiny hints of intrusion. There was a sound of glass, so he jumped out of bed and ran to the window. But he could see nothing whatsoever at first with sleep-blindness. The Cunninghams, he thought. The day of reckoning had come. So he picked up the hammer from under the bed and ran out to the landing, looking down the stairs and then calculating from the nature of the sound still in his ears that it must have come from outside.

It was the crash of car glass. Coyne ran into Jimmy's room and looked out, only to see a young man breaking the window of his car with a large rock.

For fucksake, Coyne whispered. Hatchet-man Joe Perry had finally come to claim his share of vengeance, and Coyne watched the destruction of his car for a moment before he ran back to his bedroom and put his shoes on. Flung himself down the stairs. Threw his Garda overcoat on over his bare chest and boxer shorts. Opened the door to see that Perry had already gone. The fucker had taken off and was hooring away along the pavement like a cat on E. With the hammer in his hand and his bare legs showing under his Garda coat, Coyne ran along after him, but his lungs were seized.

You slimy bastard, Perry.

In despair, he threw the hammer wildly at the shape of Perry in the distance, climbing over a wall and disappearing. Coyne walked back. It was freezing outside and he could hardly move with the sudden shock of cold air in his lungs. Must have looked a right sight too – in his Garda coat, with no socks and no trousers.

He examined the car and found that Perry had smashed the front window on the driver's side. It was as though the damage Coyne had caused to Berti Cunningham's car was returning to him inadvertently by instalments. Though Perry could hardly be working for them. Breaking windows wouldn't be their style. Too mild. In a great burst of resentment and emotion, Coyne began to formulate soft plans for killing. He would have to eliminate his enemies or be eliminated himself.

In his shocked and dreamy insomnia, he saw himself dealing with the obstacles in the world like a benevolent dictator, saving the nation and saving the planet. Not like an eco-fascist, but a saviour kicking the ass of the globe back into shape. Coyne's revolution was coming. But when he climbed back up the stairs of his house, the scale of his plans was reduced by a feeling of utter despair and helplessness. The whole world was committing suicide.

Carmel had not even woken up. She was fast asleep, with one arm hanging over the side getting cold. He covered it up, treating her like a child. Then he put on his clothes. Went in to the children and stood there, just watching them for a while, sleeping out their tiny dreams of wild animals and elephants and, of course, the swing. He stood another ten minutes over Jimmy's bed, silently saying goodbye to them all.

He walked out of the house with some vague idea that he would drive around the streets and find Joe Perry. But it had already just become a minor detail in a grand disaster. He brushed the glass off the driver's seat with his arm and drove off with no clear idea where to go, just relying on the motion of the car to convince him that there was some sense of direction left in his life.

In the meantime, Fred had received another call from Naomi. This time she wanted to tell everything, so Fred told her to get into a taxi and gave his address in Dublin Port.

She arrived and made the taxi driver wait for her outside. Told Fred she didn't have much time, so he sat listening carefully, nodding his head at every word as she told him the story of her life. About the big drug deals, about the killings. Mentioned the crucifixion of Dermot Brannigan and said he died with a plastic bag over his head.

I danced him to death. They made me. And they're

going to kill Vinnie Foley too. They'll make me dance for him.

Are you willing to testify to all of this in court? Fred asked.

But that scared her. That was too much to ask.

I don't want the Gardai, she said, afraid she had already gone too far. I just want to save Vinnie's life.

Think it over, Fred urged, speaking like an oracle. You have the power to change the world. In your grasp is the key to a new destiny.

But Naomi wasn't taking any of it in. She had been preached out for one lifetime by her parents and all kinds of counsellors who had lined up to have a go at her over the years. She was seen as a social worker's dream. A challenge of a lifetime to the person who could convert her from rags back to riches.

I'm not going to the cops, if that's what you're after.

Who said anything about the cops? All I'm saying is that you're standing on the bridge of no return. Get the Cunninghams off the streets and you can start a new life.

Fred asked her where she came from. She started talking about her childhood and where she grew up in Church-town. Said she could never go back to her family. But she wanted to go back to college. She was nervous and kept looking back out the window to see if the taxi was still there.

You'll have to start listening out for the dogs, Naomi.

What dogs?

The dogs of illusion, Naomi. They're after you. If you cross the river, you can escape them. If you don't, they'll be howling after you all your life. The dogs of illusion, can you hear them?

She looked at Fred as though he had gone insane. She feared this kind of talk more than anything else, as though he'd been trying to hypnotize her and open up a huge new vista in her drugged intellect. Wide open prairies of game flashed across her mind. Shallow lakes with thousands of pink Mikado biscuits flapping their wings like flamingos. Her eyes were strangely bright and empty, as though she was already looking at packs of dogs coming after her.

He'll kill me, she said, beginning to shiver. Then she got up suddenly and went out to the waiting taxi. She asked to be brought back to the Fountain.

Drummer Cunningham was at the club waiting for her. He had sent Mick and two of the bouncers out to Dun Laoghaire to take Coyne from his home. Carmel woke up with a terrible noise coming from downstairs as the front door was pushed in and bounced back off the hall table with the force. Heavy footsteps came rushing up the stairs. She reached for Pat and was horrified that he could be missing from the bed. It was after four, and in the muddle of half-sleep she thought he was on night shift again.

Two men, wearing balaclavas, came bursting into the bedroom. It was all like radio reports, and Carmel heard herself giving a small inaudible gasp of shock. The terrifying presence of strangers in the house. The feeling that all the windows and doors were open to the elements.

Where the fuck is he? a man shouted.

He's out, Carmel said instinctively.

But then one of the men reached into the room towards the bed to drag her on to the floor by the hair. The sudden pain made her want to scream: leave us alone. But she was too frightened. Or maybe she had made an important calculation, that any sign of her fear would impact on her children and send them into hysterics. She was hoping that Mr Gillespie next door would have woken up with the noise.

Then the phone rang and nobody would go to pick it up, even though it was ringing for ages. It was Fred, trying to contact Coyne.

The man standing over Carmel in the bedroom was wearing thin pink rubber gloves. She had heard a squeak as he pulled her hair. His mate was quickly going through the jewellery case on the dressing-table but was obviously disappointed because he threw it on the floor along with all her underwear.

The man with the gloves pinned her back to the wall and showed her the gun, with its matt black gleam along the side. Moved it slowly from her face down along her body. She had fallen awkwardly, naked from the waist down, and felt the gun making its way swiftly along her thigh, between her legs, seeking out a place of invasion. She tried to move away and prevent it. Sitting up straight in order to assert her decency, keeping in mind that she must not scream. Must not frighten her assailants either, even as the cold tip of the gun entered her. He stared into her eyes, then drew away the weapon and sniffed it. He took out his mobile phone and made a call.

He's fucked off somewhere, he said, and waited for instructions.

We're going to wait here, he then said to her. If we don't find him, we'll get you and your kids. You'll get my bullets, missus.

Jimmy stood silently in the doorway, as though he was there to replace his father. Ready to protect her.

Coyne was already driving towards Leeson Street. He had decided he was not going to let them come to him. He would have the show-down on his own terms. He had driven around the streets of Dublin aimlessly until one side of his face was cold from the broken window, until he was

217

hardly in touch with the physical elements any more, like an amphibian whose body didn't matter. He had stopped twice for coffee. Hardly talked to anyone, except for one man who recognized him and said: Good-night, Guard. Then he drove up to Fred's place, but failed to get inside. Found it strange that Fred was not there, as though he wasn't letting him in any more. His old world had suddenly become out of bounds. Coyne was in exile.

He had no alternative but to bring the battle back to the Cunninghams. He drove past the house in Sandymount and found it empty and moved on to the night-club, where he left the engine running and stepped out. From the street, he shouted down at the bouncer below in the den of dickheads, Get that bastard, Cunningham, out here.

Realizing that it was over his head, the bouncer obediently decided to refer this personal message directly on to the boss, who was inside in the VIP lounge at the time, idly pushing the stem of a broken champagne class into Naomi's breast, asking her where she'd just been to.

I was starving, I went for chips, she said.

Chips, me arse, Chief said. You can't trust her, Berti.

They were waiting for Mick and the men to come back with Coyne. But Coyne had come to them instead, like a fool surrendering himself voluntarily. Coyne the noble islander, giving himself up and presenting himself for due punishment when told to.

But when Drummer and Chief came out to the door of the night-club and looked up the cast-iron stairs, Coyne was raging like a possessed cleric from the railings above. Cunningham would love to have had a gun in his hand at that moment, but it would not have done justice to the hatred he felt for Coyne. He held Chief back with his hand and waited to see what Coyne would say.

Berti Cunningham, you're the greatest piece of dried-out, calcified shite that was ever shat on the streets of Dublin, Coyne shouted down from his pulpit. So lyrical and full of passion, it was like a bard's curse, like something Seanchan would have roared at the woman who stole his socks.

You're nothing but a donkey shite and a puffing hole, Coyne added so that it almost sounded like he wanted to be Cunningham's friend. Look, you can't even spell. Nightclub. It's N-I-G-H-T, night.

Coyne had said all that in front of some late-night customers going along the street and then added the further libel of an ignominious spit which landed like a cheap demoralizing coin at Drummer's feet. Then Coyne got back into his car and drove away again.

Dried piece of calcified shite. Drummer Cunningham, the archetype of all Irish waste, had been called many things in his life before, but the graphic eloquence of this defamation made him feel like so small, so basic. This was tribal. He had been slandered on a sectarian scale and could not rest until he had put an end to the author of such abuse.

They pulled Naomi out of the VIP lounge and got into a Mazda 626 parked on the street. Mick had taken the Pajero. Drummer didn't have to go far, however, because Coyne was waiting for him at the end of the street, revving the engine of the Ford Escort, throwing his arm out the window as though he had some kind of death-wish. With the Mazda in pursuit, Coyne drove through the back streets, down laneways, across car-parks, showing off his command of Dublin cartography. He led them on a chase through the least travelled arteries of the city, even managed to pass the laneway where he had made love to Naomi, hooting his horn in three short barks like a coded signal to her as she sat in the back seat beside Drummer.

Coyne was leading his killers down to the river. The two cars raced along the docks past the cranes and containers, with the river flowing like a slit wrist out of the city, red and yellow lights reflected along the surface.

Coyne considered another duel along the docks, like the one he had conducted with Joe Perry. He was sure to win this time. But the thought of Naomi in the car made him think again. In any case, it was impossible to put enough distance between the two cars, they were right up on his tail all the time. He drove along the quays, giving a kind of farewell speech to his audience.

Telling his inner public what he would like to be remembered for. The warnings which nobody took seriously. His prophecies.

Drummer Cunningham considered firing his gun at the car in front, but felt it would attract too much attention. And Coyne had already done a handbrake turn and driven into a sort of corral, where he found himself trapped. A fatal choice. He had half expected to find another opening at the other end of the quay but discovered only chains and bollards blocking his exit. Coyne had given himself up.

Amid shouts and commands from the back, Chief took the opportunity to drive across the opening of the corral with the Mazda. Coyne was cornered at last. He had reached the terminus, parked the car in a dignified and orderly way along the quay and switched off the engine. He got out of the car and thought of making a run for it, but Drummer and Chief were already stepping out of the Mazda. So he got back into his car and sat looking out at the river, pulsing by beneath him. At least he had made the swing for his kids.

The men walked as if there was no hurry, approaching Coyne's car with all the time in the world from two separate angles. Berti Cunningham with a gun in one hand and the other arm in a sling. Now we have the bastard. Come here, fuckhead. Come here and feel pain.

Naomi was left behind in the car watching this final show-down and waiting for the order to come out and dance. The dance of dockland is what it would be, in among the containers. Or maybe Berti had somewhere else in mind, like the VIP lounge back at the club. She lifted up a mobile phone left on the front seat of the Mazda and quickly dialled a number.

Drummer opened the passenger side door of the Ford Escort and found Coyne sitting inside, looking up passively. He seemed to have surrendered everything now, just waiting for death. Drummer pointed the gun in at Coyne, looking him over cautiously to make sure that he was unarmed.

Watch her, he said to Chief, and then got into the car beside Coyne. Chief walked back towards the Mazda.

So you want to talk to me about spelling, Drummer said to Coyne.

Coyne sat motionless in the car, hands on the steering wheel as if he was waiting to be told where to go. Like he was going to be Drummer's chauffeur from now on. Drummer hit him across the side of the head with his gun, then slammed the butt into Coyne's stomach so that he let out an involuntary grunt. He was winded.

OK, you have two choices, my friend, Drummer said. We can settle this here and now by the river. Or you can come back to the club and settle it there in comfort.

Coyne looked back at him with a stoic expression, defying the pain in his eye from the blow he'd received. Ready to demonstrate his hatred for Cunningham.

That's one choice, he said. You've got it wrong. Two

choices would mean three different things to choose from at least.

Well, that said everything! That summed up human existence all right! It was clear that Coyne had given up any respect for his own life at this point, because there was no choice. He had been cheated out of his extra choice, so he would accept nothing. Drummer just laughed at him. Thanked him for the information and told him he might like to know something else.

We've got your wife and kids, Coyne. Come on. Let's go, he said, and Coyne obediently started the car with the point of the gun sticking into his heart.

Outside Coyne's home, there was a large force of Gardai. Several squad cars parked at angles across the street and three men were being led away from the house, among them Mick Cunningham.

Inside, Carmel was sitting in her dressing-gown in the front room, with her three children around her like refugees. A number of uniformed Gardai and detectives were in the room with her. And Fred was there too, holding her hand, trying to assure her that everything would be fine. The Gardai were taking care of it. But their presence in the house and the shock of her ordeal left her pale and frightened.

He's in trouble, she said.

It will all be right in the end, Mrs Coyne, Fred kept saying. The Gardai will sort these people out. Wait till you see. Fred was the fountain of authority and reassurance. Offered to make tea.

I'm afraid Pat will do something, Carmel said.

He'll do no such thing, Fred insisted. Pat is a good lad. He'll be all right.

Naomi saw Chief coming back and dropped the phone. She was talking to the Gardai. She had that look of betrayal on her face.

You fucking bitch, Chief shouted as he reached the car. But in the same moment, he turned around and looked behind him at the Escort. Heard the engine racing with an angry whine. Coyne had reversed back, but instead of coming towards the Mazda, he put the car in first gear and raced straight towards the edge of the quay, rushing forward with a desperate grin on his face. Drummer had no time to react and sat in the car like a helpless passenger as Coyne's car went over the side into the river. Mr Suicide, bejaysus. Chief ran back to the edge just in time to see the roof of the Escort sloping forward at an angle in the water, headlights shining down through the thick, green-brown river. The engine acted like a plumb weight, pulling the front of the car down. There was a dull gunshot from inside the car as the red wounds of the brake-lights began to disappear. It was all over within seconds, it seemed. Bags of air escaping to the surface containing the echoes of Drummer Cunningham's final curses.

Coyne felt the impact of the water. First like a concrete wall. Then like a soft pillow on which the car sank down swiftly. Berti Cunningham shouted beside him, holding the gun up towards Coyne's head. But Coyne ducked instinctively and in the moment of crisis judgement, the shot fired aimlessly out to sea, smashing through the windscreen, bringing the river right in on top of them. Drummer then tried to free himself from his sling, certain that he wouldn't need it any more in the water. Tried to open the door but was prevented from doing so by the pressure of the water which rushed in all around them like a cold bath. Pockets of air remained trapped in Coyne's clothes. His foot was still on the accelerator and his hands were on the steering wheel as though he was going to carry on driving wherever Cunningham wanted him to go, as soon as the car settled on the bottom of the river. He felt the cold water reach his armpits.

The engine cut out. So did the lights. It was utterly silent and Coyne could only think of Carmel right then. There was an extraordinary moment when his body began to panic and fight against the invasion of water, releasing his mind into a strange state of tranquillity where he thought back to when they were making love, only hours ago. He could see it clearly as the water rushed around his head and up his nostrils – Carmel's presence, the unforgettable absence of words, the lucid feeling of eternity as he felt her belly against his. I love you, Carmel. The words he had never been able to say before, the words he had substituted in a million different ways with a million other gestures, hurried up in tiny urgent bubbles to the surface.

The force of the tide turned the car over. Even before it crashed into the slimy silt floor of the river, it had drifted some distance seawards, finally coming to rest on the bottom, lying upside down on its roof. Coyne felt Cunningham's hand on his arm in a dead man's grip, like they were going to be the best of friends from now on and into eternity. He struggled in the sheer darkness to get away from this new companion. His legs kicked involuntarily and he reached out through the window, clutching at the door. The priority for air had eliminated any other thought at this stage.

Coyne felt the water churning around him. He was unable to move, surrounded by millions of beige bubbles, like the ascension in a pint of Guinness. He was escaping from this world into another, floating up into a higher state of being – a creamy head. His soul was leaving his body,

swallowing black mouthfuls of the river. Carmel, I love
you.

Chief ran to find a lifebelt and came back to the rim of
the quay. A head had surfaced on the river like an unsink-
able water rat. He heard the hoarse shout of Drummer in
the water, a hollow, desperate sound, which echoed back
from the far quay and lodged in the tall corridors between
ships and wharf. He threw the lifebelt out and began to
rescue his leader. Had to drag him along in the water to the
next set of steps where Drummer could come back out
again.

By then, however, the blue lights of squad cars were
already flashing across the surface of the river, racing along
the docks to where Naomi stood on the quay beside the
Mazda, waving.

Drummer appeared over the edge, wet and exhausted,
only to find the Gardai waiting for him. The river and the
whole of dockland had become festive with the amount of
lights. Squad cars everywhere. Drummer told himself not
to panic. He'd survived worse scrapes than this. Gave
himself up, knowing that his grasp of the constitution
would save him again.

But then he saw Naomi being escorted away by a Bangarda. He looked back at her, just as they placed the
handcuffs on him and pushed him into the back of a squad
car. Their eyes met and he knew that he had been betrayed
by her in the end. Shivering and coughing up the oily water
from his lungs, he understood the depth of her infidelity.
He knew that she had made love to the law.

At dawn, with the grey light seeping up from the mouth
of the river, the Garda subaqua team located the vehicle
on its roof, already half submerged by silt. Mobile cranes

were brought to the quay and the car was eventually dragged towards the bank. Carmel was there, waiting. She had left the children with her mother. Fred and McGuinness stood by her for support.

Other people had gathered there too. People on their way to work stopped to see what was going on. Two young men with a video camera set on a tripod, waiting for the crane to start lifting. And as the chains tightened and the wheels began to emerge, Carmel first thought this was the wrong car because it looked so dirty and discoloured. Plastic bags and slimy, grey debris clung on, making it look like an ancient wreck. The roof was dented and crushed down so that she could hardly see anything. Expected to see the shape of her husband upside down inside, slumped over the steering wheel. But as the water gushed out through the windows and the doors, she saw nobody. She could identify the registration number alright. But Coyne was missing.

He had managed to climb up a steel ladder along the wall of the river. He had hidden himself among some of the containers, saw the lifebelt going out to Berti Cunningham and ran through some of the side-streets leading back towards the inner city. He had coughed up so much salty water and spit that he felt light-headed. Felt as though he had swallowed black washing-up liquid. A bad pint maybe. Thought he was already in the afterlife as he dragged himself along the deserted streets, all wet and dripping. Trousers clinging heavily to his legs as he walked. Frozen with the cold.

He had shed his old persona. As he wandered through the early-morning streets with the commuters flooding in to work, he was absorbed by a feeling of personal triumph. Coyne was a new man. He had survived. He had abandoned the one possession which had troubled him most. He had shed his private car like a shell. He could now make a new beginning.

At a men's shelter in the city, he was given a change of clothes. Nobody recognized him out of his uniform, even though he had often delivered homeless men to the door. He was given breakfast and stood there surrounded by these familiar faces, drinking his tea with them and talking to them about the river. He was one of them now and they were listening to his story, how he had dragged himself up the ladder, how he had been washed clean. Told them he had abandoned his car. In the river he had become a new man, because he had got rid of that burden. There was too much privacy, he told them. We are all victims of somebody else's privacy.

They were dumbfounded. Each of them chewing quietly or muttering to himself in agreement. Somebody hummed *The Rocks 'a Bawn*, then stopped again. Each man preoccupied with his own troubles, deep in his own exclusive thoughts. Coyne's message washed over them like the words of a prophet. He was saying what they had all discovered for themselves many times over, but were no longer able to express, because it was so long since anyone wanted to listen to them. They were a silent bunch of people, not used to saying much to anyone any more, except to ask for the price of a drink, or a cigarette. They watched Coyne, the voice of the new homeless, talking about laughter. It was all about who was laughing at whom. They sat or stood around gazing at him in such silent agreement. Some shuffled around, thinking about that. Laughter! None of them was laughing. One man stood with a stack of newspapers under his arm, eyes wide open in complete amazement, waiting for him to say more. Coyne had found his audience at last.

There was a quiet sense of euphoria too in walking through the streets again. The fact that he was travelling on foot in another man's clothes made him feel light-headed. He should not be alive at all. And perhaps he wasn't. He was existing in a kind of twilight, a life after life, or some kind of angel state beyond death, marching with great Gulliver steps in the opposite direction to the general flow of commuters. He seemed to be heading into the wind, moving like an unseen ghost while the traffic rushed past him. He saw faces peering out through the windows of a bus as if they were blind and could not see him. He thought of waving at them but then moved on, heading out along the railings of Trinity College, along Merrion Square, stopping briefly outside a shop to watch people coming and going, buying newspapers, Kleenex, Polo mints for the office. People rushed up granite steps and disappeared into Georgian buildings. Drivers fought over the last parking places while Coyne slipped quietly out of the city. Further out he found himself waiting for a bus, facing out over an endless stream of cars. It was almost silent. As though the sound of the traffic all around him had stopped or been substituted by the crashing of waves and he was standing on the last outcrop of rock, facing out to sea. This was the afterlife. Coyne standing at the bus stop, raising his arms into the air, blessing the rush-hour tide. When his bus came at last, he went upstairs, a solitary passenger on the upper deck.

Fred told Carmel they normally find the body within ten days. As he drove her home, he asked her if there was anything he could do to help. He said he would stay at the house for a while to keep her company in her grief. This was a great tragedy. A moment when the whole nation stood behind her, he said. Carmel collected her children from her mother's house and went home. The house was empty when she got there. Detectives had already taken fingerprints and left. One unmarked Garda car was still outside, keeping vigil. And as soon as they got inside, Superintendent Molloy phoned to offer his condolences, insisting that the Gardai would make all the arrangements for the funeral. Coyne was a contemporary hero, as far as he was concerned. He had fought the worst enemies of the city. There would be posthumous medals. Molloy said he was coming over to pay his respects, personally.

Mrs Gogarty sat down in the kitchen and began to cry. The children wanted to know why. What was wrong? And Carmel was preparing to tell them – your father had to go away for a while. But how could she explain that he would never come back. They measured his absence in shifts until they saw the dark blue shape of his uniform through the front door. Words like forever and never were concepts that only Coyne could explain.

Carmel gathered the children around her by the kitchen table. Your Dad, she said. He won't be coming back.

Mrs Gogarty looked at them all red-eyed, waiting for the shock of the news to appear in their eyes. Carmel had to hold all their hands. They looked puzzled. What did she mean, he wasn't coming back. They looked around at the solemn faces, Carmel, Mrs Gogarty, Fred, waiting for somebody to tell them what was going on.

And then Nuala looked out through the glass in the back door and saw her father on the swing outside. He was rocking back and forth, staring at the sky. Unaware that they had returned.

He's out in the garden, she said, laughing. He's hiding outside, on the swing.

Everone stood up and saw Coyne sitting on the swing in

his ill-fitting clothes. Tears instantly sprang to Carmel's eyes as she opened the back door. Then she couldn't help laughing. This was ridiculous, she thought, as they all stood looking out at Coyne wearing another man's suit. He was smiling at them. Testing the strength of the ropes. Making signs at her to come out and sit on his lap.

So she ran out and sat on his knee, holding on to him.

Why don't you draw me on the swing? he said, putting his arms around her.

What, in those clothes? she answered, looking him up and down, feeling the bristle on his face and running her hand through his matted hair.

Jimmy came out and began to push them, rocking his parents back and forth slowly. Nuala and Jennifer ran over to help him, all three of them pushing as though they could never allow the swing to stop. As though they had to keep the swing going for ever to make sure that Coyne and Carmel would never get off. To make sure they remained locked in their embrace for ever. To make sure Carmel would never stop kissing Coyne's face. At the window of the kitchen Fred and Mrs Gogarty looked out in amazement. They were joined in the same moment by Superintendent Molloy, who stood aghast at the back door, holding an enormous bouquet of flowers in his hand. Next door, Mr Gillespie watched these new antics with great concern. Sad bastard, he muttered to himself, as he leaned down to pick a ball out of a hole in the ground.